The
Rocket Girl's
Tale

K. Hippolite

THE ROCKET GIRL'S TALE

iUniverse books may be ordered through booksellers or by contacting:

iUniverse
1663 Liberty Drive
Bloomington, IN 47403
www.iuniverse.com
1-800-Authors (1-800-288-4677)

ISBN: 978-1-5320-3152-6 (sc)
ISBN: 978-1-5320-3153-3 (e)

Library of Congress Control Number: 2017913398

Print information available on the last page.

iUniverse rev. date: 09/27/2017

CHAPTER 01

THE LETTER

Reiki shielded her eyes from the streams of sunshine dancing in a hazy sky as she struggled not to lose sight of Jude in the crowd. The scrunched-up letter in her hand was addressed to her, and she'd been dying to read it all afternoon. Nervous jitters prevented her from even prying it open for a peek.

"Come on, Reiki. It's about to start!" Jude made it sound like they were about to miss the greatest moment of their lives when he traced his way back to fetch her.

Reiki gripped the letter tightly and hustled along after him.

They climbed stone stairs to reach an overpass where they could gaze across the sea of heads to the fortress. Jude grabbed Reiki's hand and tried to pull her faster than she could manage in heels. Only by dropping the precious letter did she avoid a spectacular fall. She retrieved the envelope from a pile of snow gone concrete-grey from fluorine exhaust and cigarette ash. Meanwhile, Jude ran ahead.

"Slow down, Jude," called Reiki. "I'm gonna wipe out."

Jude ignored her and climbed to the top of the stairs. He propped a foot on a wall and peered out as Reiki caught up to him.

Chaos reigned the city streets right now, where a caravan was being loaded under the ministrations of far too many hands. Regular traffic was at a standstill, which only acted to increase tempers and make the caravan horses skittish. As for the fortress, though Reiki could make out the high towers and parapets, the courtyard remained obscured by the press of bodies.

Jude sniffed the air. "Smell that? Burning upholstery. The mobs must have a really big fire going."

Reiki glanced about as others ascended the stairs and pressed in around them. From the looks on the faces of the women, Reiki knew she was not alone in wanting to be far from here. She decided on a last minute appeal.

"Jude, do we really have to watch this?"

"Relax." He turned to face her and gathered her in his arms for a kiss, but they got jostled by a man in a grey overcoat and matching bowler cap. Jude released her to shoulder back. "Watch where you're stepping, old man. You near elbowed us over the edge."

"Stars take you," came the angry response. "If the ladies weren't here I'd just as soon bash your upper lip right now."

"Jude," cried Reiki. She threw her arms about him before the fight could escalate. Jude liked to draw his pistol far too frequently, and she didn't fancy having to watch a shootout.

The man left them, a string of curses sounding in his wake.

"Come, come, Reiki," said Jude. He grabbed her by the hand and rushed her along the overpass.

They passed beneath dripping store signs, of which one advertised an electric winepress. Having no experience with wine-making, it looked like a butter churn to Reiki, only with motors and gears on the arms. An open panel prominently displayed the fancy vacuum tubes that connected to the control-knobs.

Reiki shook free of Jude's hand and stopped to check her reflection in the store window. A pity she had curls no hairpin could hope to tame, all lively and frolicking at the barest motion of her head. She wore her locks seaweed green this week–an error on her part from using too much concentrate in the juice-crystals. But she'd grown bored of the red it went when it wasn't pink lavender, eggplant magenta, or recently, what she called 'hushed teal'. She shook slush from the hem of her ruby-coloured dress and sighed.

I've got to work up the courage to open that blasted letter.

"Reiki!" Jude had climbed to the top of the walkway and now held a precarious lookout perch over the edge of the stonework, clinging to the trunk of a brass statue of an elephant. Behind him, the shoulder-height clockwork part of a downtown power core turned and clicked. She could barely look at him for fear of seeing him get his jacket caught in the teeth of that gear.

Reiki made her way over, past the dozen other people gathered at the rail. If Jude thought she was getting that near the edge, he had best rethink his plan.

From here Reiki had a clear view of the fortress grounds. Five gallows stood before the booing throngs on the street. An overturned car and a pile of wood formed the nearest source of the smoke she'd smelled earlier. People tossed shoes, store awnings, and broken panes of glass into it. The flames reached almost twice her height.

No guard seemed daring enough to set foot past the protective wrought-iron fence. They clustered inside, looking apathetic and afraid that the mob might find a way through. The gates shook and rattled under the hundreds of hands that heaved at them. If they toppled, Reiki imagined all sorts of chaos would break out.

"There she is," said a boy who wore the checkered leggings of an elementary school student.

Reiki looked where he pointed and saw the woman with the hangman's noose looped over her shoulders. After a brief six-week appointment as chief tax auditor, she'd managed to wrangle herself into this bind by accusing Lord Välenus of fraud—or, so the morning paper would have Reiki believe.

Välenus was First Elika of Hillvale, second only to the Namika. He hailed from the old order of leadership in a time Reiki's father often described as 'equally corrupt as the present, but at least back then corruption made sense'.

Lord Välenus himself was present to watch the proceedings. His long white beard trailed in the wind just like his black robes which flapped about his large golden necklace and medallion. He was a squat and portly fellow, unlike his waifish daughter who stood beside him. And he looked gleeful, which rubbed Reiki the wrong way.

If the accountant noticed the commotion around her, she gave no indication. She kept her eyes straight ahead as Välenus gave the signal to the hangman.

Reiki turned her back so she wouldn't have to see. Jude hopped down from his perch and came to hug her against his chest.

"Look at them, Reiki. This is what happens to people who get above their station."

The baritone clang of the power core making a load change drowned out any immediate response Reiki could hope to offer. Facing away, she knew when the executioner pulled the lever from the expressions of those around her. Some cheered. Some looked horrified. It was a strange energy that gripped the mob. Barbaric. That was the only word she could pin on them.

Jude ran a finger down her cheek. His eyes remained glued to the scene below as he caressed her hair. Reiki normally enjoyed looking at him; he had such beautiful brown hair and nice thick sideburns. Today, those blue eyes were cold and impassive.

Reiki rested her head on Jude's shoulder and tried to draw warmth from the dry cold winter sun they all knew as *Sol-Domice-Terrus* from the old tongue. Home-Star, as they called it now, stared back, uncaring. A funny feeling in her spine made her wonder if she was in the place she needed to be.

The frigid cold-season air drove Jude indoors and, thankfully, away from that horrific sight. They took a carriage to the warehouse district since Jude wanted to see the big fight. He was so eager to get there that they skipped dinner and arrived early. Jude left Reiki on the upper deck and ran off downstairs to get in on the wagers.

The warehouse stretched out to the distance, so the boxing ring looked a diminutive canvas raft in a lake of metal chairs. A scant hundred or so people occupied the room under lights all misty from the light haze of cigar smoke. The ceilings were tall, and the ventilation hummed, but Reiki imagined once they got the place filled, the air would go blue with smoke.

About twenty men shared the upper level with her. They sat on the ground in two groups, playing poker and slapping down gold and silver with careless abandon. Their jackets, bowler caps, and top hats lay strewn about them as they played and shouted. It drove Reiki to take a close look at the people on the main floor.

Yep. I'm the only woman here. Stars save me.

Reiki wandered away from the games and over to the railing as she fished the letter out of her purse. She held it in both trembling hands for a moment, then turned it over and used a finger to peel the flap open. The typewritten letter looked on the meagre side before she even had it unfolded.

Dear Miss Reiki.

We regret to inform you that your application to our program cannot be processed, as your GPA does not meet our eligibility criteria.

In much respect,
Professor Uru

Such a small handful of words for such a resounding rejection. Everything she'd studied for gone up in smoke. Her ninety-six point five percent GPA trailed at the bottom of the class. In other words, Reiki had just flunked.

Jude came rushing back carrying an armful of wager-strips and a foil wrap.

"Here, eat," he said as he shoved the foil bundle into Reiki's hands. He began to sort the wager-strips.

Reiki peeled back the foil and found he'd brought her

a spiced sausage bun. It was dressed in the usual garnishes and felt cool to the touch. She grimaced.

"Hey, eat already. I thought you said you were hungry."

"I meant for dinner. This..."

"It's food isn't it? Here, hold this."

Reiki accepted some of the strips, so Jude could fold the remainder and pocket them. She glanced over the strips she held. Twenty-two gold. She could pay almost a year's rent from the money he'd spent on these.

"Jude, it's a letter from the Academy," said Reiki. She held the letter before his eyes.

He shrugged after giving the letter a casual glance-over. "Stars take 'em. You don't need 'em."

"What?" she cried. "Of course I do. I studied two years to get this chance."

What else could Reiki do? Now that she was twenty, starting over in a new vocation looked expensive and troublesome. What else was a failed rocket scientist to do? Reapply on the off-chance there would be a second trip to the moon?

"I need to flip some coin in a hurry. Let's go hit up those suckers playing cards," said Jude.

"Jude, no."

He ignored Reiki's plea and took her by the hand to the nearest group of poker players.

"Gentlemen, gentlemen," said Jude. "Have I got the wager of all wagers for you."

The men looked up in annoyance at the interruption. Most of them had thick moustaches, bushy, greying hair, and large cigars hanging out of their mouths. They eyed Jude with a mix of irritation and Reiki with looks of speculation and hunger. She would have fled right then, were Jude not holding her hand.

"Scram, kids," said the dealer. "The men are busy here."

"Not until you see this." Jude pulled Reiki into a spot in the ring, displacing a man in doing so.

They had newspaper spread out for seating, but it looked way too grimy to Reiki. Faced with no choice, she set her purse down and knelt on it. She gathered up the hem of her dress and tucked it between her ankles and her thighs. All during the process, she felt the men's eyes drinking in the sight of her and was glad for her jacket.

"I'm going to take this deck of cards and shuffle it," said Jude. When he set his hand on the cards, the men actually growled. Some picked up their jackets and slid into them since their pistols were probably in their breast pockets.

"Jude," whispered Reiki.

"Next, I'm going to ask my man there to shuffle the cards." Jude handed the deck to the dealer. "What's your name there, guy?"

"Danton," came the gruff response as the dealer shuffled the deck.

"I'll ask Danton to fan the cards before my beautiful wife's eyes."

Wait, when did this wife thing happen? There was no time to ask though, since Danton flashed the cards at Reiki. She forced herself to concentrate on them in order to memorize the order.

"Lastly, Danton will spread the cards out and select one."

Danton made a wide arc of the cards and selected one from near the middle.

"Now gentlemen. You saw that neither myself nor my

wife has come into contact with the cards after they were shuffled." Jude fished in his pocket and produced five gold coins which he slapped down on the ground beside the cards. "I say Reiki can tell you what card Danton has. Who's against me?"

The men laughed a roar of disbelief and tossed coins down. They made a small mountain compared to Jude's pittance.

"Okay, go," said Danton, eyes locked on her.

"Diamond Naiskarin," said Reiki.

Shocked, Danton threw the card down. Everyone leaned in to see her statement was true.

Laughing, Jude swept the pile of gold over his, but the men began to argue.

"Hold on, she cheated somehow."

"That's impossible."

"Bet again. Double or nothing."

Jude laughed again and shook his head as he began to rise. "Now, now, gentlemen. We won fair and square. Them's the rules, right?"

The clicks of five pistols told Reiki the men disagreed. The group had their guns all trained on Jude's heart.

"Sit back down," said Danton. "We'll play again. And if you've been cheating, things won't go well for you."

CHAPTER 02

INTRODUCING REIKI

"Check them for cheats," said Danton.

The men who weren't holding guns grabbed Jude and yanked him to his feet. They got his pistol out from his breast pocket and dropped him after patting him down for more weapons. Someone grabbed Reiki's purse, and she thought better of fussing about it as the men dumped it out on the floor beside her.

A big, hairy fist rummaged through her makeup and accessories. He dropped her resinboard cutters, glass protractor, and a makeup brush with a sharp handle into the purse and stepped away with it tucked into a giant, meaty hand. A heap of Reiki's life stared back at her on the floor there, with a tampon crowning the top like a cake.

Could this get any worse?

Three men took turns shuffling the deck, and Danton fanned the cards before Reiki as he had done before. This time, when he spread the cards out, all the men who had shuffled it drew a card. By some silent agreement, each held his card away from the other.

"Double or nothing," said Danton.

"I'll have to throw in my pistol or these wager-strips," said Jude. It was the first time Reiki could remember him running out of money. He really must have broken the bank on the betting.

"Pistol's worth maybe two gold," said Danton. "Throw in the bird and you got a deal."

"Done," said Jude without hesitation.

"What?" Reiki made to stand, but rough hands landed on her shoulders and prevented her from rising.

"Slow down, birdie," said Danton. "Get the cards right and you walk outta here. Guess wrong and you get to entertain us before the match."

Panicked, Reiki thought back to the deck. Two of the cards were easy, but Danton had inadvertently covered the edge of the third card while fanning them. She knew it was a club, but she'd have to guess the value by elimination.

"Two of clubs," she said as she indicated the man she was unsure about. "Five of hearts, and Namika of spades."

All three flipped their cards over. Reiki allowed herself to breathe again.

Jude swept the large pile of gold onto a few sheets of newspaper and balled it up as Reiki got to her feet.

"You chaps wanna throw me back my pistol?" he asked.

"Take the gold and run before we change our minds."

Reiki heeded that advice and fled. Someone shoved her purse into her hands as she raced out of the group. She didn't even stop to collect her accessories.

The hall had been filling up during their distraction, so now about a hundred people stood in the upper decks. Streams of people poured out of the stairs. Reiki would have to push her way down for now. She was about to do so when Jude caught up with her and blocked her path.

"Jude, let go of me. I've got to get out of here."

"Don't hurry so. We're safe now."

"You're mad," said Reiki. "You almost got me raped or shot or both."

"Nah, we had it under control. Nothing we can't do, you and me."

Reiki wanted to scream. She punctuated her next words by slapping the back of her hand into her palm. "You got me robbed."

"It's just stuff. We can buy it again."

Reiki shook her head. "Look, I just want to go home. I'm going to make a steaming cup of apple cider, curl up, and wish this letter and this whole day never happened."

"Burn the stupid letter." Jude snatched it from her, tore it in half, and hurled it over the rail.

Reiki leapt for it. She almost fell, but Jude dropped the bundle of coins and caught her by the waist. Her hand closed about one of the halves. The other half vanished into the darkness of the assembled crowds below.

Jude pulled Reiki back to safety, and she collapsed in his arms a quivering heap.

"You almost jumped over the rail after a letter you don't even need," said Jude. "Now who's the mad one?"

Reiki stashed the half of the letter she had in her poor, thinned-out purse. She was certainly not going to burn her greatest achievement, even if that was a failure.

"Slow down, girl. Don't kill yourself over some star-forsaken Academy that doesn't want you."

Jude spoke as he got her sitting down.

Wait. His knee? Oh, he wouldn't.

Out came the ring, and Reiki slapped herself in the face. *That's* what the wife reference was about. And the sudden lack of money. How blind could she have been?

"Reiki, I wanted to ask this after the match, but I think you need some cheering up. Will you marry me?"

No way to come out of this without looking like the worst person ever born. Reiki burst from Jude's arms and ran for the stairs.

She made the lower level as an exhibition match started. When Reiki glanced to the middle of the warehouse, she saw the forest of arms and fists that accompanied the roar of a thousand cheers.

People bustled past her, eager to reach their seats. She was caught in a river of tweed jackets, overcoats, boots, and fistfuls of wager-strips. More than once she was shoved or elbowed off balance. No one even stopped to say sorry or showed any sign they knew she was there.

Dejected, Reiki made her way to the nearest wall and tucked herself into a shadowy recess that may once have been a ticket booth. Dry paper crunched under her heels, and the place reeked of stale urine, but it was clear of fast-moving elbows.

Reiki took a moment to sort through her purse. She had lost all her money, so taxi home looked out of the question. In the morning she would need to get new ID ordered. And new apartment keys cut. She'd have to break into her own window tonight. The cost of repairing it would come out of savings earmarked for books.

Guess I don't need books any more.

The crowd thinned out as the last of the stragglers ran past. Still no sign of Jude. Was he upstairs bemoaning a broken heart? Perhaps throwing a temper tantrum and getting into fights? Maybe Reiki ought to check on him to deter him from doing something stupid.

Maybe he needs some time to work through things.

Reiki emerged from hiding and stumbled into the women's restroom near the front doors. She ensconced herself in the middle urinal, made to use it, then remembered she had no coins to stick in the dispenser to get toilet paper.

Shades! One thing after another.

Running footsteps slammed into the restroom door, and someone rushed into the urinal beside her. A black, hard-soled shoe appeared under the steel partition. A man's shoe, to go by the size and grey pant leg. A leather folder plopped down on the floor beside the foot. As it flopped open, Reiki saw a list of what looked like addresses, names, and accounts numbers typewritten on yellow paper.

The man on the other side expelled a deep breath of exhaustion. Someone on the run? Reiki had no idea. She tried to keep her eyes off the book, but she'd always found numbers mesmerizing. It was when the man sighed again that she managed to regain her wits.

"Excuse me, sir. Are you okay?"

There was a long, uncomfortable pause on the other side. Reiki thought he was surprised to find out he was not alone. He swept up the folder and lifted it out of sight.

"It's been a terrible day, milady."

"How so, sir?"

"They murdered my wife today, those bastards. Put her up on the gallows and took her life."

Reiki opened her mouth to speak, but found she had nothing to say. Here was the husband of the accountant from the afternoon's execution. What words of consolation could she offer such a man? Her own bad day paled in comparison to his. She thought hard.

"Milord knows the stories, I'm sure. They say when a beloved soul goes to the stars, it will result in a joyful reunion some day."

Only heavy breathing told Reiki the man was even listening, so she pressed on.

"She's watching you, milord. One day, you'll be together with her in a world where there's no pain. Only light and skies and song."

"Aye. I do believe it, I do."

More footsteps sounded outside, and someone heaved a shoulder on the restroom door. Already alert and scared, Reiki pulled her feet up, lest anyone should see her, but the man beside her made too much noise and was heard.

"There," came a gruff voice.

Bodies heaved at the urinal doors to the stall next door, and they gave with a bang. There was scuffling. Punching sounds and groans. An unnerving quiet moment followed.

Reiki trembled in fear, but managed to not make a sound. Not even a scream would help this far down Industry Road, since it was rarely policed.

For all I know, these are the authorities come to fetch him.

The tableau of silence broke with that same voice.

"Bring him."

Dragging noises followed the sounds of a half dozen men leaving. Reiki allowed herself to breathe and prayed silently for the man and the soul of his wife.

CHAPTER 03

INTRODUCING ARTHUR

Arthur Galenden was a little bit lost the evening he saw the green-haired damsel skulking around in the shadows.

So far, he found Hillvale difficult to navigate. The roads weren't made with cars in mind; they tended to make sharp turns or merge in unexpected places. One street even had steps. An actual two-step staircase that mopeds could rumble over and horses picked their way up.

It all contributed to his being lost. The directions to the charity auction failed to account for the Lansdale being unable to pass down many of the city's streets.

Thus, when Arthur spotted the young woman, he turned over the book in his lap and held up a hand to signal a stop. When they slowed down and pulled over beside her, Arthur rolled down his window and called out.

"Sweet lady, directions if you please."

The woman had just sped up when the car arrived, but now she turned and did a double-take. She had long, shapely legs and a figure that bordered on buxom. Her fingers were long, ended in unpainted nails, and bore no marriage bands. Her roundish face, all peppered in freckles, was etched with worry and strain.

Hard to blame her for worrying. Arthur glanced at the industrial-type warehouses with their upper floor lights gleaming against the deep blue darkness of the sky. The sewer grates along the sidewalk oozed billowing clouds of steam while bats clustered around the only clock tower in sight.

It was the kind of edge-of-town street Arthur would think twice about traversing unarmed. He'd seen a fair number of men in caps and matching jackets gathered in the archways of the warehouse exits in his travels. They cast dice for silver and glared at the Lansdale like they wanted to rob it. Arthur wondered how this young lady could pass here unmolested.

"Directions to where, milord?"

Eric climbed out of the driver's seat, walked around the nose of the car to meet her, and showed her the directions he had scrawled on a folded up sheet of paper. She glanced at it and shook her head.

"You want to drive to the Conningway Hotel, you have to go back, around to the clock tower, and hop on Ghets Avenue from the north."

Arthur found himself lost just watching the way she twirled her arm out when she pointed. This woman was mesmerizing. He wanted to talk to her more. Even if nothing came of it, this was a rare opportunity.

Eric, having received the directions from her, bowed and returned to the driver's seat. Instead of moving on, the woman remained where she stood and drank in the sight of the car. Now was Arthur's opportunity.

He leaned back out the window. "Your name, milady?"

"Reiki," she said.

"Would you like a lift, Reiki? We seem to be headed the same way."

Her eyes slid past the car and to the cluster of warehouses behind them. Whatever Reiki saw there, Arthur imagined it was part of her decision.

"Um... okay."

She walked around the car and climbed in.

Eric started them off as soon as Reiki was settled. Aside from the startling green hair that dropped past her upper back, Reiki wore a clingy red dress cut a daring three spans above the ankle. Her shoes and purse were muddy and speckled in slush, much of it frozen on.

"You look really cold," said Arthur. "Thanks for accepting the ride. Maybe you can thaw on the way."

Reiki shook her head and seemed to fold in on herself. "I don't feel the cold. Cryokinetic. Rank four."

"Ah, a very uncommon power." Arthur smiled to comfort her while mentally going through his list of phrases to draw her out.

Reiki surprised him by taking the lead. "May I ask your name, milord?"

"Arthur to you, Miss Reiki. Arthur Galenden. What do you do?"

"I'm a student and part-time seamstress," she said. "And you?"

"Our family business is oil. But I'm in town to bid on outstanding tenders for the moon project."

Her eyes went wide in surprise. "Really?"

"It's so indeed," said Arthur. So, she was impressed by things like fancy cars and rockets. That would be a perfect in. In a few moments, he'd have her stockings charmed off.

"I assume you're drilling for your oil then," said Reiki. "You look Gedanese, which is a shale-type region with heavy oils. I'm guessing you use steam injection for your tertiary recovery."

Arthur quirked his lips in surprise. Reiki knew a lot of facts about a demesne halfway across the continent. This wasn't going to be as easy as he'd thought.

"Oil prices are high, but nowhere near high enough for the effort of tertiary recovery," he explained. "When the well ceases to be profitable, we plug it and move on."

"Oh, I see," said Reiki in what sounded like reserved acceptance.

She looked out the window, and Arthur followed her gaze to a warehouse surrounded by people. Though the ancient bulb-laden sign claimed it was a clothier, he was willing to bet some quasi-legal activity was going on in there.

"Dog fighting?" he ventured.

"Boxing, but it's just as bad."

They passed a pair of electrokinetic guards using their powers to carry a man in a grey jacket. The way he hovered between them, he looked like he might be sleeping, but the red splotch on his chest told tale of a gunshot wound.

The Lansdale stopped to allow the men to cross. The headlamps reflected bright against their ceremonial robes and flashed off the golden tips of a conspicuous black ledger the lead man carried.

Reiki had her head down during the proceedings, and Arthur hoped she'd missed that bit of ugliness. As the men whisked the body off to the morgue, they drove on, trapped in a conversational lull. Arthur decided to take the direct attack to stir things up.

"So, Reiki. Are you married?"

"No, I uh... Had a boyfriend until just now. Things weren't working out."

Arthur saw a picture of a lover's quarrel at the boxing venue. She'd wanted something more serious, but he had liked things simple. They'd quarrelled, and she'd thrown the promise ring at him.

"You're free to come to the auction with me, then," said Arthur.

"Oh, I... I can't."

"Never say can't. Can't is for people who've given up."

She smirked at his proverb. "I didn't mean it like that. What I meant is I'm just not having a very good day and wouldn't want to dampen your evening."

What to tell her? That even that slight grin was a ray of sunshine peeking through a stormy night? That would be coming on a little strong, though Arthur felt it in his heart. He decided to take it slow. Women like Reiki were worth the wait.

"All right, we'll drop you off at home to thank you for your help."

He would also send flowers in the morning to cheer her up. During a lunch date the next day Arthur would close the deal.

"No thanks, I'm good. There's the hotel up ahead, so you can drop me off here."

Arthur gave Eric the signal to stop as he looked around. Brownstone apartments surrounded them on a busy downtown street. A mix of cars and bicycles rolled by, as well as two horse-drawn carriages.

Reiki climbed out as soon as the Lansdale stopped moving. Since she was street-side, the open door drew an angry ding from a cyclist. She ignored it and poked her head back inside.

"Thanks for the lift, Arthur. Good luck at the auction."

She was gone before Arthur could think of a way to extend her stay. Reiki walked around the back of the car and took an alley over which metal fire escapes formed an unholy arch. Down that brick path, Arthur spotted the headlamp of a motorcycle parked behind boxes of garbage that was likely home to a family of rats.

Reiki turned to glance back before the night swallowed her. Passers-by closed the gap, and the traffic ambled on in a sigh of release. Arthur frowned in Reiki's wake. This one that got away, she was beautiful, mysterious, and at one with the heartbeat of the city. By the stars, this encounter was far from over.

Arthur travelled the rest of the way to the Conningway Hotel and disembarked under a large, heavy-looking portico of brass railings and halogen lights. The people gathered to the sides of the red carpet were a mix of velvet, white canes, top hats, and expensive jewellery. Hotel porters and valets wore tuxedos in baby blue with black belts and visored caps.

Among those porters was Mallen, Arthur's chief accountant. He approached as Eric walked up on the other side.

"Shall I return around ten?" asked the latter.

"Make it eleven," Arthur replied. "I bet this auction will run a little late, and there might be a wine and cheese somewhere along the line. What do you say, Mallen?"

Mallen gave a nod and a smile. He wore his wavy black hair cropped close to his scalp on the sides and bunched a little higher on top, which made his dimpled smile look warm, smart, and friendly. Arthur tended to wear his hair short to medium-length, but since his was straight and sandy brown, he leaned towards the loose long-fringe side part.

"Lots of good pickings tonight," said Mallen. "I spied out a Süffite high family with an unmarried daughter going in. They got her under lock and key, but with some effort, I could swing an arrangement."

"I got an even more interesting one for you," replied Arthur. He pointed an elbow back down the street. "Mysterious green-haired woman about seven blocks back. Wanna see if you can get her address for me? Her name's Reiki."

"No last name? Is she a serf?"

"Didn't offer one. She might be. Still, see what you can get."

"You got it." Mallen took a step away, then paused and turned back. "By the way, the lady in the doorway behind me is Iliara Välenus. Her father is in charge of the region while the Namika is off fighting a war somewhere. Had some tax auditors executed today. You'd best avoid her if at all possible."

"Interesting," said Arthur.

Colour-matched iron pins held Iliara's long brown hair in a star-shape that must have taken an army of stylists to create. She wore a petal-shaped dark blue dress and a simple necklace of large pearls. Her toothy smile reminded Arthur of a crocodile. And she had eyes on him through the glass doors. Despite Mallen's warning, he was not going to be able to sneak past her.

Might as well face the music. Arthur bid Mallen and Eric safe travels and made his way to the door. A young lady in a cream-coloured gown materialized from the onlookers and looped her wrist through his arm. They walked forward as the doors parted in unison under the porter's hands.

Once through the second doors, the majesty of the vestibule cloaked them. A large, six-jet fountain filled the centre of the room, over which hovered a telekinetic woman in a sequin-studded body suit. The chandelier had enough bulbs on it that Arthur was sure it needed its own generator. Everywhere he looked, he saw beige rose marble, flecked with granite, or varnished mahogany trim, or guests in expensive linens.

Iliara Välenus was already homing in on him as the inside porters collected his coat. The young woman who had walked him down the carpet palmed him a business card and made herself scarce. Arthur glanced it over.

Glowing Embers
Overnight, Emergency, and Performance Services
Hillvale, Downtown West
Telephone: 23-511

Her name was scrawled on the back in red. "Xandri" with a little heart over the "i". No doubt it smelled of perfume, though Arthur pocketed it without sniffing it since Iliara was almost upon him.

"Arthur Galenden," said Iliara. She stuck out her hand for a kiss. "So pleased to meet you."

"I'm honoured. Iliara Välenus, isn't it?" Arthur spoke as he delivered the kiss to her palm. No gloves, he noticed. The stylistic choice sent a message.

"Perfectly right," said Iliara. "I notice you came alone, Mr Galenden."

An honorific on his name when technically she outranked him here. It was a plea, almost. If he rejected her, the snub would shake social circles all over town. She would make him pay for that. Arthur decided to play it safe.

"I am. Would you be willing to act as gracious usher for me?"

"Absolutely. Come."

Eyes followed them from behind wine glasses and martinis. It was like being in a tank of piranha. Arthur decided to ask about it.

"You're very popular here, Iliara."

"My father is First Elika," she replied. "He stands next in line for the throne should ill befall our illustrious leader."

"And he has a stunningly beautiful daughter."

"Arthur, do stop. You're making me blush."

Iliara's tells were a bit of flush to the face and eyes that seemed unable to settle. Arthur noted that for future ammunition should the need arise.

They walked down a hallway, toward open doors through which Arthur saw an auditorium with seating for five hundred.

Iliara stopped them there and turned to him. "This

charity auction is such a brilliant way to raise money for those poor Graalites, don't you agree, Arthur?"

"Mmm," he said. There were a lot of pretty faces in attendance for the auction. He cursed his luck getting stuck so high up the food chain of the local aristocracy. Iliara's presence would winnow out his chances of finding welcoming arms to wrap around his shoulders tonight.

"The Conningway is the oldest hotel in Hillvale," said Iliara as she led them through the doors into the auditorium.

It was a bit gaudy, really, but Arthur bit his tongue on that reply. Instead, he offered a few words of praise as they found themselves seats.

In the audience, Arthur picked out the five wealthy high family members that he had come to meet during his week-long stay so far. Others were various stakeholders in the upcoming moon-landing project, such as the founder of the Academy, sitting in the front row with his wife. Apart from Academy scientists, there was the usual assortment of guild craftsmen, Süffite merchant princes, and other rich aristocrats trying to vie for high family status.

All the high family present, including himself, would be competing for the precious open tenders on the moon-landing project. The lucrative contracts were more than worth the trip north from his homeland. He would know from this auction just how much competition he faced.

There were only five people who could potentially outbid him. Once he ran the bourgeois out of coin, the choicest pickings would fall to Arthur. All in all, tonight's catches should prove worthy of having to tolerate Iliara.

"You'll want to be careful around the man in the fur coat in row two," whispered Iliara. "He's Mr Megerin.

Recently named to the bottom dregs of high family. Made all his coin in creative bookkeeping during his long stint as a tax auditor. A lower court justice now, but I guarantee you a man of his persistence will make high court within three years."

Ok, so another potential competitor, since the new Megerin dynasty would need to prove its financial leverage in order to gain status among the houses. If Iliara planned to keep giving him tidbits like this, she might even make herself useful.

Two men emerged from a door near the front platform, rolling a cart with some sort of device bolted into it that looked like a phonograph with the lid removed.

One man took the cart and rolled it to the centre of the platform while the other stepped up and turned to face the crowd.

"Ladies and Gentlemen. Thank you for coming," said the man. "May I present the world's first stereo electronic radio, donated graciously by the founder himself. Ah, my first bid, I see."

"Five gold," called out someone in the crowd.

"Thank you sir," said the announcer. "But may I suggest that this prototype is a one-of-a-kind masterpiece of new technology. It is absolutely unique and will never be produced again."

Several hands went up, and the auction began in earnest.

Most of the items up for bidding were fairly run-of-the-mill: a silver-plated toaster, designer shoes by some master cobbler, a few other technological prototypes from the Academy. No people for sale, Arthur noted. That meant indenture really had been abolished in Hillvale. Very interesting.

He participated in the event, bidding with the conservative restraint of a man unsure of the value of the items presented. Once he had driven the price on the more expensive items up to a suitable figure, Arthur cooled off on bidding, as if he had overextended his coin.

He did buy one item about halfway through: an Orionite hand fan of which the slats were made of ivory and leaves of green feathers. It was a gift that would impress Reiki. By now Mallen would have discovered Reiki's address, and Arthur would be able to have the fan delivered in the morning.

Green feathers to match her hair. Ivory was rare enough, what with elephants being on the verge of extinction. Overall, one hundred forty gold well-spent.

The purchase of the fan caught everyone's attention. Arthur saw the Süffite high family a few rows ahead observing him with interest. If the family patriarch sat among them, Arthur knew he would be sought out after the auction. He'd drawn the interest of just about everyone except the blonde in the back row who studiously ignored him just now.

The next item was the deed to a farm. Arthur supposed it was as close to indenture as Hillvale came these days, because a man near the back put in a low starting bid. The type an owner might offer if he were bidding on his own lost property.

"Land assessment went up on the farms bordering Credd," whispered Iliara. "Word is they're planning on widening the highway. All that land is skyrocketing in value."

Arthur nodded. The farmer had been unable to pay the new taxes, so he had been forced off. A common occurrence for the serfs when a minor demesne like Hillvale suddenly started expanding.

Megerin had put in a bid for twenty gold, doubling the farmer's offering. Arthur smirked and raised his hand for thirty.

They alternated back and forth, pushing the price up to a hundred gold, which Arthur was willing to bet, was around the true value of the farm. Megerin showed no signs of relenting.

"Good! You're really killing him," said Iliara. "That jackal deserves it. But you'll want to ease off now, or he'll back out."

Instead, Arthur signalled for double, driving the price to two hundred gold.

"Two hundred and twenty," said Megerin, suddenly. He stood up and turned to face Arthur.

Arthur took to his feet as well. "Four hundred."

A bit of applause rose from the audience at that announcement. The farmer, ashen-faced, removed his hat. Arthur graced the crowd with his businessman's smile. There would be a lot more people seeking him out after. The Süffite patriarch would do well to take a number.

"Five hundred," said Megerin.

"Six," said Arthur.

"Seven," said Megerin.

"One thousand."

The crowd fell into a hush. It was a ridiculous number. Almost half the purchase price of the Lansdale. Perhaps two decades of salary in any skilled trade.

The announcer might as well have ceased to exist for all Arthur paid attention to him. The world became the dark-eyed stare of one Mister Megerin.

Regal-looking in his red velvet robes, and holding his varnished cane, Megerin looked like he belonged on the Namika's throne. Arthur could picture those thick, greying eyebrows raised in stern reprimand. Megerin would be a perfect high justice one day.

A young woman sitting beside Megerin tugged his sleeve. Too far to hear what she said, Arthur pictured it as 'Daddy, why are you bidding so much on a piss-poor farm like that?'

So, there's more to this farm than a few coins of unpaid taxes. I see through you, Mr Megerin.

"One thousand gold, going three times," said the announcer. All eyes in the room settled on Megerin."

The daughter complained again and stomped her foot. Startled, Megerin looked about, appearing surprised to be on his feet. He sat down without further comment.

"Sold!" called the announcer. "To the man in the Gedanese jacket beside the most gorgeous woman in the world."

Arthur nodded as he sat down. Iliara was a celebrity here. He would have to have his people research her when he had a chance. As for Mister Megerin, Arthur would have to thank the daughter for adding pressure to the situation.

"Why, in stars name, did you buy that farm for so much money?" asked Iliara.

"Call it buyer's intuition," replied Arthur. He patted the back of her hand.

The auction was almost over, and Arthur could feel the

subtle shift in the room, as people sized each other up for the chance to approach him. He hoped the farmer didn't escape in the chaos, because he wanted to be the one to say that the farmer and his entire family would be staying on the property for as long as they cared to.

Perhaps Arthur could gift the farm back to the family in his will.

"Ohh, Megerin is absolutely livid," said Iliara with a giggle. "I love it. More than worth the price. I hope you've not managed to bankrupt yourself out of that eye-catching car of yours."

"Nah, that purchase won't hurt too much." Arthur stopped short of telling her about the family's three oil wells. Their estates bordered a large underground reservoir, and several high family operations had bought into the area. With the world's increasing dependence on oil, Arthur was already turning a thousand gold a month on exports.

Much better if Iliara remains convinced I'm into flipping properties, thought Arthur. If she knew his true value, she'd redouble her flirtatious efforts and make a nuisance of herself.

"And there's the last item getting sold now. Get ready for the welcoming committees." Upon pronouncing this, Iliara looped her arm through his.

She certainly knew the nature of the meetings that would soon take place. She would be foolish to let him get away now. And if she wanted to play volunteer shield, Arthur had no reason to deny her the chance.

Besides, if he had not been mistaken, the blonde from the back row had just jotted down her address on a slip of paper torn from a notepad. Arthur only needed to work his way over to the potted plant where she stood and he'd be able to devise some excuse to bend over and fetch it from wherever she was about to drop it.

For now, Arthur and Iliara rose to shake the hands of the assembled guests.

CHAPTER 04

THE LISTING TROGLODYTE

After Arthur dropped Reiki off, she made her way through the alley while sounds of city life drifted from behind.

Should have gotten him to drop me a little closer to my building, she thought. *But he was so intense. Way too creepy. 'Rather walk half an hour than show him where I live.*

"Hey, sweetie-pie. Come back, won't ya?" The voice behind her was male and from a second-floor balcony.

Reiki walked on without looking back. It was early yet, but the way the apartments reached skyward around her, only shadow and starlight shrouded the lonely alley. Very easy to find her way into some even more dangerous situation if she was careless.

Up ahead, Reiki spotted a nightclub she knew. The burnt out wiring in the Listing Troglodyte's sign had gone unrepaired so long that the neighbourhood knew it better as the Trog. One of Reiki's clients worked there; Reiki dropped by regularly when she needed sewing work to pay her tuition. For now, it would serve as a place to rest and gather her wits.

The neon sign over the backdoor showed a feminine form in red wavy lines with a protruding white leg ensconced in a golden shoe. Metal trusses supported an aged and withered doorframe, and the brass door handle was tarnished brown with age.

All class, this place, thought Reiki as she walked inside.

Rarely had Reiki been there at night, so it was a pleasant surprise to see the mirrored stage fully lit. The heat from all the rows of bulbs on the stage floor was enough to push back the cold season chill. On special nights, three women would perform flourishing high kick dances up there, but tonight only Loretta occupied it. She was in the middle of a song when Reiki arrived, voicing the notes to a slow jazz number, as a man in a show-time hat crooned a sad harmony on his trumpet.

The Trog's stage-side seating was packed with men. From their rapt attention, Reiki was willing to bet they liked the show. Their enthusiasm was possibly due, in part, to Loretta's red bustier top with all those sequins catching the spotlight. The mounds of sparkling costume jewellery on her shoulders was tamed by a white boa, only to be set off by the golden tiara perched in her bushy black hair.

Unnoticed, Reiki made her way to the bar and slid onto an unoccupied stool at the back. The barman came to call on her.

"Nice evening, Reiki. Results from the big exam in?"

Reiki let a sag of the shoulders preface the news. "The good news is I'll be dirtside making more outfits for Loretta."

"Oh, fiddlesticks. You need some cheering up. Vermouth and a pinch coriander, as usual?

"No, sorry. I just dropped by to talk to Loretta."

The reality was that her purse held no ID, no apartment keys, and more importantly, no money.

Charlie seemed to read Reiki's turmoil from her face, for he tapped the bar with both hands. "Don't worry. It's on the house. You make yourself comfortable and get some warm courage in ya."

"Thank you, Charlie!" Reiki did as he suggested and watched Loretta fill the air with her voice. Loretta had that opera-singer build and diaphragm to back it up, so her music more than enveloped the club... in a way she became it.

While she watched, memories of the yellow pages of the ledger crossed her mind. Reiki couldn't help it. Her brain tended to memorize random numbers she saw, and parts of Loretta's song acted like mnemonics to reinforce it.

"Clayton-clocktower-two-six-power-hour," said Reiki in tune to the music. She took a sip of her drink, then set her hands on either side of the glass so she could use her powers to cool it. Being a cryokinetic had a few advantages. If only it were possible to make a living freezing things. Sadly, it was one of these rare powers people had yet to find a way to monetize.

There were so many topics to ponder. School. Jude and the proposal. The hanged accountant and her husband. Reiki's mind bounced from one to the other while Loretta finished her set.

"Reiki, Reiki, nice to see you." Loretta approached and took the stool that Reiki's neighbour vacated for her. Charlie placed a wide-mouthed glass of orange liqueur on the bar next to her. "You just come from school? You have more dress designs? Bring, I look. Maybe I find something good to wear."

"No, Loretta. I'm just dropping by," said Reiki.

Loretta gave Reiki an expert once-over. "Your face shows lines of stress, and your shoes see better days. You fight with boyfriend, neh?"

Reiki sighed. Keen-eyed Loretta had sniffed her out.

"He proposed to me today. Caught me by surprise."

"You no have ring. Things not work out."

"Oh, Loretta. I like him. But I just don't love him."

"You two break up? Is not good day for you." Loretta's fingers made a clinking sound from all the rings on them when she picked up her glass.

"Not exactly. I kinda just ran off."

"These high family boys. They too much stress. Look there, down bar. See that gentleman there? He mechanoid repairman, very nice. Come here all the time. No, no, wait, hear me out."

Reiki closed her mouth over the brush-off she'd been about to give.

"He marry before, but lost his wife in the riots before new Namika declare. He young, maybe twenty-four. No kids, poor fellow. You stay tonight, meet him, neh? Give him a chance. Maybe something become of it."

"We'll see," said Reiki, though she doubted she could stomach that after the night she was having.

Loretta shuffled closer and leaned in. "Ooh, there's another gentleman for you. He come when I finish last song. Sit near back door now. Very tall, dark curly hair. I think he's in love with you."

Was someone following her? Reiki straightened up, but she didn't dare turn to look.

"You must smile, girl. Try not to look so terrified."

Reiki forced herself to relax. The men from the restroom couldn't know she'd seen the page of ledger accounts. No one would think she'd memorized it. By now, they were certain that their secrets were sealed away.

Still, I'm getting out of here.

"Loretta, can I use your washroom?"

"Is no problem. You know where?"

"Yes, upstairs. I remember."

"You hurry. When you come back, I arrange meeting."

"Thank you, Loretta. I'll think about it."

Reiki got up and walked to the door marked women. The dark-haired man in the back followed her every move with his eyes. The door blocked him off, but it felt like his gaze accompanied Reiki to the top of the stairs.

The lights were out, but Reiki found the dressing room by the red glow of the front sign. She saw the fire escape outside the window and pushed the coffee table over to it. When Reiki picked up the magazines to put them aside, they left coffee rings behind. She grimaced. Forget resurfacing that table; Loretta needed to push it to the curbside and hope someone absconded with it during the night.

"Why I need new table?" she asked aloud in a mimicry of Loretta's North Rionite accent. "This one do job. Is good enough, neh?"

Oh, Loretta. You're a second mom in so many ways.

Reiki stopped to trade shoes with Loretta. These heels were already killing her feet, and she could pick them up in a few days. The tennis shoes she slid on were a hideous companion to her dress, but the closet held no practical clothes that fit. Satisfied that she could at least run if she needed to, Reiki slipped out the window and closed it behind her. She descended to street level and fled the alley.

Thanks to the change in footwear, Reiki covered a lot of distance and widened her head start on the man. She figured she would have ten or fifteen minutes before he realized she was gone and came out to investigate. Plenty of time to get off the streets.

Her mind went back to Jude as she walked. Proposing to her at a boxing match. Words failed to describe how she felt about that. Kajo, her high school sweetheart, had dumped her stone cold and refused to listen to her many reasons for getting back, but even he wasn't that thoughtless.

Reiki glanced back to the towers of the fortress wistfully when she reached an intersection. After four years of her teenage life spent pining for him, Kajo had gone on to become Namika. As ruler of their demesne, he had no time for her foolishness. And Reiki, having recognized it as that, had thrown herself at Jude in the hopes of forgetting him.

Except, she had to admit, the Jude plan had not worked out.

Tomorrow morning I have to face Jude and tell him we're done forever. A clean break and no more getting back.

Motion caught her eye. Not physical motion, but a change in heat patterns. All the way down the wet flagstone street, Reiki saw her footprints in rainbow colours. Red where she stood now, yellows farther out where they had cooled. And blue in the far distance, fading to obscurity.

The red glow of heat leaked out from between two

buildings. It was man-sized, and at rest for now. But since Reiki hadn't seen it in approaching, it must have arrived from behind.

The man from the Trog, no doubt. Reiki bet she could follow his footprints right back to the door. Just to make sure, Reiki hurried along and took a couple of turns. Her shadowy stalker copied every one.

Reiki chanced across a police box as she walked. It was closed up, and no lights shone in the windows. Whoever was in charge of manning the one-storey office was off on errands or walking a beat. She thought better of waiting around and moved on.

If they think I have something worthwhile to tell the authorities, they'll shoot me and have done with.

The Naldine overpass loomed ahead over a roundabout, lights forming a ten storey crochet hook in the night sky. Squat electric lampposts dotted the final roundabout before the foot of the access, and a horse-drawn cart was the only vehicle in sight. A city worker laboured behind the cart to clear snow from the roadside.

She crossed the roundabout, by-passed the access, and walked along the stone embankment that formed a canal for the Salthan River. The water level ran about a body-length below the street level at this time of year. Stairs carried Reiki to a small ledge at which rowboats could moor. The ledge would be submerged come spring, when the system carried more water. For now, Reiki could pass, only getting the toes of her shoes wet at the edge of an abyss of black water.

This place would be perfect as long as Reiki's stalker made the mistake of following her. And from the sound of scuffling from the street, she thought she might get a lucky break.

He came in at a hasty run, panting as he skidded to a stop. He probably thought he'd lost her. So much the better.

As he charged down the stairs to the lower walkway, Reiki held out her hand and concentrated on all moisture she could reach with her mind's eye.

At her command, the damp stairs went icy. Caught off-balance, the man slipped and fell. He landed in a confused heap of limbs at the base of the lowest step.

Reiki froze the river water in a circle around him. Stalagmites of ice exploded in a ring, and water crawled up their spines to knit into a cylindrical wall. Veins of impurities within the ice glowed an eerie blue light that filled the canal. The ice began to sublimate on contact with air, so that a fog curled out from it and poured out over the thin walkway.

The man clambered to his feet and rubbed what would likely be a bruised backside. He grumbled an oath and stumbled blindly before noticing he was trapped. He locked gazes with Reiki.

"Wait, Miss!"

Oh, now he wants to talk?

Reiki walked onto the surface of the water. Everywhere she stepped, ice crystalized and spread out enough to support her weight. Before long, she had a cantilever-style bridge, though it was quickly overrun by the heavy mist that curled up past her ankles.

"I'm not here to harm you, miss. I was sent to protect you."

"From what?" she asked as she formed stairs of ice so she could climb back to street level. The inside of the man's prison was too smooth to climb. Her stalker was trapped until he could use a sharp object to chisel his way free, or until morning, when the fire department might chance by and lower him a ladder.

"From the city. You needed help. I've been sent."

Yeah right. Some help he was, following me like that.

"They should have sent someone to protect you from me," said Reiki. She crossed the last step of ice and regained the city streets.

The glow from her psychothermic shift faded, and darkness once again became master of the recesses of the canal. Reiki walked away and left her stalker down there.

The only sound that followed her was the stranger's howl of despair.

CHAPTER 05

HOME

[*** Seven Years Ago ***]

"This will be dangerous," said Kajo. "You have to promise not to tell anyone."

Reiki nodded her understanding. At thirteen years of age, danger still meant thrill. Terms like cardiac arrest and system shock were foreign concepts best left to biology class.

Kajo gestured at the door of the school's storage room, and the surrounding bricks stitched themselves over the frame.

"Sealed to lock in sound," he explained. "And it's five minutes to Still-Hour, so there won't be anyone to hear. You can scream if it helps."

"I won't scream," said Reiki.

But she did when the burning started. Cells disintegrated or were transplanted. Root cells were reprogrammed and ripped from deep bone marrow. Despite Kajo using his powers to dull her pain nerves, Reiki had the feeling of passing through an oven.

He told her afterwards that she'd spent a minute

clinically dead while he sang to her heart in a desperate bid to coax life back into her body. Reiki didn't remember that part. She remembered everything else from that point on. Every last second, every detail. Backwards, forwards, there seemed to be nothing she couldn't recall if she put her mind to it.

As for the cryokinesis, Reiki was certain she'd always had it, though the night of her transformation had brought it into focus. Telepathically, she was useless. A battery of connections she was told. Other telepaths could make connections through her head like a switchboard, but Reiki herself could neither project nor receive a single thought.

The burning pain of a transforming body made way to fire, followed by blue arctic ice. It was the only way Reiki had been able to cope–by mentally crawling into a cold place. Ice made way to dreams of flying in warm skies, then falling...

Reiki started awake. Sunlight streamed through her apartment windows, and she was sprawled across the sofa in her street clothes.

Alerted by her stirring, Mister Kittles jumped onto the backrest and mewed impatiently. Reiki set a hand out to pet him, but instead of responding with a purr, he used a paw to bat her hand.

"Calm down, Kittles. I'll feed you soon enough," she said.

She stumbled to the bathroom. On the mirror, Reiki found a note tacked on by a magnet.

'Dropped by to see if you got your acceptance. I'll look you up tomorrow.–Mother.' said the note in scribbled Hillvalian printing.

Ah, yes. Her friends and parents would be waiting for the news. With any luck, the world would come to an abrupt end before Reiki had to face that ordeal.

Jude was right about one thing: Reiki needed to burn the Academy's rejection letter and get it out of her life. And somewhere along the line, she had to solve the whole ring situation. She was going to have to tell a rich, impatient, upper-class male that she wasn't that into him. Things could only get ugly from there.

However, Mister Kittles started head-butting her shin. Reiki hurried into the kitchen to feed him.

The kitchen was done in a bare-bones design with an island type counter that divided her open-concept apartment. In the living room, Reiki's five shelves were so overloaded in books that two of them leaned on the other three for support.

Reiki walked through the living room to reach the front door. She had to step over her replica astronomical sextant that pinned one tip of an unrolled starmap. Pens, pencils, slide-rule–they all formed a treacherous field of objects to slip on. New mail littered the floor by the mail-slot in the door.

"This place is a mess, huh, Mister Kittles?" Reiki opened the front door, picked up the bottle of milk that awaited her outside, and turned for the kitchen, allowing the door to swing shut behind her.

As Reiki stepped over the stream of mail, the upcoming announcement ceremony came to mind. Professor Uru had put together a dinner-dance for the presentation of the acceptees. It was scheduled for this very night, which put it in the middle of the liberation efforts for Graal, but Reiki knew the rocket would not wait. Not even for a war.

Mister Kittles cried plaintively and rubbed up against Reiki's shin. She fetched a saucer and poured milk in it for him, then tossed a second dollop into a saucepan so she could start cornmeal porridge. While she stirred the pot, Reiki thought about the invitation.

Of course, she had to attend. Janan and her other classmates deserved her congratulations. But who would be Reiki's plus-one now that things with Jude were on a downer?

Maybe I've judged him too harshly. After all, he does want to marry me when he has all those rich girls competing for his attention.

Reiki was also consciously aware that she needed his strength to get her through the announcement ceremony. Easy to overlook some of his rougher tendencies when she was like this.

As if summoned, there was a knock on the door, followed by Jude's voice.

"Reiki, you in there? Open up."

She froze, unsure what to do. The sound of the key in the lock decided for her. She had omitted to relatch the chain when she'd fetched the milk. Blasted oversight on her part.

The door swung open, and in came Jude. He wore a shirt under an unbuttoned jacket, and the curious lump over his breast told Reiki he had already replaced his stolen pistol. He smelled of the citrus shampoo she had once been so fond of. And there was jauntiness to his stride. The betting on the big fight must have gone well.

"There you are. Why didn't you open?"

"You didn't give me a chance."

Jude walked around the island to join her in the kitchen and smiled. "Hey, look. On the way home last night, I got you something."

He tossed a handful of gold-wrapped Selanese coconut chocolates on the counter and leaned beside them so his hair covered one eye. Such a cheater he was. He knew very well she loved that type of candy.

Reiki took a deep breath and forced herself to focus on the problem.

"Jude, I'm going to need that key back."

He slapped himself on the forehead. "Of course. You lost your key. How'd you get in, anyway?"

"I made a stick out of ice and used my protractor to carve it. I remember what the key looked like and all."

"Right, right. I'll go have a new copy cut."

"No, no. I need that key back."

Jude looked puzzled when she pointed at his pants pocket. She decided to be clearer.

"Sorry, Jude. I'm breaking up with you."

"What? Why would you do that? Everything's going great."

"No, no. This just isn't working out."

Jude looked shocked for a moment. Then his eyebrows went up, and he smiled.

"I get it. Marriage is a big step. You're nervous. Overwhelmed, right?"

"It's not that at–"

"What's that smell?" Jude tilted his head and raised an eyebrow. "Are you burning your breakfast again?"

"Shades!" Reiki stirred at the pot but it was too late. Charcoal at the bottom. She set the pot aside and turned back.

"Jude, I—"

"No, Reiki. No need to apologize. I forgive you. I don't blame you for making a scene back there. If anything, I deserved it."

Reiki sighed. This break up was getting more convoluted instead of simple.

"I just need my key back," said Reiki. "You're..."

An asshole? An inconsiderate jerk? What name could she pick that would leave it irrefutably clear, yet not get him all defensive?

"Go ahead, Reiki."

"We're not right for each other."

Okay. So she'd just wimped out. Stars forgive her.

Jude stretched out his arms to hug her. "Don't be silly—"

"I mean it, Jude. We're through. Give me back my key and leave."

He stared at her a long time, and Reiki put on her best 'I-mean-it' face. He hesitated a moment longer, then nodded and lowered his arms.

"I get it. You're upset. You need space."

He was following the ritual. They'd broken up so many times, it was practically a script.

"The key, Jude."

He fished in his pants pocket wordlessly. The crushing and awkward silence was broken only by the jingle of keys as he removed hers from the set. Reiki remembered one of them usually started crying at this point.

Please, let it not be me this time.

"Guess, I'm going, then." Jude ambled to the door. He set his hand on the doorknob and turned as he used the other hand to clear his hair from his face. "I'll be back on the weekend. We'll work it out. We always do."

Reiki shook her head. "No, Jude. This is good-bye forever."

He mouthed the words 'I love you' and slipped out the door. Reiki followed him and relatched the chain. She leaned against the door and tried to force her mind to relax. Jude. Accountant. Breakup. A marriage proposal. Announcement ceremony. The concepts all danced in her head and threatened to overwhelm her.

As if pulled by puppet strings, Reiki retreated to her room to cry it out.

CHAPTER 06

DINNER

City lights scrolled past the window of the Lansdale as Arthur studied his date.

Xandri was an unusual sight by any comparison to the women back home. Her dress, already a blinding shade of yellow, was banded in a crimson red sash with white sigils scrawled all over it. Brown was likely her natural hair colour, but she had it in hot pink tonight. Along with expensive contacts that made her eyes an unnatural bright green.

"You'll remember to spell my name with an X, won't you?" she asked.

"Absolutely, Xandri," said Arthur. He took up her hand and kissed it. Strong hands, at least. Probably related to her harp, which was stored in the trunk. Her hair brushed her shoulder when she tilted her head at him, a serious look in her eyes. Her face was painted so heavily that Arthur doubted she could smile if she wanted to.

"Please don't forget," said Xandri. "There's already a Sandra, a Sandri, and a Chandri in my neighbourhood, and I'd hate for anything addressed to me to land in the wrong lap."

Arthur guffawed at her cheeky assertion. "Ha, and what makes you suspect there would be anything from me in the mail?"

A hummingbird would be jealous of the rate she batted those eyelashes. "Forgive little Xandri for assuming on the grace and zeal of Master Galenden."

Arthur sighed and looked out the opposite window to hide his grimace. This escort was worse than a paid sycophant. Still, if she kept Iliara off his back, she was worth every penny of the five gold a night she was costing him.

At least he wouldn't need her services for the overnight because he still had that address from the blonde woman at the previous night's auction. Eric had driven Arthur by that manor earlier today, and Arthur had spotted clinging vines on the eastern wall. He was good enough at climbing that he would have a warm bed for the night.

"We're almost to the fortress now, Master. Have you been inside before?"

Where did this master bit come from? Arthur shook his head.

"It's quite lovely from inside," continued Xandri. "All majestic and artsy. But I've only ever been to the concert lounge once. They don't normally allow commoners– er... us to the upper floors."

"I can see it from here," he said. "It's quite the tower."

"It was built four hundred years ago as far as we can tell. Did you know there are runes and marking on the doors that come from a language no one can identify?"

Arthur frowned. Xandri sounded like she was reciting from a textbook. Perhaps she had memorized little snippets of facts in some far-flung hope of sounding intelligent by regurgitation.

"Xandri has displeased you, Master?"

Again with this master thing?

He set a hand over hers on her thigh. "Please. Just call me Arthur."

"Arthur." She said it slowly. As if his name were a large stick of licorice she could rub between her legs in the privacy of her room.

Yep. He had no idea if he was getting ahead or falling behind with Xandri. Best to hope he had just broken even.

"Finally here," said Xandri, oblivious to Arthur's confusion.

He glanced out the window as the Lansdale coasted to a stop before a lush red carpet. The fortress beyond arose like a lump of eerie, misshapen, dark-grey stonework. Uneven staircases encircled the outside walls, most of them dying out as if the remaining flights had slithered off. Doors hovered on walls with no access, and some windows were bricked up from inside. No one particular wall looked complete, but rather, each segment of support looked to have been laid by a different builder working for a new, untested architect. The very mortar changed colour depending on where the eye travelled or what spotlight shined on it.

"This is the ugliest building I have ever seen," said Arthur.

There were six local guards posted along the carpet to keep pedestrians from treading over it. They had double-barrel rifles looped over their backs and large hunting knives strapped to their waist. Very unassuming. And not a single war-type mechanoid in sight. Hillvale probably didn't see a lot of battle.

While Arthur watched the scenery, Xandri had managed to touch up her makeup. He extended a hand to her and smiled.

"Shall we?"

The ceremony Arthur ended up attending ran overlong, with name after name being called onto a raised platform to shake hands with Academy heads. It was enough that the Maitre D' ordered the appetizers brought out as the last quarter of the names were being called.

An announcer off to the side named the people summoned, and explained what their contribution to the faculty had been. Fully, a hundred fifty people were summoned, which seemed a lot because Arthur's agents had told him only fifteen were going up in the launch.

Seating came in the form of tables for six. The hall was large enough for all two hundred tables, plus the stage, and there was even room for a dance floor, all glossy, varnished, and inviting.

All high family ended up seated near the stage, so Arthur spotted Iliara a stone's throw away. He wondered after the man sitting beside her. Xandri might know. Come to think of it, Iliara probably had the means to figure out Xandri's occupation–if she didn't know already. She might store that information in her growing arsenal of useful tactics.

Fortunately, Iliara ignored him during the entire presentation and dinner.

Xandri ate about a third of each plate set before her during the five course meal. She helped stoke the conversation across the table with the other four high family members facing them. Through this, Arthur was able to glean that all the choicest contracts had been all-but-decided in secret backroom meetings.

No worries. He could bid on sceptic and disposal systems. Arthur imagined few other families or guilds would want to deal with that, but his people had become adept at stopping oil by-products from leaking into the environment.

Free from having to converse, Arthur was able to scan the hall to get a feel for the other guests. He was about halfway through his sweep when he managed to spot Reiki.

She sat at a far-off table with four people her age dressed like students. Why was that chair beside her empty? Had her date stood her up?

Reiki laughed at some quip the students must have made. Not a polite high-family-style giggle, but the full out belly laugh of someone happy to seize every inch of life.

In his excitement, Arthur set his wine glass down in the wrong spot and made an impolite clink noise with the edge of his plate. Xandri eyed askance of him, but he ignored her to stare at Reiki's table.

He wanted to go over there and sit in that empty chair beside her. *Excuse me Miss, mind if I watch you laugh?* No, no, no, that wouldn't do at all. He needed a better line like *Boy, is it chilly here sitting beside the hottest demoness this side of the ten hells.*

Arthur jumped when Xandri pinched his leg.

"Quit staring," she said.

"I have no idea what you mean," said Arthur. But he put on his disinterested-face none-the-less. He checked and was relieved to see Iliara was still distracted.

During salad, minstrels arrived and began setting up beside the dance floor. Five violins, almost as many violas and cellos, a piano and a woodwind band, and Arthur predicted an evening of ballroom dancing.

During the yogurt dessert, the back of Arthur's mind screamed at him to wait and assess his situation before moving. He really should be taking advantage of a post-dinner social hour to ply his skills and score a promising tender. Problem number two was that empty chair beside Reiki, and whatever man had stood her up.

Nah, he told himself. *Just a few minutes with her won't hurt.*

Maybe a dance, if she agreed. Hopefully, he could find out what neighbourhood she lived in, as Mallen hadn't been able to follow her home from *The Listing Troglodyte* that first evening they'd met.

Curious story, that. Mallen showing up late at night, shivering from cold. Arthur had yet to coax the story out of him, and he still had no address. The post office had been unable to deliver the fancy green fan without at least a neighbourhood. Very frustrating.

An elbow from Xandri reminded Arthur to chip into the conversation at the table. It felt like forever before the Maitre D' approached the microphone to invite everyone to stay for more entertainment.

The minstrels began to play, and a flock of blue-clad servants descended upon the tables to clear the last of the dishes. Most of the guests were already on their feet, pairing off, and approaching the floor.

Reiki bid farewell to her cluster of students and made for the door. Of course. With no date, she wouldn't stay for the dancing. Stars fall if Arthur was going to let her escape so easily.

Arthur turned to Xandri. "I need you to talk to her and delay her."

Xandri smiled coyly and batted her eyelashes. "My guild is still billing you. Even if you shack up with her tonight. And it's extra hazard pay if I'm to play jealous girlfriend."

"Just delay her a moment. We'll work it all out after."

"Mmhmm." Xandri rose and left in a rustle of skirts.

Arthur hurried to the servers' staging table and approached a woman in a white box-style chef cap setting up the dessert buffet. She looked up as he approached and winked.

"All is quiet in the kitchen so far, milord. No juicy gossip yet."

"I have a new mission for you," Arthur told her. "See the girl in the purple dress?"

"That's maroon, actually."

"She needs to have an accident. Chocolate cake should do. Get it on her back so she can't reach it."

"Will do."

Arthur went to stand by a stack of towels to wait.

CHAPTER 07

DANCE

Reiki made it through the announcement ceremony with none of her friends suspecting her inner turmoil.

Her classmate, Janan, sat beside her on the other side of the conspicuous empty chair and joked with her throughout the evening. Janan's scores in metallurgy and fluid dynamics had earned him a spot as chief engineer on the rocket. Reiki thought that was a perfect job for him. She could think of no one who had worked harder to get it.

Once the dinner was finished, and the last certificate handed out, Reiki decided to head home. She saw no point in sticking around and being the seventh wheel when all her fellow students were paired off. Unfortunately, when a pink-haired woman stopped to ask her questions about the green in her hair, a server stumbled and spilled cake on Reiki's back.

"Oh, dear! I'm so sorry about that." The server looked horrified at what she'd done.

"I can't see, is it bad?" Reiki twisted, but the stain was on the small of her back.

"It's only a smudge," said the server. "There's towels over there. Don't worry. It'll come out."

Beside the towels stood Arthur Galenden from the fancy car last night. That corner of the room was not exactly the place Reiki wanted to be with chocolate cake on her back.

"Please hurry," said the serving woman. "I can't bear the thought of the dress being ruined."

It was Reiki's fanciest dress. She couldn't afford to lose it, so she steeled her resolve and approached. Who knew? Maybe Arthur had forgotten her already. He probably saw hundreds of faces in a given day.

Reiki approached the table in quiet footfalls. Arthur had his eyes on the dance floor. Maybe she could sneak in and out before he even turned around.

Please don't let him see me. Please don't let him see me.

Wishing failed her.

"Reiki," said Arthur with a heart-melting smile. "What a nice surprise to see you."

"Arthur Galenden," she replied. Reiki offered him a half curtsy while her mind raced. *Distract him. He won't stay at the dessert table for long.* She just had to keep him talking until he made an excuse to leave. "Did you like *The Tale of the Sinister Storm*?"

"You remember my name and the book I was reading in the car when we met." He bowed his head in appreciation. "I am truly honoured."

"It's one of my favourite books. I couldn't help but notice." Reiki realized, by Arthur's thoughtful look, that he had yet to finish it. "You were on page... thirty-two, I believe. It's rather long, isn't it?"

"I gave up on it halfway," said Arthur. "It had structural problems."

She blinked at him in surprise. "Do you mean the point where the protagonist thinks the prince has become an ugly frog and wishes to kiss all the frogs in the world in the hopes of finding him? Some analysts have called that a maimed allegory for courtship. It really hits you over the head like a blunt hammer, doesn't it?"

"I like my literature with a bit more finesse," said Arthur. "The competing main character prince is completely out of his breadbasket."

Reiki knew she stared open-mouthed. Jude never liked literature, much less love tragedies. Here, this beautiful, well-read man happened to share her opinion about an obscure character in a book written a thousand years ago. Too good to be true. She wanted to ask him a million questions about what he thought of the other characters. And questions like why he'd chosen such a difficult book as a leisure read. Did she dare?

No, keep it simple or he'll take fright.

Reiki settled on the first question that came to mind.

[***Arthur***]

"Please tell me you enjoyed *Lahkmoor* by Master Armen Tellnayen," said Reiki. She cupped her hands together with excitement. "You know it was written as a response to the *Sinister Storm*. And the two writers were contemporaries."

Again with the dusty old tomes? It made Arthur wish he'd really read any of these books. *Ok. Open ended guesses. Feel her out a little.*

"*Lahkmoor* was a long time ago," said Arthur. "We might have studied it when I was a young teen."

"The book with the swamp around the castle," supplied Reiki.

Swamp stories always had evil critters in them. Arthur only needed to guess what type.

"And the evil trees?" he ventured.

"Thorn bushes. The writer was very specific in that regard."

"Ah, yes. I'm not sure I liked that one either," said Arthur.

"Not sure you liked? That story was beautiful –"

Arthur set a finger across Reiki's lips, and she went so doe-like, he worried that her eyes might roll from her face.

"Reiki," he asked. "Would you like to dance?"

[*** Reiki ***]

When he asked her to dance, her heart went to thundering so hard, Reiki was certain her ears had turned red.

There had to be something wrong with this picture. A high family man of his stature sought her company for a song? Was she dreaming? Was he a demon seeking a taste of her soul? Whatever the case, he was waiting for her answer, and his eyes spoke of fleeting hope that she would agree.

Chocolate cake, you fool! You need to wipe off the cake! Decline on the dance or you're going to look totally foolish.

"Y-yes," said Reiki. It was all she could manage, for her throat constricted and tied itself into a knot.

He took her hand and started to lead her to the floor, but stopped and frowned.

"Oopsie, it seems you've had an accident. Here, let me."

Mortified, Reiki could only stand there and let him dab at her back with a towel.

Close your mouth. You look like you're having an orgasm.

"All done. Not so bad."

"Thank you," she said while trying to work out an explanation for the cake that looked heroic.

Again, words failed her, and Reiki quietly allowed Arthur to lead her to an empty spot on the floor. The couples were engrossed in the Selanese flip step. It was a tactile version of the Cha-cha. She had read it once three years ago... recently enough to be able to perform it.

Reiki set her hips in the opening sequence, and Arthur matched her toe-to-toe. At that point, the rhythm of the music took over, and they began to dance.

[*** Arthur ***]

Shades, Reiki dances like an automaton.

Her motions were precise and spot-on. No flourish or stylistic decisions. Flawless, textbook dancing. Her hands were cold to the touch, and her face serene. Reiki must have studied dance under a very harsh regime.

Okay, get her talking and figure out her interests. If they matched his, things would get more comfortable.

"So what brings you here?" asked Arthur.

"I– I tried to make the A-list you saw. I mean, on stage there. Of students." She tripped over her explanation so much that Arthur had to piece together what she was saying. "I wanted to go up on the rocket. To the moon."

"But they didn't take you."

"No, I... uh. The others, they... out-performed me."

She seemed to be agreeable to having been beaten out on what was surely a once-in-a-lifetime opportunity. Arthur wondered what the criteria had been.

"Were the final examinations in your core subject area?" he asked.

"I... don't really. I just bend my mind around problems and I work things out. Sometimes I do it fast. Most of the time I take too long."

"Nothing wrong with taking your time on a problem."

"It's huge when you're writing a test and you can only allow yourself five minutes per question."

"I see," said Arthur.

They swirled among the other couples for three stanzas before the violins came in with a blend of slower waltz. Reiki maintained proper position throughout, so Arthur refrained from trying to pull her close.

White and blue were the in-colours, it seemed. Blacks for the men, including Arthur. Dressed in red, Reiki was a spotlight on the dance floor. A show-stealer she was, in her elbow-length gloves that were so far behind the times it looked new. Arthur decided to comment on it.

"You look stunning in red, you know."

Arthur must have touched home on a distracting topic, for Reiki babbled up a glimpse of her mind.

"Thank you. I chose fabric the same colour the rocket fuel takes once we condense it and turn it into bricks for storage. It settles really heavy when you get the concentrate right and looks almost like a strong red wine. It's that strength that gives the rocket the required escape velocity." On that pronouncement, Reiki's eyes widened, and a very unlady-like oath escaped her lips. "Shades, I'm boring you, aren't I?"

Boring him? With scientific talk when he was in town to bid on the rocket project? He could listen to her all day. Arthur let his mirth show in his lips and shook his head.

"No, Reiki. You're absolutely wonderful."

At last, she closed the gap between them.

[*** Reiki ***]

That was new. All her life she had been called ugly or beautiful, wacky or sexy, depending on what people wanted from her.

No one had ever called Reiki wonderful. No, wait– Jude had once, forty-four weeks ago less a day, while she was straddling him. By now, he had probably forgotten. A brief geyser in a shallow, tepid lake of passion.

They were technically into song number two. Did Arthur realize this bordered on impropriety? Reiki hoped he didn't care. She wished emotions could be snapped into perfect recollection so she'd have this night with her forever.

"What's your favourite colour?" she asked. Anything to stretch the moment.

"Sand," came Arthur's reply.

What a strange answer. Did he mean mineral sand or coral sand? Or perhaps that was an allegory to some piece of literature he wanted to evoke in her mind.

While Reiki racked her brain for a match, she felt him try to ease her backwards into a dip. Caught off-guard, she resisted, so that they two remained upright while all the other couples on the floor swooshed in a cascade of twirling fabric.

That looked difficult. How would she ever do that? And for a dance she was a novice at.

The second twirl was coming, and Reiki didn't think she could do it. All she needed here was to slip from his grasp and make a fool of herself by crashing to the floor.

But Arthur's eyes were calm, and his touch was sure.

Reiki closed her eyes and let go.

[*** Arthur ***]

Once he felt her body relax, they dipped with the other couples. The motion looked so second-nature to Reiki that the fingertips of her trailing hand almost kissed the floor.

Back on her feet, Reiki placed her cheek on his shoulder. Arthur felt her heart beating wildly, and her hands were super cold. Probably worried that her dance instructor would learn of her little deviation from the lessons.

Arthur glanced to the tables where Xandri waited in the shadows cast by plastic palm leaves. A gentleman came to talk to her, and she slipped him a business card.

Good. Xandri's keeping herself occupied. Very efficient on her part. But wait... You're forgetting that blonde from the auction.

The thought made him chuckle to himself. Those who knew him would be disappointed to hear his thoughts right now.

You go through women like you throw out socks, his friends would say. *Why are you suddenly in the mood to dance all night with this clumsy duckling?*

Arthur knew they would die laughing at his answer, but it was true: Miss Brilliant hadn't existed until now.

[*** Iliara ***]

Look at them there, dancing like they own the place. I bet they don't even realize the rest of us are here. Three songs too. Why don't they just make out and get it over with?

Iliara narrowed her eyes at Arthur and the green-haired woman he danced with when he was supposed to be dancing with her. Everyone in town knew by now Arthur was a reserved man. Who did this whelp think she was? Did she not know Iliara's clique was watching?

Standards, you man-thief. Hands off what's mine.

A slow sigh of frustration welled up in Iliara's throat. The mess with recovering the ledger and destroying it before anyone got hold of the account numbers within had proven expensive. Every murder Iliara had to arrange set her back eighty gold. Surely, by now, she had spent enough to make all her problems go away?

"Just one more," she whispered. "One more body, and I swear I'll go on the level."

Death to the man-thief.

[*** Reiki ***]

Oh, song number three, where did you go?

Once the last of the violins stopped playing, everyone would applaud, and the fast music would start back up. Arthur would bow in parting and be off to seek another dance partner, ending the moment forever.

To think she had craved the Jude-free solitude of her apartment all evening. Now, all she wanted was to stay up all night talking to Arthur. Fickle? Yes, Reiki had to admit. Impossible? Sadly so. All Arthur saw here was a dance. And that moment of paradise was drawing to an end.

The song was in its final measure when Arthur cleared his throat. Reiki's head turned into a cyclone of thoughts as she tried to come up with something to say.

"Once you helped me in the street, I knew I had to get you something in thanks," said Arthur. "I'll mail it to you if you would tell me where to send it. I wouldn't want to impose upon you to stay until the end of the night so I could get it from my car."

Impose? Hardly. But Reiki knew what he meant. He wanted to get rid of her so he could find another partner. She'd be holding him back if she stuck around all night. It made her sad, but she recognized the necessity.

"Address it to Reiki, by way of Downtown-South," she said. "I will get it."

"Oh good. Women like you are so hard to find."

That got her attention. The cyclone of thoughts died to a murmur.

[*** Arthur ***]

"Wait, what?" she asked.

The music dwindled out, and people started to applaud. Arthur clapped with them and awarded his smile upon Reiki.

"In life, I mean. Hard to find women of your calibre."

"You've been following me, haven't you?" she asked, eyes widening in fright.

He laughed and set his hands about her as invitation to stay for another song. In doing so, Arthur caressed her shoulder to try to ease what must be a bit of fright. "No, not exactly. I merely wanted to reward you for being such a nice person."

But Reiki looked dubious. There were questions in her upturned eyes. He opened his mouth to assuage her fears, but she spoke before he could form the words.

"That curly-haired man who followed me to the Salthan River. He was working for you, wasn't he? You've been after the ledger the whole time."

"Huh? Oh, Mallen. A ledger? I really just wanted to send you my gift."

"He sure put a lot of effort into following me."

This conversation was getting off the intended track. Arthur decided to put her off-guard. "You are stunning and irresistible. Please forgive me my forwardness, but I thought you were in danger that night."

"Oh," said Reiki, gaze flickering down. But then, she looked up, eyes flashing. "Tell me who Calexus is."

"Who?"

"Calexus. She's a principal character in chapters five and on in the book you claim to have read halfway through yesterday."

"Oh, that Calexus," said Arthur, racking his brain for an excuse. Here a half-truth would help. "But I didn't even like that book."

"You haven't read it. You... lied to me." Reiki turned

away and pressed her shoulder to his chest. "I thought you—I mean, I thought we…"

Instead of finishing the sentence, Reiki's body began to shake. When Arthur tried to look into her eyes, she set a hand on her cheek so that all he saw was an open palm.

This would take some explaining.

"Reiki, I'm sorry. When I saw your smile back there on the road, I needed desperately to reach you. To talk to you."

The palm never wavered, but at least the strains of the next song were starting up. Maybe she'd stop fussing if they danced again.

"Reiki, please. Look at me."

"Unhand me, sir," said Reiki. "This is too much for me."

Arthur released her from the embrace of the dance and watched Reiki dash away. She ran headlong into another couple, barely pausing to apologize, before fleeing the dance floor with her face in her hands.

And he remained frozen in place, not daring enough to follow.

CHAPTER 08

GENTLEMEN, SHE'S WITH ME

Arthur stood at the edge of the dance floor. He looked to Iliara like a lost puppy. He was so intent on the doors that he failed to register her approach before she laid a hand on his chest. He started as if jolted awake from slumber and set a hand over hers.

"Poor Arthur," said Iliara. "Flighty, little commoner girl broke your heart?"

Arthur laughed. "Hardly. But I can't get over the suspicion that it may be me who broke hers."

"She'll live. In the meantime, how about dancing with a woman instead of a girl?"

He accepted her invitation and linked arms with her. They caught the beat and finished the second half of the song as Iliara's clique watched on in approval. Arthur seemed to be able to read her movements like a telepath. He missed no steps and was at her side for every twirl.

I hope the rumour mill is getting an eyeful of this.

The song came to an end, and violins hinted at a slow

song to follow. Iliara drew up to Arthur in preparation, but he held her back at the shoulders.

"Thank you for the song, Iliara. And I'm terribly sorry, but I must duck out on you."

"What?" she asked, though she remembered not to frown. Anger led to surges in her aura, which led to burnt out wiring... the tribulations of being the daughter of a powerful electrokinetic.

"I can't get over the feeling that I somehow made her cry," said Arthur. His eyes looked clouded and wistful. Like he actually believed that nonsense he was spouting.

"She's play-acting, silly boy. What woman turns into an emotional firecracker after three songs? She's a complete faker."

"No, no. Reiki doesn't come across that way. That's not how fakers play the game."

Oh, so Reiki's her name? Excellent.

The slow song was in full swing now, but Arthur kissed her hand in parting.

"On that note, I bid you farewell."

"But my other songs–"

Arthur was off before she could complain. Reiki had warranted three songs. That meant Iliara was supposed to get four. What an embarrassing affront.

Iliara followed him off the dance floor, but she remained on the carpet, staring at the doors. In her peripheral vision, she saw her clique form ranks behind her. But they knew not to bother her right now. Instead, they busied themselves preening.

For several long minutes, Iliara stared at the doors.

Rejected after just one song because of Reiki. This Reiki needed to be contained. Tonight, if possible.

A grin came to Iliara's lips. She knew lesser men would throw themselves from great heights to see such a smile. The plan she had... it was perfect.

Reiki's days were numbered.

Arthur dashed outside and ran to the street where guards milled about before the gates. He saw no sign of Reiki.

He turned to the nearest guard. "Did you see a green-haired girl pass here just now?"

"Milord, she went in there."

He indicated a five-storey tall building on the corner of the facing block that looked like a giant metal furnace trying to engulf a greenhouse. The hulking vertical sign ran from the ground floor to the roof, prominently displaying the words "Atrium". Balled up bits of newspaper formed the welcome trail to ominous, banded steel doors. And several men of questionable repute huddled under the one working light, having a smoke.

"Milord," said the guard when Arthur brushed past him. "The Atrium is a little rough around the edges."

An excellent hiding spot. Reiki had chosen a place she didn't think he would follow.

"I'll be okay," he told the guard. "Thanks for the tip."

Arthur crossed to reach the Atrium and stood before the doors. He felt the sidewalk depress under his shoes, and the doors squeaked as the bands slid apart under hidden cogs. When the doors shuddered open, he was surprised to be greeted by a draft of warm air and the gravelly sound of an electric tube piano. About fifty people danced to the noise, as five percussionists beat a chaotic accompaniment on racks of pots, pans, and metal buckets.

Arthur stepped inside, and the doors shut behind him. The inside of the Atrium was made up of wire-frame mesh walls and indoor grow-lights. Vines and leaves grew through this foundation, seeming to form living walls, particularly thick near the light sources.

The lights dangled from high ceilings and swayed in time to the music as men and women gyrated their hips and pumped their arms. No sense of dancing partners or choreography prevailed. The scene was alien. It was a room of bodies writhing to expel demonic possession.

Young men of rainbow-coloured hair clustered at the walls and stared at Arthur as he looked about. If Reiki was hidden in this crowd, she would blend in fairly easily. He spotted metal stairs leading up to the second floor. Arthur gambled she was up there and took them.

The cacophony of music faded to a murmur as Arthur made his way down the poorly lit passage. Floor-to-ceiling windows lined little alcoves along the way, but they were designed for natural sunlight, so the evening's darkness filled many of them. In some alcoves, old men clustered around tables playing dominos. In others, men in top hats discussed matters with the gravity of elected magistrates.

Reiki turned up on the third floor in an alcove lit from wall-mounted fluorescent tubes in each corner. Moths fluttered around as they buzzed to the melody of an artificial waterfall that formed an indoor creek. Reiki sat with her back to the hall, at a metal table covered in fist-sized potted cacti that squirted bubbles in the air.

"You followed me," said Reiki without troubling to turn around.

"I came to apologize," said Arthur.

"Oh." Reiki's response was casual and disinterested.

He took that as permission to enter and sit across from her.

Reiki's eyes looked puffy, and her mascara had streaked down her cheeks. Arthur grimaced. His suspicions were correct: she had been crying.

She seemed to divine what he was thinking and shook her head.

"It's not you. It's just that this has been a very terrible week for me. I guess this was the icing on the cake."

"You probably feel a little played," said Arthur.

"I put a lot of expectations on you. When you turned out different from my imagination, I heaped all the blame on you."

That was a remarkably open admission. Reiki's dark brown eyes darted back and forth as she said it. Arthur took a moment, lost in them while he decided on a reply.

"Have you ever wanted to impress someone so much you were willing to stretch the truth a little?" he asked.

"Mr Galenden, with your resumé, I doubt you need to make up things you've read to sound interesting."

"You get what I mean, though. It was a part of your life, and I wanted desperately to engage in it."

Reiki had no response for that. She became interested in her thumbnail.

He pressed on. "So can we go back to Arthur instead of

71

this mister thing? In fact, maybe we could just forget tonight happened and start all over?"

Reiki looked up. "I could do that, you know. I can make myself forget things as easily as I can remember them."

Arthur chuckled at the thought. "Nothing so drastic. Instead, I vote we finish our dance."

She temporized as tiny cactus-bubbles crossed the air between them. When Arthur reached across the table to take her hand, she drew back.

"I don't even trust myself, right now," said Reiki.

"Come, Reiki. I want to hold you. There's no one else in the world I could imagine spending my evening with."

Reiki stared at him in shock, but then her cheeks creased into a smile that transfigured her face into an image of happiness. She allowed Arthur to take her hand and lead her to her feet for a brief hug.

"See? Not so bad. Wait, you're not crying again, are you?"

"Oh, no. I'm fine." She wiped at the edges of her eyes with her knuckle. "This stupid makeup really burns your eyes."

"Well, the night's ahead of us. Let's get you back to the dance."

"Wait, I can't go back in there. I'm a mess."

"Oh, don't worry about that. Xandri has her makeup with her. We'll get you fixed up in no time."

"Xandri? Wait a second." Reiki frowned and cocked her head. She blinked rapidly a few times in concentration. "You were sitting next to a pink-haired girl. The same one who stopped to ask me about my hair."

"Yep. That would be–"

"It was planned, wasn't it?"

"Huh?"

"You had them spill cake on me on purpose, didn't you?"

Arthur backed off as she advanced on him menacingly, but the rocks of the waterfall blocked his way.

"It's not like how it sounds," he said.

"You've arranged this whole thing. I bet you even knew I would come to the Atrium."

"No, no. The guards told me."

Reiki lashed out and grabbed his tie. She pulled her other hand across it and, with a 'snik' noise, she cut it in half.

"That's for ruining my dress, you worthless flake of chimney ash."

She threw the severed tie in his face and retracted the blade on her resinboard cutter. Arthur tried to stop her from leaving.

"Reiki, wait."

She rounded on him. "No. You just can't help lying to me, can you? You had me eating out of your hand right there. Well, no more. You know why? I hate you."

"Now, Reiki. Calm down a—"

"I despise you, Mr Galenden. Be gone from my life and never return."

The music stopped downstairs, and Reiki tilted her head to the floor as if she could see through it, a frown slowly clouding her face.

Compliment her? Beg her to stay just a moment longer? Arthur felt his options draining from between his grasping fingers.

"Shades," breathed Reiki. She fled the room.

Arthur followed her to the hallway as he undid his

severed tie and let it fall to the floor beside him. Reiki had a penchant for coming up with the unexpected.

Shouts and thundering steps arose from below as Reiki made it to the far end of the hall. She slipped out the window and took a fire escape before a crowd of men ran up the stairs. By the light of other alcoves, Arthur saw they carried pistols and leather saps. And judging by Reiki's reaction, they were after her.

Any sane person would stand back and allow Reiki's sordid past to catch up with her. Interrupting these men could prove fatal. Forget Arthur's diplomatic immunity and that these men would want to avoid killing him at all costs—a stray bullet would be undiscerning in that regard. Very easy to find a quick exit from this life if he got involved.

Yep. Best to just walk away right here. Not worth risking your life over this one.

Against all possible logic, Arthur reached back, grabbed the nearest metal chair, and carried it to the hallway. He brandished the chair like a shield, and the charging men skidded to a confused halt in front of him.

"Gentlemen, I hate to tell you, but the lady's here with me," said Arthur.

The crowd of men filled the hallway. Arthur estimated at least ten of them. Maybe twice as many on the stairs. He was hopelessly outnumbered and outgunned. His only advantage was their moment of confusion.

The men parted by pressing their backs to the walls, forming a corridor of bodies that gave way to the landing of the stairs. At the end, Arthur saw one of Iliara's friends.

Doli Stanton. He had done his basic research on Iliara's goon-squad. She wore a white ballroom dress as she floated down the hall. Her long black hair seemed alive, the way the tresses snaked out to touch metallic objects as if magnetized to them. Her eyes glowed an unnatural white in the darkened hallway and her red lips were curled in a grotesque rictus of a smile.

She chuckled. A low, rumble of a laugh that made her head bob in a creepy fashion. Even her own men were unnerved by it.

"Shades," said one near Arthur. "Stanton's in rare form tonight."

The chair in Arthur's hands erupted into orange flames. He dropped it in surprise. When he looked up, Doli had her hand extended to him, and her palm glowed with the same infernal energy as the chair.

Ok, so Doli's a Lightning, then. Those powerful electrokinetics, who could harness energy at will, ran minor demesnes like this. The most powerful Lightning, known as the Namika, ran the entire region, but the Namika for Hillvale was away at war, leaving the unsightly underbelly of his organization in charge.

"Cast him aside," said Doli. "Continue the search."

An army of hands grabbed Arthur and hurled him into the alcove. He landed on his side and feigned unconsciousness for a moment.

His antics had bought Reiki maybe half a minute. As scores of men rumbled past the doorway, he wondered if that would be enough. And in his mind, he warred with his options.

She hates you, and you've just risked your life to help her. Cut your losses here, old chap.

Arthur shook his head and got to his feet. Forget whether

or not she would ever love him back, or would even know he was involved. Reiki needed help. Arthur would respond.

Safely, though. He heard Doli in the hallway instructing the remainder of her thugs.

"I sense Reiki went upstairs to the roof. You four head back down and make sure the exits are blocked off around the building. You others, check if there are neighbouring buildings she can get to."

"Yes, Miss Stanton."

Shuffling followed, and Arthur deemed them distracted enough to make a break for it. He clambered to his feet and dashed into the hallway. He was at the window before a cry sounded behind him. He made the steps outside the window before they could respond.

He met a shoe near the roof. A high heel belonging to Reiki. So great was her haste that she'd given up her shoes. A sure sign of desperation.

Looking out from the roof, skylights formed a forest of glowing lanterns, as chimneys and vents gushed a melange of smoke and steam into the starlit sky. Yelling and sirens punctuated the cool air. Many of the shouts were from the rooftop level. It was like a sonar signal to Reiki's progress.

From the direction of the yelling, Reiki had jumped to a different roof, and was now running perpendicular to her initial direction of flight. Arthur was unsure why she'd be doing so, unless she had run out of rooftops and had been forced to change directions.

It made his life easier. Arthur cut diagonally in her direction.

To cross from one roof to another, Arthur had to climb onto a fire escape and leap to the opposing metal rails.

Traffic honked many storeys below as he did so. A quick fall to the death flirted with all of them on this chase.

Arthur got within sight of Reiki on the next block, where the buildings were so close together that he could jump from one to the other. Two of the most athletic men were close. He could see that they would run her down before long. All the other men were so far behind, they were inconsequential. Arthur doubted the majority could even see her.

He ran up to them and met them mid leap over a skylight. When Arthur crashed into the trailing man, he threw the pursuer off-balance enough to send him crashing through the glass. The other landed clear and continued the chase. Arthur raced after him.

The last man leapt for Reiki just as Arthur moved to tackle him. Arthur caught his ankles, and his grab fell short of her. They tumbled to the ground as Reiki took a graceful and magnificent leap from the edge of the building.

The man kicked free of Arthur's grasp and tried to follow, but skidded to a stop at the ledge. When Arthur ran up beside him, he saw why.

Reiki made her way along the trellis that branched over the waterworks of the Conningway. The ledge she stood on was narrower than her feet, so her toes dangled out over free fall. She had her back to the wall as she inched along, and she grasped the bolt-end of the rivets for purchase.

"Girl is crazy, what?" exclaimed the man who stared beside Arthur.

More men came rushing up behind them and stopped to stare as well. Someone drew a gun on Reiki, but the others stopped him.

"Are you nuts? Kill her, and she'll leave a traceable corpse. Doli will have our heads."

Below Reiki, the various fountains were still, and the pools were covered in canvas for the season. Stone monoliths arose under ground-based spotlights, looking like a field of spikes from their vantage point.

"There's our boys on the Conningway side," said someone. "We got 'er trapped now. She can't come down from there."

Reiki came to a metal jaguar welded into the trellis and climbed onto it so she was perched on its behind, hovering over the pit of spikes. Oblivious to the healthy amount of thigh she had on display, she looked back and forth in a clinical assessment of her position. Her eyes were lost to Arthur in the distance and poor lighting, but it felt like her gaze settled on him.

She mouthed three words at him.

I hate you.

Arthur had no training in lipreading, but those were the only words that made sense.

Reiki leapt from her perch after that. She spread her arms in a swan dive and splashed down in the waterworks, vanishing into a gap between the sheets of canvas. The water immediately froze, catching her splash in an unnatural point as tall as the stone monuments around it.

Awed, the men argued among themselves.

"Did you see that?"

"She's dead for sure."

"We gotta report this."

They dispersed, seemingly forgetting Arthur. When the last of the men had vanished down the fire escapes, he sat on the ledge to watch the Conningway Hotel porters arrive to chip at the ice. It did no good–the ice was too thick. They would have to wait until next thaw to find out if Reiki was under there.

But somehow, Arthur doubted it.

He looked at the starlit sky and wondered what had become of her.

CHAPTER 09

CALL GIRL

Arthur stood before the window, staring at the moon as Xandri sat on the bed behind him, playing her lap harp.

Gone. Reiki had fled from him and would never return.

Face it, Arthur. You've found a woman that your looks and fortune can't impress. You've played her, and she hates you for it.

Unfair. He needed someone to invent a time machine and fix this mess before he got himself this deep in.

Arthur turned to face Xandri.

The lamp light traced her slender arms, framing her fingers in gold as they rippled in a magical dance. She had her eyes closed, mind lost in song or perhaps in some other plane of existence.

After such a chaotic night, he found her playing very soothing.

Does Reiki play any instruments? Would she be impressed by my basic piano skills?

He regretted now giving up piano lessons so young. But the lure of other activities had been irresistible to a teenager with so many options before him. Falconry, equestrian jumping, hang-gliding... Arthur had them all under his belt.

Get over Reiki, already. There are more willing fish in the sea.

The music stopped. Arthur looked over to see Xandri watching him under a hooded gaze. Her fingers remained pressed against the strings in playing position, but her chin rested on the neck of the harp.

"You okay?" he asked.

"This is where most of my clients start negotiating what happens next."

Arthur sat on the bed and patted the other side.

"You've played long enough. Come lay down."

Xandri placed the harp back in its case beside the bed. She took her time closing the lid and fastening the clamps into place. She flicked off the lamp, and Arthur heard the scraping noise on the carpet as she pushed the harp to the side.

Job complete, Xandri sat back up and shuffled closer, with her back to him. She became a mound of fabric as she pulled her dress over her head, stripping down to a white shift more suitable as sleep-wear.

"Little Xandri requires help unlacing, sir."

Arthur leaned to his side and did the honours, tugging at the loops on the bindings for her corset. He was well-practised at that activity and unwound it in moments.

Xandri sighed in relief. "Oh, so nice to be able to breathe again."

The corset felt unusually heavy to Arthur. When he held it up to the moonlight, he noted iron rods sewn vertically through the lining.

This thing belongs in a dungeon, he thought.

They shuffled a bit as Xandri lay over Arthur's outstretched arm and rested her head on the other pillow.

Reiki's easily a fist taller than Xandri, noted Arthur with a tinge of sadness. Maybe Xandri could make use of the shoe if he never managed to slip it back on Reiki's foot.

He drew breath to ask about shoe sizes, but Xandri set a finger on his upper lip.

"You've talked about her for two hours already," said Xandri. "Let's talk about something else."

That reminded him that Reiki had studied peak oil theory. It wasn't exactly a secret, but the oil producers tended to be hush-hush about it. A commoner would have had to go out of their way in readings to randomly come across it, much less fully understand the numbers behind the projections.

Xandri had started a distracting squirming motion against his shoulder. Arthur got up and unrolled the top sheet to cover her, but she kept at it.

"Sorry," she said. "Xandri's breasts are very sore."

"Oh, okay. It's probably that torture device you were wearing," he said. He tossed the corset to the floor so they could hear the rattle of the iron rods. "You should probably go up a size or two on it."

Xandri reached across him, grabbed the top of his ear, and put her face up close to his.

"Ow!" yelled Arthur, for her fingernails bit deep into flesh. He tried to pull free, but Xandri's strong harpist's fingers offered no slack. "Ouch! What are you doing?"

"Are you calling me fat?"

"Ow! No, lemme go."

"Ahem?"

"Okay, you're beautiful, thin, and elegant. Now, let go of me."

She released him and set that clawed hand on top of his head. Arthur ran his fingertips over the offended ear, but felt no missing chunks.

"Here's the deal," said Xandri, ticking off fingers on her left hand that hovered close in Arthur's field of vision. "Traditional style is three gold, two more for the bum, and I don't take it in the mouth. Oh, and under no circumstance will I answer to the name Reiki."

"Ah, I can drop you off home if you like."

Xandri looked at Arthur as if he'd gone off the deep end.

"Oi, my guild will charge me an early cancellation fee if I'm back before dawn."

"Can't we just lie here and talk some more?" asked Arthur.

"Talk doesn't put sweet-corn on my table, buster."

"Okay, I'll pay you five to stay."

"Shades, you're crazy." Xandri squirmed over his hip a little. "And you're not even hard. You're not into boys, are you?"

"What? Of course not."

"Whatever. Just so you know, if my guild finds out nothing happened, I'm claiming impotence."

The morning found Arthur leaving his hotel to meet Eric standing beside the door of his car. A frost had set in overnight so that the ground made a crisp crunching sound under the soles of his shoes. It seemed to match his mood, for Arthur felt refreshed and ready to take on the day's meetings at the Academy.

"I take it that we'll be seeing the young missus to her guild on the way to the meetings," said Eric when Arthur reached him.

Arthur turned and glanced back to see Xandri standing within the hotel lobby. She was talking to an adolescent porter as she indicated the harp-case on the floor by her feet. She then pointed back inside, where Arthur assumed her other suitcases remained.

"Eric, how many suitcases did Xandri bring?"

"Four milord, counting the harp. Why do you ask?"

"I could swear it seemed like more when she vanished into the bathroom this morning for an hour."

"Perhaps they're multiplying?"

Arthur laughed. "Yes, I fear she was detained that hour culling the herd."

"There's a second porter on his way now carrying the rest," said Eric. He walked to the trunk to wait as Xandri emerged from the door, backwards so she could offer instructions to the porters.

The morning rush-hour traffic made its way past as Arthur waited. The six-lane road was a mishmash of horses, carriages, bicycles, and mopeds. There were five cars in sight apart from his. Four of them were smaller, more economical sedans, but one car, in the price-range of the Lansdale, was parked ahead of him with two young men in the front seat.

As the driver of the car had a glare fixed on Arthur through the rearview mirror, he paused to observe it closely.

The car was painted white, with arched fenders, and a curious third light on the back trunk that made the curled bumper look like an up-turned mouth. A little car, not much higher in status than a regular sedan, but pricey for its design. Arthur smirked. His car dwarfed that little crate.

The driver of the little white car broke the staring contest by climbing out. He slammed his door so hard that his unbuttoned jacket flapped about, revealing a holster for the archaic pistol he had strapped to his waist. The man who climbed out of the passenger side looked about the same age. Arthur guessed them to be in their low twenties.

"They're upset because my car is longer," whispered Arthur to Eric with a wink.

"Milord, if either of you unzip right now..." but Eric left the thought unfinished, as the pair had drawn within earshot.

Arthur held his ground and waited. From the corner of his eye, he spied Xandri approaching. The porters carried her luggage between them: one carried the harp and the other, the three carry-alls she had brought. Pity. With Xandri here, he would have to act civil.

The driver of the car gave Arthur a bow with one hand sweeping down so that a lock of his dark hair flapped over his eyes. Those strong sideburns he sported would be great with a black top hat. Perhaps Arthur could recommend him a haircut and a good haberdasher.

"A pleasant morning to you sir," said the young man, tossing that errant lock back into place with a flick of the head as he rose. "I heard that a gentleman such as yourself made my wife cry last night, and I've been looking all over town to find out if this story of villainy is true."

His wife? And here we have the answer to that empty chair beside Reiki.

"Much obliged," said Arthur, not bothering to deny the incident. Iliara had no doubt informed this man in the hopes that he would put Reiki out of Arthur's life. "May I ask who you might be?"

"Jude," said the man with another half-bow. "Jude Tavenern."

"Well-met. I'm Arthur–"

"Galenden, yes, I know. The breaker of hearts."

"And who might your stooge be?"

"Lucius," said the second man, who had placed himself in Xandri's path. "Now answer my man here, or I'll knock those perfect teeth out of your Gedanese face."

"I see," said Arthur. "Well, Mr Tavenern and Mr Lucius, I must admit I'm not certain I buy your claim of husband status with Reiki."

"What?" grumbled Jude, fists clenching.

"Not so fast, gentlemen," said Lucius. He extended an arm to block the porters from interceding.

Xandri stepped aside, a disinterested look written on her face. And Eric popped the trunk in the background, which Arthur thought was a wise idea.

"If you were her significant other, you might have found time to be by her side for the awards ceremony," said Arthur with a shrug. "She described it like the blackest day of her life. And she never once mentioned you. It seems what you see between her and yourself is a fairy tale."

Jude's face contorted into a mask of rage.

"Why you–"

"Sirs, sirs! Please, calm down," one of the porters moved to get around Lucius.

Lucius turned, snatched the harp-case from him and hurled it away.

The case carved a graceful arc as it sailed. It landed hard on the sidewalk and split open so that the delicate harp crashed pillar-first on the gravelly, grating sidewalk.

Xandri's mouth made a strange warbly shape—the first true expression Arthur could recall seeing from her.

Chaos erupted.

With a wail that matched the scream of the dying harp, Xandri launched herself after her instrument. The porters attempted to push past Lucius, who turned and grabbed both of them around the ribs to hold them back. Eric tossed Arthur his long-barrelled pistol from the trunk, and in one smooth motion, Arthur had it pointed for Jude's temple.

At the same time Jude drew his gun and trained it on Arthur's chest. They glared at each other but they were at an impasse.

"And now you would use violence to steal another man's woman," muttered Jude.

"As you would draw a gun to keep her. Why don't we ask Reiki what she thinks of that?"

They continued their staring match. Arthur noted Jude's steady firing arm. He had a good poker face. The type of person who would act blindly if called out on a bluff. Firearms were probably the choice duelling weapon in these parts, so he was versed in them.

"So what shall it be?" asked Arthur. "Will you fire on me in the middle of the street? Or will you crawl home, grow a chest hair, and dust off your sword?"

In the background, the grunts of the struggling porters

continued, and Xandri made a single "meep" sound, lying all curled up on the sidewalk with the harp in her arms.

Jude stared a moment longer before lifting the gun. Arthur matched motions with him.

"Lucius, let's burn a trail," said Jude. He backed off two steps, but kept an eye on Arthur.

"You don't wanna blast his head in?" asked Lucius as he gave the porters a final shove.

"Nah, I don't kill sissies," said Jude.

Arthur shrugged as he watched them leave. That parting shot wasn't even worth a rejoinder. Instead, he went to Xandri who looked to have gone catatonic. She blinked but once when Arthur touched her arm.

"Eric," he called. "Help me get her in the car. We need to find a master harpsmith if one exists in this demesne. No price is too high."

Xandri had suffered harm for his sake. Stars granting, Arthur would set things right.

CHAPTER 10

OUT OF OPTIONS

Reiki spent the night huddled beneath all her sheets and blankets.

It was a lucky break that few people knew the Conningway's waterworks connected to the city aqueducts. The escape, a soaking wet run home in freezing temperatures, had burned her psychic 'batteries' to almost null, leaving her groggy and exhausted.

But life fears kept sleep at bay. Reiki napped in fitful spurts and rose well before sunrise to shower. After rubbing petroleum jelly on the soles of her poor, bruised feet, Reiki washed every last bit of green from her hair. Such folly, that, trying to be something other than a redhead. She supposed it was because her hair could change texture, adapting to the colour she put in it. That made it almost a challenge to try every colour as often as possible.

Sadly, Reiki's freckles and skin complexion were a dead giveaway to her natural looks. Way back, when Kajo had changed her, he had given her this perfect body but omitted to fix skin blemishes.

"Should have asked him for perfect hair and teeth, too,"

Reiki muttered to herself as she stared at the bathroom mirror.

I like your tangly hair and crooked teeth as they are, Kajo would have said. Reiki knew this because he had said the same of her body in regret after the change. He would have changed her back if it were possible without killing her.

She emerged from the shower and combed out her hair as dawn prodded a finger of light through her bedroom window. Jude would laugh if he were here now. He'd remind Reiki that her hair would be back to its normal curls after a few hours despite all her efforts. Then she would throw the comb at his head, and they would laugh it off.

If only Jude was more empathic. If only he could be just like Arthur in temperament.

How can you say this? You've known Arthur for perhaps fifteen minutes.

An imperious Mister Kittles head-butted her shin, reminding Reiki that a hungry cat understood nothing of quiet-time. She walked to the living room.

No milk awaited her outside the door today. Usually the milkman delivered by sunrise, but perhaps he had been held up.

That meant dry bread crusts for Mister Kittles. Reiki knew he would make his displeasure known. All movable objects would be knocked off her shelves today. Experience with his rampages meant Reiki's breakables were stored on lower shelves.

"You better not be naughty today, Kittles," Reiki warned. "I have to get those accounts to authorities, and this place better not look like a tornado passed by while I was gone."

That was a good plan. Reiki could still recite the account numbers from memory. She would put them in the hands of someone she could trust. The captain of the guard, for example. Except he'd be at the war front just now. There would have to be someone.

At the moment, any action was better than none. It would only be a matter of time before they figured out her new hair colour and came after her.

Reiki picked out a black and white checkered dress and shoes she could run in, just in case she was spotted. She opted for a blue winter jacket with a large fur-lined hood.

Satisfied with her chances of passing unnoticed, Reiki set out for the Namika's fortress.

Not three blocks from her building, Reiki came across the milk van, which was pulled over in front of a small group of townsfolk. There seemed to be some argument between them and the milkman. Reiki slowed as she passed by to listen in.

"I promise you the depot's run clear out," the milkman was saying when Reiki drew within earshot.

"But you had some earlier. I saw you," said a man who wrung his scarf in his hands.

"Is there some sort of privileged list of who gets deliveries first?" asked someone else. "I wanna be on it."

"There's no list," said the milkman. "Milk runs out, it's out. When they solve the Graal problem, everything will return to normal."

Reiki paused to consider. Hillvale lacked the arable land and pastures needed to feed itself. She knew most grains and vegetables came from the southern lands of Süff along the access near Credd. Could it be that Graal was a major food-provider as well?

What else did Graal make? Perhaps she should stop by the market and stock up on non-perishables.

No, she was too late on that idea. On the way to the fortress, Reiki passed Market Street where a mob of angry people already clustered. By afternoon, pandemonium would encircle a city block.

"Not pretty," said Reiki as she passed by. A quick mental inventory told her that she had only three or four days' worth of food in her cupboards. Reiki would have to bus to the bottling plants near her parents' neighbourhood in the suburbs and buy as many canned goods as she could carry.

Her next steps took her by the post office, so Reiki popped inside to have her address unlisted. They might think to mail her something imprinted and use telepathy to follow the mailman to her apartment. Lord Välenus was powerful enough to force the post office to give up her address, but Reiki thought it unlikely he would want to expose himself that way. To foil any attempt at finding her, Reiki had all her mail forwarded to a post office box and left with the key.

The fortress turned out to be all ablaze in activity when Reiki reached it. Three guards, rifles in hand, barred entrance to the front doors against a loose scattering of townsfolk. Normally the guards kept the compound clear all the way to the front gate, but with most of army tied up in the war, Reiki could see how order might get lax at home.

Reiki bought herself a copy of a thick newspaper and found herself a bench across the street, facing the fortress, where she made herself comfortable. She sped-read the entire paper during the next fifteen minutes, allowing her mind to seize on the important concepts as it would. The first thing she learned was that the war was almost over. With the food situation worsening, Kajo, the Namika, was expected to return from the battle front and enact legislation to combat prices.

Everything else was rumours and speculation, but Reiki digested as much as she could. One thing came out clear: Kajo was on his way back home to a small parade of welcome. Reiki only needed to find a way to get him alone.

"Reiki!"

That was the last voice Reiki would have wished to hear. She turned to see Sanny, her secondary school friend, approaching.

To look at Sanny, it would be impossible to tell she was a commoner, for she carried the air and dress of high family. Her father was a loan officer, and he made a decent living from commissions, so she could afford the fancier things like a fully stocked wardrobe. Like her high family counterparts, Sanny still lived at home and proclaimed pursuing marriage to be her full-time job.

"Reiki. I just heard the news. What in the world are you doing?"

Ah shoot, she knows about that too.

"Hi, Sanny. Nice to see you."

Sanny came up to the bench and paused to lay down a handkerchief which she sat on. "Why would you go and break up with Jude? How many times do you think he'll wait around for you to make up your mind?"

"This was the last one, Sanny. I'm tired of the cycle."

Sanny rested her fur-lined gloves on Reiki's hands.

"Look. I'm your friend, so I'm going to level with you here. You're never going to do better than Jude, so you can give up looking, okay?"

"No, that's not it at all. He's just not right for me."

"Who's right, then? Harry, with his junk collection?"

"Oh, lud," said Reiki. During one of her breaks from Jude, for some reason, she'd thought to date a scrap metal recycler. A three-day fling she didn't care to remember.

"Your problem is you're waiting for some sort of magical love to fall in your lap," said Sanny. "Jude likes you. You like him. Do you need a flashing neon sign?"

"It's not a question of like. I just can't connect with him."

"All because he asked you to marry him at a stupid boxing match? Wake up, Reiki. It's not like you have a line up of suitors in the wings."

"Sanny, I–"

When Reiki raised her hands Sanny caught her at the wrists. "You're giving up a marriage a lot of women would give a kidney for. You're going to die alone if you walk away from this, Reiki. Is that what you want?"

It was too much for her. Reiki felt tears well up in her eyes. She tried to blink them back to no avail. Sanny handed her a spare handkerchief and put an arm around her shoulders.

"There, there. Now I want you to repeat after me. Ready?"

Reiki nodded.

"I, Reiki, hereby vow to go make up with Jude, and be happy for the rest of my life."

"Gleh," said Reiki, for her mind rebelled against the idea. Why not just stay single? Start the post-moon-flight career she would have had to start even if she had been chosen go up. Forget the social requirement for marriage; she'd sort that out after she got herself established.

Yet, she managed to nod, since Sanny was expecting an answer. While she dried her eyes, Reiki noticed her Academy classmate Ferra emerge from the front doors of the fortress.

Ferra thanked the guards and took the path for the street where Reiki sat. She wore white pants and a light blue jacket, as usual. It went well with her blonde hair cropped close to her scalp and her red scarf.

When Ferra reached the street, she crossed to Reiki's side and drew to a halt, watching them.

"Reiki. You've been crying. Is it about flunking out of the Academy?"

"What?" cried Sanny.

Reiki groaned inwardly. Now that Sanny knew, the news would spread to friends and family. Not quite the way she would have wanted them to find out.

Still, she could at least congratulate Ferra for making it.

"I heard them call your name, Ferra," said Reiki. "You're going to the moon. Shouldn't you be buried in studies?"

Ferra fixed a blue-eyed gaze on Reiki and shrugged. "No need. I learned already everything I need to know. You must study more. Your memory is very good, but you're not so smart, so studies must fill the difference."

"Yeah, I guess," said Reiki, unsure if Ferra was speaking as a matter fact or with intent to offend.

As propulsion expert, Ferra held the vital, yet thankless job of the Verifier, double-checking Mission Control's dirt-side calculations. In some ways, the role of the Verifier outranked the ship captain, since it would be Ferra's job to countermand an order that might jeopardize the flight.

Saddled with that much responsibility, Ferra could be forgiven a fair bit of brusqueness.

"I go now," said Ferra. "Early morning meeting for all Academy faculty tomorrow."

"Ok, Ferra. Thank you."

"Bye, Reiki."

They watched Ferra, with her brisk, long-legged stride, charge down the sidewalk.

Sanny turned back to face Reiki. "Well, she was a little bit rude. Why are you smiling?"

Reiki shrugged. Academy faculty meant a hundred fifty graduates plus professors, dirt-side engineers and more would need access to the fortress. No one would notice Reiki if she snuck in with them—she was technically still Academy, after all.

The thought brought an even bigger smile to her face. Ferra had given Reiki the keys to the fortress. By this time tomorrow, she'd have the entire problem of the ledger solved.

CHAPTER 11

THE END

Iliara Välenus was in her private suites with Doli Stanton when she heard the chimes that meant a guard needed her attention.

She expelled an exasperated breath. Booboo's talons still needed work, and she had only just gotten the falcon to settle enough for her to file them. She wondered if she might be able to ignore the guard long enough to make the interruption go away.

"I'll get that," said Doli, who sat in a high-backed leather easychair. She made to set down her needlework, but Iliara shook her head.

"I don't want Booboo getting antsy from people moving around. The guard will just have to wait."

Doli laughed. She had a deep-throated laugh that Iliara found annoying. As the daughter of a second, Doli really needed to practice a polite lady-like giggle. Same way she stubbornly refused to dye her hair and curl it. Black hair belonged to a peasant woman leading a donkey along a dirt path, not to someone of higher birth.

"Shush, you," said Iliara. "Your sniggering is upsetting Booboo."

"Good! I hope he bites you like Poopums."

Iliara grimaced at the reminder of her last falcon. She'd wrung its neck for that. That made her sad; she'd liked that one.

The chimes sounded again, and Booboo fidgeted a little. Iliara set down her file and turned for the door.

Doli followed her in a rustle of cloth since she was already dressed for court. Iliara was still in her morning wear–she preferred not to greet the day until noon. The sun could get way too bright in the mornings, and her perfect skin needed taking care of.

"Yes? What is it?" asked Iliara as she flung the door open to see a slothful man from among her paid-off loyalists. The guy was easily into his third decade, which made her grimace. She didn't like old people.

"Milady, there's ah... ahh..."

He glanced at her nightgown, flushed, and forced his eyes up. Iliara wondered if he was going to faint from glimpsing her partially undressed body.

"Speak, fellow. I'm a busy person."

She was about to slam the door in his face when he found his tongue.

"That green-haired woman you had the boys looking for two nights ago. We think she's here."

Iliara drew up in surprise and the guard quailed before her.

"What? Here?"

"You said her name was Reiki, right? She came in with the Academy students this morning."

"Are you sure?"

"We wouldn't have even noticed, but her classmate Ferra managed to get a message out."

"Mmm, I see," said Iliara. This Ferra thing was working out really nicely. Best to encourage strong bribe-susceptible relationships like that.

"Your orders, milady?"

A smile of happiness lit up Iliara's face.

[*** Seven Years Ago ***]

"I don't get this at all, Kajo."

Reiki bit her lower lip and set her hands on her hips.

The escarpment overlooked Hillvale, and behind her, Kajo sat cross-legged on the low barrier wall. He toyed with the brick she'd just thrown at him.

"Sticks and stones won't fix this lopsided relationship, Reiki."

She whirled to face him. "Lopsided? It wouldn't be like that if you'd allow your heart to feel for a change."

"We're thirteen-year-old kids. What would either of us know of feelings?"

"You're being ridiculous. Of course we understand love."

Kajo lowered his gaze. "This isn't love. It's dependency."

"Okay, fine! Call it dependency. Walk away from it. Never see me again. Would that make you happy?"

He had no response for that. By the way he avoided her gaze, Reiki knew she'd found a chink in his armour.

She pressed the advantage and gestured across the cityscape. "See all this? One day, this could be yours."

Kajo chuckled. "I have no plans to take over this city, Reiki —"

"It will," she insisted. "And I want to be by your side when it happens. Why are you pushing me away?"

He closed his eyes and lowered his head. "What I did to you... it wasn't right."

"It's not like you gave me your spleen."

"I changed you to fit a societal ideal. If you stay with me now it's because you think you owe me."

"Absolutely not. I dated you before the change and I'll date you after."

He sighed. "It's going to be many years before you'll understand."

The finality in his words crushed her. For a moment, Reiki could only put her back to him while she struggled to keep her composure. This was far from over. She hoped he knew that. One day she would prove herself to him. He would see her as a match if Reiki had any say in the matter.

She turned back to face him. "Well, if you're going to insist on this, I want one final kiss. This much, at least, you owe me."

"If I kiss you, I'll never have the strength to leave you. Here, take this."

Wind rushed past them, and the air grew heavy. A mist coalesced about Kajo's hand and formed into a heart made of water.

The heart floated over to her. Reiki set her hands about it and froze it. She clasped it to her chest as Kajo leapt from the wall.

"Come," he said. "I'll fly you home."

The heart had never melted. Reiki dug it out of her purse as she wandered the halls of the fortress. It had lived in her top drawer for the last seven years along with her other keepsakes. But now it would come in handy.

Reiki checked the rest of her inventory as she explored. Sneakers today, in case she had to run. A green dress, thick stockings, and a black, checkered coat made her look the perfect role of Academy grad. She still needed to replace her lost accessories, but she could do all that this afternoon after the ledger accounts were delivered to Kajo.

Several guards stopped her along the way, and Reiki had to repeat her story of being sent by her professor to attend legislature. Through the chaos of people coming and going, the harried guards ended up giving her directions to the balconies and managed to overlook her lack of a pass or certificate. Before long, she found the entrance she wanted.

Court was in session when Reiki stepped onto the balcony. Kajo sat on his throne, flanked by his Elika, and courtiers milled about to the sides. The men who occupied the middle of the floor looked like captured soldiers from the war front. Several prisoners stood there, hands cuffed in front of them, and surrounded in guards.

Oh, so that's why security was so lax around here. The guards are overwhelmed with the influx of prisoners.

It mattered little how many guards were around just now. This next part of Reiki's plan was going to be discreet.

She got the frozen heart out of her purse, slowly, so as not to draw the attention of the four people who shared the balcony with her. Reiki gripped it in both hands and broke it.

Kajo glanced up at the balcony right away. If he saw her,

he gave no indication, but it would be enough. Reiki only needed to hide in a washroom until court was over. Kajo's seventh sense would guide him to her.

She turned and left the balcony with a rough plan of locating the nearest washroom, but four guards blocked her path.

"Miss Reiki?" said the nearest guard. "You'll have to come with us."

Okay. Play it cool. They had probably figured out she wasn't here with the Academy. They would question her a little and kick her out. Even if they locked her up, Kajo would find her. Better she went with them quietly rather than cause a scene and draw unwanted attention.

Reiki was surprised when they indicated she should extend her arms for fancy brass-plated manacles. She considered an indignant protest, but settled for a passive approach as they clasped them about her wrists.

"I'm sorry if I broke some sort of law. I was a little lost and wanted to see what was going on."

"Save the speeches. Unless you enjoy being gagged."

Oh, this sounds serious. Reiki put up no further resistance, and walked between them to a steel lift.

They took her a few floors up and then along a hallway. The last door took them to some sort of reception hall, with an oak table that would seat ten. At the head of that table sat Iliara Välenus.

Iliara's hair had that fresh-out-of-the-shower look, and she had her arms flat on the table, self-styling as a high merchant guilder in casual dress. She had her mouth set in a humourless line that sent a shudder down Reiki's spine as the guards pressed her into the chair on the far end of the table.

The room had windows on one side and a stand-up divider on the other. Someone was hidden behind that screen. A telepath, no doubt. Waiting to draw any secrets he could from her public mind. Iliara would toss questions out and if Reiki so much as thought of the answers, they would have the secret of the ledger.

Iliara refrained from the expected questions, opting to place her elbows on the table and rest her chin on her hands.

A brief respite before the interrogation would begin. Reiki thought fast.

She could lock the memories away to a keyword like 'Kajo', but Iliara might think to say that. Anything else Reiki might think of could be drawn from her. The keyword would have to be something Iliara wouldn't know.

"What is your name?" asked Iliara.

"Reiki, milady." On the tail of that response, Reiki felt a heavy disorientation. She put her hands to her head as best she could in the manacles. They said telepathy felt like vertigo or déjà vu.

"You're not going to lie to me, are you?" asked Iliara. "That could have serious consequences."

"I don't understand, milady. Why am I here?" It was a stall tactic. She needed a moment with them playing defensive.

As the dizziness abated, she tossed all her memories into one lump and locked them away. Name, address, past relations, she dumped anything that could identify her or the ledger accounts out of her conscious mind and sealed it up tied to her transformation event. Kajo would know that one. He would bring it up when he found her.

There was no time for caution. Reiki was one question from dooming herself by thinking the wrong thing. She wrestled against the next wave of disorientation as she got the locks in place. Most fortunate timing, for her mind rebelled to the telepathic intrusion, and a wave of chaotic thoughts engulfed her.

CHAPTER 1

THE LETTER

Her name was Reiki–the scrunched up letter from the bottom of her purse told her so, though she wondered if there might not have been some mistake.

As she stood on the sidewalk in the frigid winter air, one of hundreds of spectators to the final preparations for a parade, Reiki found she had several questions that she was unable to answer. Questions such as who was she? And where was she? And who in the world had torn up this letter and left it for her?

She searched her purse one more time. No ID to be found. Three gold coins to her name. A retractable resinboard cutter, protractor and a single makeup brush. Only these items in what was a handbag that looked like it might hold much more.

"I've been hit over the head and robbed," she surmised. She had no idea how she'd even come to be here. Everything until a few moments ago was a blank.

The banners rising in the street fluttered, their beautiful reds, golds, and blues, proclaiming victory in some place known as Graal. That meant the other flags proclaiming peace were talking about here. Hillvale. Her home? Or another land.

The energy of the crowd quickened Reiki's pulse. She was unsure how, but she felt it, tangible, like heatwaves shimmering over a radiator. Twirling like a weathervane in a windstorm. It was both awesome and terrifying at the same time.

Reiki uncurled the letter and read it one more time, hoping it bore some clue she had missed the previous times.

> Dear Miss Reiki.
>
> We regret to inform...
> to our program cannot...
> not meet all of our...
>
> In much...

Her own address was gone. Torn off on the other half, wherever that was. This made Reiki sad because she might have been able to at least follow that address to her home. The rest of the clues to her life were probably there if she could only find it.

"Excuse me sir," said Reiki, accosting the stranger beside her who also watched the parade. "Can you tell me where I am?"

He looked at her as if she had gone off the deep end.

"Lady, I don't have any coin to spare."

"No, it's not that at all—"

The man twisted away from her and left in a hurry. Reiki sighed. How, by all the stars, was she going to get help?

A quick glance about the crowd told Reiki that few

were paying her any heed. One man, a block away, had an unpleasant glare for her. She must have run afoul of him in the past or something. With his shoulders set just so, and his hands buried in the pockets of his overcoat, he looked like he was very upset.

Definitely not the person to talk to if she could help it.

Reiki made her way the opposite direction, weaving through the clusters of people. She skidded a little on a sloped part of the pavement and glanced at her feet. Sneakers, stockings and a conservative green dress. Was she a student or something?

She glanced behind and saw that the man happened to be travelling the same direction and pace as her.

Yeah. Not likely. I'm being followed.

Reiki turned at the first corner she came to, taking her away from the crowds and onto a business district. It was there that she found tall store windows in which she could see her reflection.

Shades! She looked a mess. Mascara running off the edges of her eyes, foundation wearing out to expose a mixed complexion. A forest of red hair raged on her scalp, all frothing and untamed. It was a wonder farmers weren't trying to shear it to make wool.

The body underneath all that made her blink in surprise. Maybe she was a model or an exotic dancer or something. That would explain the makeup brush she carried.

The face of the man following her loomed in the reflection, and Reiki realized she needed to move on. She forged ahead, down the lonely street, leaving the joyous shouts of the parade behind her. As the raised curbs were too narrow to travel on, she walked on the road portion, listening to the grit of sand-filled slush on the flagstone surface.

The man ambled along after her. Taking a side road away from the crowds may have been a bad decision. Reiki bit her lower lip in frustration, but she carried on.

The intersection ahead opened onto a four-lane street packed with traffic. Reiki could face the man there if she had to. Preferably within shouting distance of a guard. In fact, facing him might be a great idea if he knew her. She only needed to find a way to do that safely.

A bus was stopped at the intersection when Reiki arrived. She watched people disembark and considered boarding it before remembering that she had no idea where the bus would take her.

What Reiki really needed was a warren. That is, if there was a medicine they could prescribe for memory-loss. *Take three of these with a glass of water and you'll magically remember who you are.* Ah, would that be perfect.

The man following her stopped at the intersection to the side-road, where he glared with narrowed eyes. When Reiki glanced at him, she caught a furtive motion of his hand. The glint of some metal object flashed at her. She hoped that wasn't a knife she had just seen. Best not to find out here.

A guard's office stood on a rise in the roadway ahead. Reiki picked that direction and walked off, trying not to stand out too much by looking panicked. She was mostly ignored by the pedestrians, though some offered her little smiles. No one seemed to recognize her, unfortunately. Except a man she came across standing beside a fancy car.

The car was parked by a music store, and the man who stood near the passenger door was dressed like a high family chauffeur. He watched Reiki casually, but she saw the look of recognition in his eyes.

Finally someone who knows me. And not a moment too soon, for the man following her had closed the distance too much for her liking.

"Hello," said Reiki, as she came to a halt before the chauffeur. "I believe we've met."

"We have, milady," said the chauffeur. He tipped his hat with a smile. "The name was Eric. You gave me directions a few days ago."

"Perhaps you could return the favour by pointing me to a warren, then?" she asked.

"Reiki!"

The voice behind her belonged to a man carrying a harp case in both hands. He had sandy brown hair trimmed just above the ears, combed with delicate precision. The sleeves of his black jacket were tapered wide at the ends with stylistic ribbons sewn around the buttons. And he wore a thin red tie under a straight collar.

The look in his eyes was a mixture of hope and relief. Perhaps a bit of longing, though that part made Reiki's knees feel rubbery. How in star's name did she know a high family man this hot?

"Hi."

It was all Reiki could think to say. Did this man have time to stop and help her? How would she ask?

The man walked past her and joined Eric who had gone to the trunk and now flipped through the keys on a heavy ring. He turned a smile on Reiki that made her already rubbery knees shake. That she didn't collapse right there on the sidewalk was only by conscious effort.

"Hold on. Let me put this thing down," he said. Once Eric got the trunk open, the high family man set the harp inside. When he arose, he held a smaller, flat package wrapped in coloured paper that he brought to her. "This is the gift I tried to send you. I'm so sorry it caused so much confusion between us."

"Why, thank you," said Reiki, accepting it.

The tiny card tied to the package said "To Reiki, from Arthur Galenden."

Oh, so that was his name. An important clue.

"Perhaps I could offer you a lift," said Arthur.

"Yes, please. I would like that."

"Great! Then, please, step inside."

Reiki climbed in through the door he held for her. The inside of the car smelled newish and sported facing seats. She chose to sit facing forwards, looking at the wall that separated the driver from the rear cabin.

The artifacts of the car were a fascinating curiosity. A book called *The Tale of the Sinister Storm*, lay on the floor beside her feet. Also on the floor were a leather pouch for binoculars and a pair of new galoshes. A hump in the centre of the cabin held an octagonal plane of varnished wood that formed a table. Cool air oozed out from under the table. An enclosed space, perhaps? Maybe wine chilling in a bed of ice.

"Don't mind the clutter," said Arthur as he climbed in to sit beside her. "And thanks for accepting the ride. That man at the flower shop was giving me the creeps."

Reiki followed his gaze to see the man who had followed her. He studied a street-stand of flowers as if planning a purchase, but the way his gaze flicked from the flowers to the car told her he was still watching.

"Probably one of Iliara's goons," said Arthur. "That woman's got a mean-streak to her, and I don't want her trying to hurt you."

Reiki wondered why anyone would want to hurt her, and why Arthur might be sending her such an unusual object as the gift she held. But most important of all, it meant he knew her address.

"Would you be able to drop me off at home, kind sir?"

"I don't know where you live. Hence the trouble with the gift."

"Ah," said Reiki. "Sadly, I don't remember either."

"What, did you hit your head? There aren't any bumps or bruises that I can see."

Arthur raised a hand as if to touch her scalp, but seemed to rethink the idea. Reiki wistfully pictured him running his hand through her hair. To tame the thought, she set her hand against the back of her head.

"Doesn't feel like I have any bumps. But I really don't remember." Reiki lowered her hand and unzipped her purse. "And see, I think I've been robbed. My ID has been stolen. I'm sure I must have had a library card in here. All I have is this resinboard cutter—"

"Whoa," said Arthur. He shuffled away and covered his tie with his hands. He expelled a sigh of relief when she placed it back in her purse. "Well, I know you live in downtown south. We'll drive you around there on the way to a warren and see if anything jogs your memory, okay?"

"Sure! That would be fantastic."

"To downtown south, Eric," said Arthur.

Up ahead, through a little window, Eric tipped his cap and started the car.

They rode in awkward silence for a few minutes while Arthur tried to puzzle out the woman sitting beside him.

Her hair was light red today instead of the green he remembered, but she was just as stunning as before. Really, it was the sparkle in her eyes that made her face beautiful—the way she seemed to drink in her surroundings, as if life itself was a potlatch dinner of sights.

She had worn pink lipstick, though it was starting to fade. Freckles were starting to show under her foundation. Pretty with or without makeup. Well, cute at the very least. But she needed to tend to the mascara at the edges.

Those saucer-like brown eyes flicked at him nervously, and Arthur smiled to reassure her. How she had gone from that finicky schoolgirl in the Atrium to this becoming woman he had no idea, but he wasn't about to start questioning it.

"If you don't remember where you live after the visit to the warren, I'll drop you off at the Academy," said Arthur.

"Where?" she asked, lips bunching into a small, worried pout.

"The Academy of the Stars. You were a student there."

"Oh. I wonder what I studied."

"Math, I'm sure. Other sciences from the sound of it."

"Oh, okay," said Reiki. "I do have a lot of numbers in my head. I wish one of them was my address."

She held up a hand, stared at her wrist, then let her gaze wander over her attire. Green dress with lighter diamond prints bursting out from the hip. Half student, half-fashionista. The wardrobe was as much a mystery as the woman underneath it.

He decided to comment on it.

"You look positively incredible, Reiki."

"You're too kind, Mister Galenden."

"Call me Arthur, please."

"Thank you, Arthur."

She didn't quite manage to say his name the way Xandri could do it, but the look in her eyes was far more open and honest. Welcoming, almost. Arthur was willing to bet if he leaned over and kissed her right then, she would offer no resistance.

What has happened to her? Is this even the same person?

The Lansdale rolled to a stop before the warren.

Reiki hesitated, and Eric misinterpreted it as a sign to get out and open her door. Jolted into action, she finally climbed out. Arthur followed and gestured to the row of glass doors facing them.

She placed her hand through the crook of his arm, and they entered the warren together. Her hands were freezing, and her steps were hesitant. Arthur couldn't blame her. Warrens usually gave people the creeps.

It was something about the ceilings which were too low and ribbed like the inside of a giant mouth. Or the over-clean scent of the air. Never mind that the walls were eggshell white, and the lighting, a very soft glow from gelatinous bulbs affixed to the ceiling.

They were in a waiting room that contained a reception desk and a bio in green scrubs and cap. The man was seated in the chairs where Arthur would expect patients to be.

"Are you guys open?" he asked. "This is Reiki, and she needs urgent attention."

"Reiki, come," said the bio. When she sat on the chair beside him, he unlooped his stethoscope from his neck and pressed it into the crook of her elbow.

Arthur looked around while the biopath worked. From inside, the warren looked like they did back home. He knew warrens were grown somehow, so perhaps they all shared some common blueprint.

The bio frowned in concentration. "You are in excellent health, young lady. Why are you here?"

"I've lost my memories," said Reiki. "I think I have amnesia."

The bio pressed his fingertips to Reiki's temples while Arthur looked on. Biopaths like this one were low-rated telepaths whose powers lay in speaking to bodies rather than minds. If there was anything wrong with Reiki, a biopath would find it. Curing it would be a whole other problem.

"There is no sign of brain trauma. If anything, your brain is much more vibrant than the average person your age."

Reiki protested. "But my memories—"

"Are intact. There's no sign of telepathic blocks. Any amnesia you suffer, it's purely psychological. With no injury, I can do nothing for you." The bio looped his stethoscope back over his neck and reclined in his chair, leaving little room for doubt that the session was over. "No fee. I give you a clean bill of health."

He would speak to them no more after that. Arthur's only choice was to guide a distraught Reiki back to the Lansdale.

CHAPTER 2

INTRODUCING REIKI

Reiki burst into tears the moment Arthur got her back in the car. She buried her face in her hands, doubled over, and wept quietly.

Arthur sidled over to the middle and rubbed her back as she cried. When he tried to draw her to him, she resisted, so there they sat for several long minutes.

What are you thinking, Reiki? Frustration at not having answers? Fighting off inner demons? Arthur doubted even she knew right now.

He handed her the lens cleaning cloth from his binoculars, and Reiki blew her nose into it.

"Thank you." Reiki sniffed and dabbed at her eyes with the cloth.

"Keep an eye out for neighbourhoods you recognize," said Arthur. He gave Eric the signal to go. Having something tangible to do would keep Reiki's mind off the situation.

Reiki gave a nod of assent and wiped her eyes one final time with her sleeve before offering him a glimmer of a smile.

"Sorry about that," she said. "I guess this is really hitting me hard."

"I understand perfectly. What are your earliest memories?"

"The street where you found me. I was supposed to be doing something important."

"Don't panic. It'll come back in a moment."

"I hope so."

They drove through the city, watching the various neighbourhoods roll by. Though they crisscrossed the entire downtown core, Reiki had no clues to offer them about her past. Finally, Arthur had Eric take them around the border between the suburbs and downtown Hillvale in the hopes that something would jog a memory.

"Stars! I don't recognize this area at all. It's like this entire city is a vaguely familiar place I might have once visited," said Reiki. She stared out the opposite window and clenched a fold of her dress in her right hand.

The left hand went to her face to rub at an eye. Arthur set a hand over her right hand and found it tense. What could have happened to her to put her in such a state?

"Reiki," he said.

"I'm sorry, Mr— Arthur," she said, refusing to tear her gaze from the opposite window.

"Reiki, look at me."

He reached across to set a finger on her chin and turn her head. Ah, those eyes were red, tear-filled, and tortured. Arthur supposed he would be frustrated too if he couldn't remember where he lived.

"I'm here, Reiki. You're safe."

That had the opposite effect from what he'd intended, and a single tear rolled down from her eye.

The Lansdale rolled to a gentle stop at a suburban intersection. Rows of two-storey townhouses, stone steps, and tiny lawns greeted them. Children played and ran about when traffic allowed. The last of the evening sun gave the sky an orange hue.

Reiki trembled and shed a second tear. She was fighting it hard, Arthur knew. As for calming her down, he was uncertain what to say.

He moved his finger from her chin to the base of her jaw just under her ear. Reiki closed her eyes and tilted her head, mouth closing into kissing position. Arthur leaned into it, but a rap at the window interrupted him.

"I'm sorry, milord," said Eric, when Arthur rolled down the window. "We seem to have a flat tire."

Arthur sighed and looked at Reiki. She had retreated to her side of the car, where she wiped at her cheek with a sleeve. She gave him a fleeting smile, looking as if a sudden well of bravado had banished her tears.

"I'll be right back," said Arthur. He climbed out of the car and followed Eric to the front.

"Eric, this tire isn't flat at all," said Arthur, for the front tire showed no signs of damage. Even if it did, they had two spares. One was strapped inside the trunk and another affixed to the back.

"Milord, you know I worked twenty years for your father. He and I grew up together. We were practically brothers."

Arthur tilted his head in puzzlement. "I know this, Eric. Why?"

"You trust me, right?"

"What is this about, Eric?" Arthur put his arm across Eric's shoulders. "Of course, I trust you. You're not just staff. You're family."

"Then, I must implore you not to kiss this woman," said Eric.

Arthur laughed and walked him away from the Lansdale.

"Oh, Eric I was only–"

Eric stopped them and grabbed Arthur's free arm by the sleeve. "I know what you were doing and I insist you must not."

"Ah, but Eric–"

"She's obviously out of sorts. You know she despised you a few days ago, and suddenly she's forgotten this? If you kiss her now, we both know what will happen. This would be abuse of the highest level."

"Oh, Eric–"

"Promise me," said Eric, shaking him. Arthur had never seen Eric so wound up about anything before. "I've never asked for much and I'll be by your side until the stars fall, but only this once, promise me you won't touch her until she's better."

"Oh, I see. She reminds you of..."

Arthur trailed off. The name Carrah was a taboo word between them. Eric still visited her grave every year.

Eric gave Arthur a glassy-eyed, pleading look. "Please, milord. Not while she's in this state."

What choice had Arthur but to offer something to such a dear family friend?

"Okay, tell you what. I won't go near her. Unless she goes head over heels and tells me she loves me, I won't touch her. You have my word of honour. Now what's gotten into you?"

Eric released him and seemed to deflate in relief. "Just preventing you from making the worst mistake of your life."

"We'll swing by the Academy. Her fellow students will recognize her and tell us where she lives. She must have at least one friend there." Arthur watched Eric's brows knit in consideration of that idea. "I can keep my hands off her that long, don't worry."

"It's no longer for that I'm worried," said Eric. "But I can think of no better plan."

"Then, let's have at it."

Reiki smiled at Arthur as he climbed back inside. That there had been no tire-change was obvious; he wouldn't try to hide it from her.

"Sorry about that," said Arthur.

"It's no problem," said Reiki, offering her smile to cover what Arthur could guess was a bad case of the nerves. "Gave me time to think."

"Us, too. Maybe we'll take you to the Academy. Your colleagues can help you better than we could hope to."

"Yes. That would be great. Thank you."

During the ride back to downtown Hillvale, they stayed glued to opposite sides of the seating as if some invisible barrier threatened to electrocute either party that crossed it.

Arthur wracked his brain to come up with small talk to keep her mind off the situation. He couldn't even offer a comment about the weather if she couldn't remember how warm it was yesterday. It was Reiki who surprised him by asking the obvious.

"So, what brings you to Hillvale, Arthur?"

"Me? Oh, I heard about the tenders the Academy had out and decided to make some bids on the moon-project."

"On the open tenders?"

"Yep. All they have is an empty field and a rocket. They still need support services like meals and housing for the eight hundred people who will staff Mission Control."

"Yes. It takes a lot of people to launch a rocket."

Her statement gave Arthur some hope. At least, she remembered her occupation.

"That's the Academy coming up now," said Reiki. She turned to look out the window. "I see Eric's taking us up to the main hall."

The dome-roofed building that formed the main-stay of the Academy was buried under a forest of radio antennas. White pillars supported an overhang above the front stairs, upon which almost fifty people moved.

Arthur took the students in with a wave of his hand. "One of them is bound to know you. Just walk around in the foyer a few times and wait for the magic to happen."

"Such clever thinking," said Reiki. She looked deep into his eyes.

Four seconds crawled by and they said nothing. To Arthur, it felt like four hours.

"Guess I should be going, then," said Reiki.

Her hand twitched, and Arthur considered taking it up for a good-bye kiss. He stopped to consider how practised he was at that. Allow the hands to linger in contact after the kiss just right. Throw in a suggestive look to the eye, and his dates usually melted on the spot. A shame to let this opportunity pass. But a promise was a promise.

Eric stood a discreet distance away, so Arthur gave him the hand signal to open the door for Reiki.

"Bye, Arthur," said Reiki.

"Bye."

Shades! This was the longest good-bye in recorded history.

Reiki climbed out of the Lansdale and thanked Eric. She slung her purse over her shoulder, picked up the gift that was still wrapped, and turned to give Arthur a little ripple of the fingertips.

He waved back, though she had already started off and had her back turned. Arthur slid over and climbed out her door, where Eric stood leaning on the window frame.

"Did she see someone she remembered?" asked Eric.

"No. I told her to walk back and forth until someone recognizes her."

"What?" cried Eric. "That's a terrible plan."

"It seems logical to me."

"She shouldn't be wandering around in the hopes of getting recognized. What if she runs into Iliara's people?"

"Hmm. When you put it that way..."

Reiki drew to a stop at the base of the stairs. At the top, between a pillar and a tilted bronze domino, stood a thin blonde woman in white pants and a red scarf.

"Stars and shades, but if looks could kill..." muttered Arthur, for the blonde had a glare fixed on Reiki that gave him goose-bumps. "She would have to be a part of the goon-squad."

"Call her back," said Eric. "We can't dump her here."

"I'm afraid you're right, Eric. Let's get her away from this place."

"Well spoken, milord." And with that, Eric tipped his cap and climbed back into the driver's seat of the Lansdale.

"Reiki," called Arthur.

With a look of infinite relief, Reiki turned and walked back to him. Arthur found himself admiring the sway of her hips as she walked, how her hair flipped about. He almost wished the walk were much longer.

"Yes?" Reiki, drew up. The haunted look to her wide eyes spoke the rest of her sentence: *Please, get me out of here.*

Your wish is my command, Reiki.

"Maybe you should come back to the hotel with me. I have a floor rented, and there's lots of room for you. In the morning you might feel better."

"Thank you, Arthur. I appreciate your generosity."

Arthur held the door and helped her inside.

"This will be your room." Arthur ushered her into the hotel room and flicked on the lights.

Reiki looked about. The double-bed with its wooden trim took up most of the room, underneath a counterpane that matched green, paisley-patterned curtains. The writing desk shoved into the corner looked incongruous; Reiki guessed it had been stored here from some other room. It even had a hole for inkwells, from back when students used to write with fountain pens.

"What do you think?" asked Arthur.

This room is a fashion apocalypse, but at least it's dry and safe. Reiki whirled about to face him and smiled. "I love it. Thank you so much."

She gave him an ultra-formal curtsy where a hug would have been much more descriptive. But he had been so physically distant during the car ride here that Reiki knew he wanted space.

"I'll leave you to get settled. I have some affairs to take care of."

Arthur parted on that pronouncement, though Reiki felt his eyes on her until the door had fully closed.

She kicked off her shoes and explored the room further. A door at the side led to a small washroom of high-family style, with a standup basin and urinal. Baths were probably located in some other room on this floor. She would have to ask about that.

There was a tall mirror attached to the wall above the washbasin. Reiki entered the washroom, twisted the knob on the wall-mounted light and gazed at her reflection in detail the store-window had been unable to provide.

Stars! What striking lipstick. She looked like some kind of hired escort. And... freckles, right to her collarbone. Could this get any worse?

On a whim, Reiki grabbed up the hem of her dress and rolled it up.

Red frilly panties with lace sewn in the sides? How embarrassing. I hope no one saw those!

That made Reiki wonder if she had ever had sex. Which led her to wondering if she should go look for a hand-mirror.

"Milady?" A voice from the main room surprised her.

Reiki peeked around the door of the washroom and found a hotel maid leaning in the front door. She held a

123

bundle of clothes under one arm and pulled a wheeled cart behind her.

"Ah, there you are, milady. Mr Galenden asked me to bring you a change of clothes and some tea. If I may?"

"Yes, please come in," said Reiki.

The cart was draped in a white cloth, and a silver tea pot was perched on top. Dainty teacups for four and little covered bowls formed a spoke-shape around it.

"Women's bathroom is downstairs from here. Tell the liftman where you need to be and he will know. My office is on this floor by the elevator. If I'm not in it, I should be along promptly," said the maid. She spread the clothing on the bed with one hand. "Would there be anything else at this time, milady?"

"Thank you, no," said Reiki.

"Heavens watch over you, then."

The maid slipped out the door.

Reiki went to the tea tray and picked up the lid of the largest bowl. Crackers the size of her pinky finger. Perfect—she was starving.

She ate five crackers, each slathered high in butter, almost without tasting them. Then, she made herself stop and settled on tea.

What do I take in my tea?

Reiki didn't know, of course, but she was certain that she had been about to reach for the sugar. Black tea, then, with two spoons of sugar. She would rediscover her tastes one meal at a time.

Ah, but what to do, what to do?

Her family must be in this city somewhere, worried sick about her. How would she contact them?

Reiki rose from the edge of the bed and walked to the window. She peered at the city lights through the crack in the curtains, all while wishing for some magical insight as to where she should go.

As no such inspiration came, Reiki's mind turned about, feeling much like an engine where the gears of the transmission had worn too smooth to catch.

She could go to the central library, for one. The archivists there might be able to connect her name to an address, provided there were a limited number of people with the same name living in town.

If that failed, she could try the local secondary schools. A teacher was bound to recognize her, and there could only be so many schools in this region. Failing even that, Reiki could revisit the Academy. Preferably at a time when the evil blonde woman was absent.

That's a good plan, she thought. *In the morning I'll hunt down my previous life and try to start remembering.*

Reiki left the window and walked back to the bed where the change of clothes awaited. One dress in denim-blue, a pair of thigh-high stockings with the ankles sewn-in, and a shift for sleeping.

"Okay. A bath, then sleep. Things won't look so hopeless in the morning."

CHAPTER 3

INTRODUCING ARTHUR

After seeing Reiki to her room, Arthur hurried to his suites, servants forming a buzzing cloud about him.

"Thank you, Yolanda," he said to the maid-servant who collected his gloves from a haphazard throw to the nearest sofa. And to the pageboy who rushed ahead to open his door for him, he smiled. "And you're looking dapper this evening, Vincent."

Once inside his quarters, Arthur shrugged his jacket onto the bed and made for the washroom to splash cold water on his face. He shuddered. Not nearly cold enough to wipe away the memory of Reiki looking so lost and vulnerable in that hotel room he'd dumped her in. Reiki, whom he longed to take up in his arms and kiss with all the violence of a struck match. The unusual commoner woman who faced the greatest ordeal of her life, yet still had the courage to smile and try to look relaxed.

Stop thinking about her. Remember your promise.

Such an ill-advised oath he had sworn. Had Arthur been

a bit more careful in the wording of that promise, he could go back to Reiki right now, pick her up, and carry her to the bed, where they would–

He splashed more water in his face, then slapped himself. That did the trick. She was back to the periphery of his thoughts. And his face stung.

"Milord?" asked Vincent from the main room of Arthur's suites.

"No worries, my man," said Arthur. "Just getting to a new mental state."

In about three years, the boy would probably start filling out that maroon long-coat he wore, with its silvery cuffs and button-lining. Then, he'd understand what Arthur was going through.

"The others await your presence in the study, milord."

"Ah, yes. I will join them."

Arthur strode back into the main room and found Vincent waiting there, holding a clean jacket for him to slip into. When he took the jacket, Vincent trotted out ahead of him. Arthur remained a moment to slide it on and sweep his hair into order with a hand.

Satisfied with his look, Arthur left the room and followed the pageboy.

Eric awaited him in the study, standing by the window, facing the street where the Lansdale would be parked. The furniture was mostly single-seat, high-backed easychairs whose white upholstery felt soft and feathery. Seated in one of those six chairs, facing a long centre-table, and with a teacup in his hand, was Mallen, the Galenden accountant.

In the chair across from Mallen, Arthur saw Niobus, his chief of staff.

Vincent held the door for Arthur as he walked into the room. He inclined his head to Yolanda who had just poured a tea for him at the head of the table. By the time he managed to sit down, she had added the sugar cube and cream. She swished out the door in a flurry of skirts.

"Sorry to have kept you waiting, gentlemen," said Arthur. "Just finished ratifying the deal with David McKnight. Was held up on the way back by a personal matter."

"The contract..." Mallen paused to raise his teacup to his lips. "They agreed without modification?"

"No last-minute haggling about the price at all," said Arthur. "Twenty-five thousand in trade for our services at the launch site, taking care of the sceptic systems. They've brought on another guild to handle the bathroom facilities. We'll only need to deal with what comes out of them."

"I see." Mallen glanced at the notebook that rested closed on the table before him. "The specs for their on-board water scrubbers. Do they really want us to try to build that?"

"Indeed," said Arthur. "An excellent haul, I'd say."

"Pah," said Niobus. He scrunched his dark Wyvernese features into a look of suspicion and shifted for comfort in his heavy boots, knocking his sabre over in the process. After he had retrieved it and set it back to rest against the arm of the chair, he continued. "Why do they only want two scrubbers? I'd think three should be necessary. This risk they're taking, it's enormous."

"No spare room in the weight-allowance for a third scrubber," said Eric. He turned from the window with a glass of brandy in his hand. "If the Lansdale only needs two spare tires, a rocket only needs two scrubbers."

"Another guild got the water reclamation systems project, so we only need to concentrate on removing the impurities from it," said Arthur. "We'll build their carbon-filters, and the toughest, meanest catalytic oxidation reactors we can to scrub out what the filters miss."

They remained an hour talking about the reactors, and how they were going to procure parts for them. During that time, Yolanda refreshed tea once and tried fruitlessly to coax them into a dinner break. It was on her second attempt that Arthur asked after Reiki.

"She's supping in her room, milord. 'Tis what most people do at this hour."

Yolanda set her hands on her hips in the way she often did when she meant to show annoyance. It made Arthur smirk. If they delayed much longer, Yolanda would force dinner plates into their hands and storm off in a huff.

"Good, good. We'll be along for dinner right after this meeting."

Arthur's statement provoked a long-suffering sigh and a flick of a long black ponytail before Yolanda whirled for the door.

She was passed there by a courier whom Vincent had just admitted.

Guild couriers like this one always had a ribbon of message tubes tied over their shoulder. The emblem of an opening door on his shoulder marked him for the job just as much as the wire-shaped pants and the visored cap he wore.

"Message for Arthur Galenden," said the courier, who passed Yolanda as if she didn't exist.

"I am he." Arthur rose to his feet.

He accepted the proffered wooden message tube and uncorked it to draw the single page out. Meanwhile, the courier assumed a power stance with his feet apart and his hands cupped before him.

"Your mother?" asked Mallen.

"Unsurprisingly, yes," said Arthur. "Grave news indeed."

Arthur passed the message and tube to Mallen, who unrolled it and read.

"To my dearest Arthur. I write to you with urgent news that our Ossington-site is drawing an unusual amount of gas as it pumps. It is likely that the well will dry up and need to be tapped elsewhere. There is the remote possibility that our reservoir contains a limited portion of the total supply of oil. You must return at once and see after this."

"That's absurd," said Niobus. "Prospectors told us those wells would run for years."

"If the Ossington well dries up, that's a third of our regular income gone," said Arthur. "We'll have to get this double-checked by an outside hydrokinetic to be sure."

"I will tell your mother you're on your way," said Mallen.

"Yes. My business in Hillvale is concluded. I'll set out first thing tomorrow."

Mallen drew a pen and folded parchment from his inner jacket pocket. Arthur watched him draw up a response and signed it when complete. Mallen rolled it up and slid it back into the message tube.

"Thank you," said Arthur to the courier as he handed over the tube.

The courier accepted it, bowed, and strode from the room in heavy, hurried steps.

They were silent a moment before Niobus and Mallen started arguing about the possibility of losing one of the wells. Instead of sitting back down, Arthur went to join Eric at the window.

"You've been mostly silent, Eric. Is that brandy getting to you?"

"It's Reiki that's on my mind. If you set out for Ged, what will become of her?"

"I don't really know," said Arthur. "I'd most likely leave her with a month's worth of hotel room rental. That should be enough time for her to get back on her feet."

"I suppose."

Arthur drummed his fingers on the window sill as he watched the pedestrian traffic in front of the hotel. He wondered how Reiki would fare after he left. Iliara's goons were obviously on the lookout for her.

"You'll tell her tonight?" asked Eric. "That you have to leave?"

"No, let her have one good night of sleep. Stars know it might be the last she gets. Shades! I really think... No, I shouldn't."

Eric peered at Arthur in confusion. "Milord?"

"You're still on your first brandy? Are you good to drive?"

"I am. Where to?"

"There's one more person I need to visit."

Half an hour later, Arthur knocked the door of an apartment in a high rise in downtown-west.

It was a long wait before the door cracked open, and Xandri's head popped into view. She took one look at Arthur and tried to slam the door, but he got the toe of his shoe in the way.

"We need to talk," said Arthur.

"How'd you know my apartment number? Did you have me followed?"

"Please, Xandri. It's important."

She relented and allowed him inside.

Xandri's apartment had wooden floors that felt a little sandy under Arthur's feet. The front hall was a forest of jackets, coats, and shoes, all different colours and styles, many of them fur. What mats they crossed were askew. Arthur fought the urge to bend down and align them.

With her hair back to light brown and all bunched up from sleep, Xandri looked younger than Arthur had first realized. He estimated her age to be eighteen: six years younger than he'd first thought.

Xandri took Arthur to her living room which was a cluster of furniture and trinkets. She had a glass table down the middle of it, which was covered in ashtrays and half-filled coffee mugs. Cushions and decorative dolls occupied every inch of seating except for one spot near the waist-high radio. That would be her spot, then. However, Xandri passed on it and went to lean against the mantel.

Arthur looked about for a place to sit. Finding none, he gave up and opted to stand. Xandri lit a cigarette from a metal case and puffed at it three times in rapid succession. She had a butane lighter shaped like a sparrow that she pocketed in rumpled pants.

"Well?" she asked.

"I'm leaving Hillvale," said Arthur. "I want to hire you."

"I'm in breach of contract to even talk about this," said Xandri.

"Is that a yes?"

"No."

"What do you pay in guild dues?"

Puff, puff, went the cigarette. "Seven per job."

Arthur did the math in his head. She paid her guild two gold more than the customer paid her for the night. In other words, she was under the gun to have sex, otherwise she'd come out in the negatives. Combine that with the expense of makeup, clothes and perfume, and Xandri was likely barely treading water financially.

He searched his pockets and fished out a bank note, which he laid on the table and pinned under a glass ashtray.

"That's worth two hundred gold in your hands when you get to a bank tomorrow morning," said Arthur. "I'm buying out your contract."

Xandri extinguished her cigarette and lit up a second. After a long pull from it, she asked, "Why?"

"You are now a harpist for House Galenden. Your new pay will be ten gold a month, which is less than you make now after guild dues, but anything you earn on top of that is yours to keep. One hundred percent."

Xandri stared at him, expression unreadable.

"Ged has a conservatory of music. And you'd be close to the League from there, which has a huge arts centre. I'd hope over time you could profess in your music career. But you wouldn't have to."

Puff, puff, puff.

Arthur shrugged. "Think on it. If you take my deal and work hard, I think you'll be buying your way out of my services within three years. When you've decided, you know where to find me."

He let himself out.

For a long time after Arthur left, Xandri stared at the banknote. She remained rooted to her spot by the mantel and stirred only when she came to her last cigarette.

The money would not only buy out her contract, but it would leave twenty to send to her parents.

Her family hated her. Hated her profession and everything that went with it. Yet, they never turned down the money she sent back home. Her seven siblings were expensive to clothe, and Xandri remembered a lot of lean years growing up. Maybe, if she could break out of this cycle, her parents would one day love her again.

But she didn't have to. She had to admit she loved her job. Expensive dinners, meeting high profile guests... it made her feel alive. Even the sex was fun, though the one thing she hated was having to spit. This might be a way to get out of having to do that ever again.

Go legit and boring? Give up a career that had supported her for the last three years? The choices warred in her head, but the logical choice won in the end.

Xandri looked up and smiled for what felt like the first time in years.

CHAPTER 4

HOME

The dreamless sleep of exhaustion held Reiki in its grip until late morning when the sounds of people bustling about awoke her.

People packing, she thought as she blinked sleep from her eyes. *Actually, more like an entire caravan.*

Reiki rose from bed and went to wash her face. She reached for a toothbrush and came up short as the realization came thundering back that she wasn't home and had no idea where home was.

"But I now know I'm right-handed, and I keep my toothbrush on that side of the sink."

The revelation consoled her somewhat. Hopefully she would remember more as time went on. Especially if she was deathly allergic to something like seafood. Best to recall that before eating anything that could kill her.

Thinking of food make Reiki's belly rumble. A handful of crackers for dinner. Pure folly on her part.

She retraced her steps to the bedroom and took the door leading to the hall. There, Reiki found five servants packing linen and lace-type finery into boxes.

Stars! When these people travel, they must take half a manor with them.

"Oh there you are," said the serving woman who had brought her towels after last night's bath. She'd introduced herself as Yolanda, and she looked to be in her mid-thirties. She carried a warm air of competence that matched her white uniform and the maid's hat on her head.

"Good morning, Yolanda," said Reiki.

"Come, come, you must be starved. We tried to rouse you for dinner but you were out like a sleeping Lightning."

"I must have been really tired," said Reiki.

She allowed Yolanda to guide her down the hall to a dining room that would seat twenty people at five round tables. At the moment, only two diners were present, and Reiki recognized neither of them. She scooted to the first empty table Yolanda presented.

"You like your bacon well done, I hope," said Yolanda.

"I think so," said Reiki, hoping that she wasn't a vegetarian.

Her body seemed agreeable to meat because the bacon and eggs went down with no queasiness to follow. Reiki stayed for a second serving and a tall glass of orange juice, which she was savouring when Arthur appeared.

He walked into the room, and the very air changed. The two other diners acknowledged him, and he greeted each in passing. But Reiki's table was his clear destination. Yolanda was already on her way with a placemat and cutlery.

Arthur wore loose-fitting black trousers and a white shirt with the sleeves rolled up. Was he helping with the packing? Very un-high-family-like if so. But oh, so dashing. Okay, so he was on the thin side when not wearing his jacket. An athletic build. With lithe, self-assured movements that carried a sprinkle of flourish.

Shades! You're staring. Say something.

"Good morning, Arthur. Slept well?"

"I did, thank you. And you? Any memories coming back?"

"I did and no, I'm afraid." Reiki buried her gaze in her orange juice. She knew somewhere deep down that she was standing on the edge of a chasm of hopelessness. To admit it openly would be the start of the plunge. She settled on a diversion. "There are some things coming back. I know I'm right-handed, for example."

"Hmmph," said Arthur, sounding not as encouraged as she would have liked. "Listen, I've got some bad news."

"You need to leave," said Reiki. "I know. I heard the packing."

"I live in Ged. You know it? It's about a thousand klicks south of here."

One thousand kilometres? That's an ocean away.

"No, I don't."

"A minor emergency seems to have cropped up back home. But you could stay at this hotel the rest of the month since it's paid already. I'll even leave Yolanda here with you since you're both Hillvalian and you two seem to have bonded."

Reiki glanced at the counter where Yolanda awaited a breakfast order from kitchen staff. To stay here and keep Yolanda from following her employer would be a lot of used-up karma on her part.

She decided to say so directly. "I'd be a burden to do that."

"She wouldn't mind at all. I owe her some vacation time anyway."

"I don't know," said Reiki, temporizing.

"Well, think about it. I've asked Eric to take you to a bigger warren when you've eaten. I don't need the Lansdale today, so maybe he can help you trace your roots."

"Very generous of you. But are you sure I'm not putting you out?"

"Absolutely not. I have a million things to take care of here and wouldn't dream of driving anywhere."

"Then, thank you. I will try to find my life in that time."

And so Reiki spent the morning driving around with Eric.

They went two hours north to the demesne of Rion, a high-population city with a very large warren. It was a three hour wait and a one-gold fee just to be seen, and though the bios gathered around her and prodded her scalp with their finger tips, they were unable to help.

"You might try deep telepathic mesmerism," suggested the team lead. "With no trauma to the brain, there's nothing biopathy can do."

When Reiki asked about the fees for the process, the bios named an astronomical figure, and she crossed it off the list of options. Arthur would pay it, she was certain, but it would take a lifetime of working to pay him back. Better to find another way.

There was a little bit of time left in the day as they drove back to Hillvale. She visited the post office, but they said there was no record of a Reiki anywhere. It was as if she had never lived there at all.

The archivists at the library couldn't issue new ID without an address, and central housing seemed to think she wasn't a homeowner. Boxes within boxes.

"Maybe I've never lived in Hillvale," said Reiki.

They were sitting in a small café having a tea at Eric's bequest. Reiki had picked it out because the tall windows allowed her to watch the traffic coming from the suburbs via the Naldine overpass.

Any one of those cars or carriages could be carrying someone who would recognize me, she thought.

"Eric, tell me a little about Ged, would you?"

"Ah, Ged is a prairie-type land. Very flat, you know?"

"Sounds windy."

"In spring and fall, yes. We're just north enough to avoid the worst heat of summer, but south enough that we don't have the cold season you guys have here."

"I see," said Reiki. She sipped her tea and focused on the window again. When she looked back to Eric, she noticed he was watching her with a paternal gaze and a slight smile to his lips. His grin was infectious. Reiki found herself returning it. "I remind you of someone, don't I?"

"Carrah, my daughter, yes. She was a fighter, just like you."

"Aw, but what happened if I may ask?"

"She contracted polio. Not terribly, but you could see that was why she needed the crutch. She was twelve when our Namika tried to stamp out the epidemic forcefully."

"They didn't."

"Oh, they did. Over two thousand, including some lower-house high family kids."

"That's horrible!"

"Had we known, we would have taken her to a different city. All the warning anyone had was the guards who pulled her and the others to the fortress. The Naiskarin did the task. I'm told it was like everyone went to sleep. But they never woke up from it."

Reiki couldn't help it. Tears started rolling down her cheeks. It was a few moments before she found strength to speak. Eric, meanwhile was grim. He probably re-lived that night in his head every time he closed his eyes.

"The Namika..." Reiki started to ask.

"Things got messy from there. People were screaming revolt, but he was too strong to be deposed through riots. An assassin almost got him. Gimped up his leg pretty bad. Kinda fitting, don't you think?"

Reiki reached across the table and took Eric's hand.

"Stars treasure your daughter's soul forever," she said.

"Thank you," said Eric.

They were interrupted by the dingle of the bell at the door as three men in top hats and ties entered. The noise of their hard-soled shoes on the wooden floors and the drafts of cold winter air that followed them seemed to change the atmosphere of the room.

"Three silver salesmen knock four times," said Reiki. "Three, seven, seven, Year forty-nine."

"What was that?" asked Eric.

"Huh, I'm not sure," said Reiki, releasing his hand to scratch her head. "It just kinda came out."

"Could it be a street address? Maybe you're recovering."

"There could be a zillion streets with that address. Really it could be just something random coming up."

"Don't lose faith. I think you're getting better."

Eric looked so convinced that Reiki had to smile. He was probably right. Just a bit of time, and she would recover.

CHAPTER 5

INVITED

Arthur was so busy throughout the day that he only had a few brief moments to spend resting and thinking about Reiki.

His primary order of business was getting all his merchandise packed and ready for transport. Hillvale's climate was much more supportive of ginseng than Ged, so he would be bringing home five bushels' worth. He also discovered coal on sale coming out of Graal since the mines wanted to offload product. The deal on the coal came with a deposit on a much larger order. The fast money would keep the mines running while the post-war cleanup still prevented much of the workforce from reporting to their jobs.

And there were the great devices Hillvale's craftsmen made. Belt buckles, sequins, studs, and axles–if an item could be made of metal, it seemed there was a smithy in Hillvale camping on a stash of them. What he didn't need for his daily operations he would gift away.

Arthur helped his staff package and label shipping crates that day, laughing and joking with them at times, other times making himself scarce so they could have peace without the boss's ears about. They would move all these goods by truck to Credd, then ship it by train to Ged, so everything had to be rain-sealed and resistant to jostling.

Dusk overtook them, but everything was ready, so Arthur called for supper break. He left his staff having their parting meal in the hotel diningroom and retired to his suites to wash up.

Still no word from Eric and Reiki. It made Arthur wonder what they were up to.

"Milord, Yolanda would summon you to the table," Vincent called out from the main room.

Arthur joined him there as he looped his tie through the collar of a clean shirt.

"Kindly tell her I'll be late, Vincent. I need some time to let my mind wander."

Vincent turned for the door, then hesitated. He turned back to Arthur and tilted his head. "You would normally sup with them on such an important night. Methinks you're worried. About Reiki, no doubt."

Arthur chuckled. Such a perceptive child, that Vincent.

"Well, Vincent, she seems to be lost in a forest of wolves. And the Queen Wolf is on her trail."

"You love her, don't you?"

"Ha, ha, Vincent. Love doesn't work that way." Arthur went to the wardrobe where his last unpacked jacket awaited. Vincent hastened to him to help him dress. "I only just met her. Love is something that kinda forms between kindred souls over a long period of time."

"Nay, milord, you are quite wrong. I overheard the hotel porters talking about how they wanted to love Yolanda until they found out she was married. And they only knew her a few days at the time. I'm quite sure that love can strike like lightning."

"Ahh, that does happen sometimes," Arthur admitted. He wondered which porters they were, and if they'd been filling Vincent's head with nonsense. "But don't follow their lead. They would have used and abused Yolanda, given the chance."

No use having Vincent grow up to be like me, thought Arthur with a pang of guilt. There was a trail of broken hearts behind him that he sometimes thought he had to flee.

"Nay, I think I understood their naughty-talk, barring the local words, and I think they would have treated Yolanda very well."

Just then, Vincent's stomach growled, so Arthur playfully punched him on the shoulder.

"Let's go downstairs, Vincent. My fears and worries aren't worth you missing dinner."

Vincent obediently trotted along after Arthur to the lift. They took it to the ground floor of the hotel, and Arthur saw Vincent into the dining room before slipping off to the front entrance.

"Milord's car has not yet returned," said the doorman as Arthur approached.

"That's no problem. I'm only going for a walk."

"Might I suggest you go armed? We've had a number of ruffians prowling about this evening, and unfortunately the guards have been in short supply."

"Ruffians, you say?"

Arthur pressed on through the doors without waiting for a reply.

The chill night air bit deep into Arthur's jacket as he made his way down the path to the street.

He glanced at the spot on the sidewalk where Xandri's harp had crashed. A telepath might see some glimmer there; some lingering emotion, perhaps. Unless the psychic impression had faded away once the harpsmith had pronounced the instrument healed.

What's Xandri thinking right now? Will she accept my offer?

With luck, Xandri was curled up with her harp right at that very moment. Just as Reiki would be home with her family. Maybe Reiki was thinking about him right now. Missing him.

Stop thinking about either of them. You're acting like a guiding star.

"Excuse me, sir. Some copper, please?"

The speaker was a little street urchin who looked about three years younger than Vincent. He wore a miner's cap and a matching grey jacket, which covered his hands.

Arthur smiled down at him. "Scamp, you have a home. I know your Namika doesn't tolerate people living on the streets."

"I do, yes," said the boy. "But food's been very hard to get at the orphanage these days. Our teacher tried to get more money, but there were too many other petitioners today and he was passed over."

"What?" asked Arthur, appalled.

"It's a small orphanage. Only ten of us there. We're usually passed over for the bigger one in downtown central."

The kidling was exactly what Vincent would have been had Arthur not found him many years ago in the streets of

Ged. Unable to take it, Arthur turned away and wiped tears from his eyes. He would have food left over from the feast his staff was enjoying right now. He'd see to it that each of those ten mouths was fed.

"Mister? Are you alright?"

Arthur nodded and cleared his throat to regain his composure. After three deep breaths he was ready to face the orphan again. "What's your address, little boy?"

"We're on ninety-eight Main, corner of Flenn, sir. Why do you ask? Sir?"

"Hmm," said Arthur, for he spied the Lansdale cruising towards the hotel. Reiki sat in the back. That meant she hadn't been able to find her home. "Run along home, now. I need to take care of a few things, then I'll bring you a surprise."

"Yessir, milord! Right away."

The child probably suspected what his surprise might be, for there was a certain spring to his step as he scampered off. Arthur grinned for his happiness although seeing Reiki back unsuccessful filled him with consternation. With less than twelve hours before they left Hillvale, what would they do to help her?

The passers-by shifted as the Lansdale pulled up in front of the hotel. The way the crowd slowed caught Arthur's attention. A number of people outright stopped walking and stared at Reiki. One of them looked at Arthur and his eyes glinted like a cat's under a flashlight.

A wave of dizziness swept over Arthur, and he found himself staggering. Telepathic crowd control. Iliara's work, no doubt.

High family teaching asserted itself. There were several

means of fighting telepaths, such as reciting nursery rhymes in your head, or shouting aloud when you felt the disorientation. Shifting your thoughts was supposed to help, because telepaths found unified thoughts easier to bend in crowd situations.

The pedestrians about Arthur formed into a mob and converged on the Lansdale, but Reiki surprised them by bounding out the door.

When her feet touched the pavement, the air went so chill, Arthur felt granules of frozen rain pepper his face. In a circle around Reiki's feet, the slush froze so suddenly it gave the squeal of cracking ice.

The ring of ice widened and sent the mob scrambling away. Those who were too slow slipped and took hard falls. One man lost his shoe to a puddle that froze on him. He ran away without stopping to rescue it.

Arthur staggered back onto the hotel property before the ice could seize him. Reiki seemed to ignore the slipperiness, for she ran to him and let him take her hand. Together, they ran for the doors, where the hotel porters waited in a protective barrier.

The moment they were before the doors, Reiki fell into Arthur's embrace.

"What was that?" he asked, breathlessly. "The ice after your dive at the Conningway. I forgot you mentioned it way back. You're cryokinetic."

Reiki ignored him and asked a question of her own. "Arthur, do you have room for one more on your travels?"

"Huh?"

"Take me with you. I want to go to Ged with you."

"Ah, Reiki. You need to be here finding your life. I can't take you away with me."

"My life is hidden from me, and this city is too dangerous. Take me with you Arthur. Don't leave me here by myself. I need to get out of here."

I need you too, Reiki, he thought as she pressed the side of her face against his neck. He rubbed his fingertips through the hair on the back of her head and thought it over. In some ways, the decision was obvious.

CHAPTER 6

GED

The Gedanese countryside was every bit as flat as Eric had promised. Flat and infinitely dull, but somehow Reiki couldn't tear her eyes away from the train window.

"I wonder what she sees out there," mused Mallen from the facing aisle seat.

"We've put her to sleep with our talk," said Arthur. "Look, she can hardly keep her eyes open."

"Ignore them, Reiki. They wouldn't even know if we left," said Xandri who sat across from her.

Reiki smiled for Xandri. She knew very little of the young woman who had shown up for the ride, except that she was Hillvalian and wore bright green contacts. Xandri was impeccably dressed and manicured, but she offered nothing of her past, and no one had explained her presence. Reiki was unperturbed about the mystery, but it made conversation a little awkward.

Xandri must have seen Reiki studying her attire, for she said, "Once we get you to Ged, I'm taking you shopping. That outfit just won't do. It looks like you got dressed in a blender."

"Now, Xandri," said Arthur, stepping in. "Admit it. Reiki looks stunning."

Looking at her dress, Reiki had to agree with Xandri. What a blinding shade of green. She must have been off her rocker to wear that.

She decided to voice her agreement. "There's lots of work for me as a traffic pylon if I don't get better."

"Don't say that," said Arthur. "You'll be better once you've had a bit of relaxation time."

"I hope so," she said. No use telling him she planned to do anything but relax. Coming to Ged as a dependent, Reiki was determined to find a way to make herself useful. She sighed and turned back to the window.

"You can't memorize the landscape, you know," said Arthur.

"I could if I wanted. My memory is quite good all the way back to the parade," she replied.

"You're healing?" asked Mallen.

"There's nothing before that point. Not even a trace. Everything after is crystal clear. I can even remember that there's a certain gentleman who keeps passing down the aisle and staring at me."

Arthur patted her hand again. "You're worried that Iliara's people are after you. You shouldn't. She has no idea you even came with us."

"And this is a train, after all," said Mallen. "There is only one aisle the man could use."

"If you say so." Reiki took another peek out at the countryside, and another thought bubbled up. "Say, how come I don't see any farms yet. We must be almost to the city by now."

"Farms?" repeated Arthur. "Why would we farm when we have oil?"

Reiki looked at him in surprise. "Surely, you don't import all your food."

"What Arthur means," said Mallen. "Is that farms aren't cost-effective to defend. Our farms tend to hug the city for safety. This far out, it'll mostly be ranchers and the like who can go mobile if they have to."

"Okay." Reiki shrugged. Probably with all the oil in the region, conquest was all Ged's neighbours had ever learned. She could understand the kind of greed they were used to dealing with around here.

A sign whizzed by that read "Ged, 22km." Mallen got to his feet.

"Almost there. Time to go sort our cargo. Get it packed for resale."

"And I'll go powder my nose," said Xandri after he left. She stopped at the doorway. "I better not hear any kissing noises while I'm gone."

Reiki felt herself flushing when she and Arthur were left to themselves. Why did Xandri have to go and say that? Now things were uncomfortable.

"I finally get why you bought all that produce and merchandise," said Reiki to break the silence. "It's gotta be insanely cheap coming from Hillvale compared to your gold-credit value here."

"You're quite right," said Arthur. He reached across the seat to take her hand. "Ged's almost here. Nervous?"

I'm more nervous that I'll get sweaty palms now that you're holding my hand, she thought. But she shook her head no. Arthur wore an unreadable look on his face as he watched her, eyes dark and sombre, as if being home had reminded him of some turmoil he would have to face. He was wearing formal robes today instead of his casual jacket. The look make him even more stunning, but also a shade of melancholy.

"What?" she asked.

"Hmm?" Arthur seemed to shake himself back to the present and smiled for her.

"You were lost in dreamland."

"No, I was imagining a world where all women were as beautiful as you."

Reiki laughed at his half-stab of a cover-up and turned to face the window. "You weren't, you know. I can tell. And..."

"And?"

She turned back to challenge him. "...and you're a terrible liar."

That made the corners of his mouth turn up in a grin. "I'm not lying. And Xandri was right. You have beautiful, kissable lips."

Reiki sighed. Another evasion. He really didn't plan on telling her what was troubling him. Although, he had opened the door on the kiss he owed her from when he'd been on the verge of it back in the Lansdale.

No. He's only teasing. Don't say it. You'll just embarrass yourself.

She said it anyway. "You know, you could kiss me if you like."

Yep. Now you look foolish. Wait for him to scorn you.

"That's a very attractive offer," said Arthur, taking up her bait.

He shuffled nearer to Reiki and placed his hands to the

sides of her cheeks. She was torn between closing her eyes in anticipation and watching the set of his brows.

"But I can't do it," he continued.

Reiki's heart sank. He had a girlfriend or fiancée. That's what he had been arguing about with Eric outside the Lansdale that day. She was flirting with a taken man.

"You're married," she ventured. "I'm so sorry."

"Nope, quite single." And his eyes went mischievous. "But I can't kiss you because a Galenden never mortgages his soul to a demoness."

On that pronouncement, he grasped her over the ears and kissed her on the forehead. He was gone from the cabin while Reiki blinked in surprise.

"What did you mean by that? You think I'm a demon? Demons aren't real, you know."

There was no reply. Reiki heard him outside talking to a member of his staff about storage conditions on the packing crates.

Very well. You can hide for now. I won't forget that I'm owed a kiss.

Reiki went back to sit down and watch as the first of the ranches came into view.

The ranches were unfenced, she noticed. The train likely made frequent stops to wait for cattle to move off the tracks. Inefficient, but that was the way things probably happened in Ged.

Eventually, the ranches gave way to farms with squat stone houses budding out near the road. Then, farms made way for a row of lookout towers, and the train began a sudden descent into Ged.

Arthur reappeared in the doorway as the panorama

opened up before Reiki's eyes. Ged seemed like it was built inside a crater, with stone housing crawling up the inside walls. Most of the city was in shadow as the setting sun cast its fleeting rays on the last few rows of buildings near the top. That, and the smoke stacks of a gargantuan factory near the centre seemed to cast a cloud over the city.

"We call it the Old Man because of the way the pipes form a face," said Arthur who took his place beside her. "It's an oil refinery, as I think you've guessed. Ged handles all of its own processing."

"What are those leaning metal towers there?"

"Cannons... six metres long each. They have a range of about three thousand metres, and twelve of them ring the city."

"Ged must have some very determined enemies," said Reiki.

"We can hit them before they get to the farms. With luck we can even shoot down dirigibles." Arthur pointed out a small airship belching purple smoke high overhead. Reiki shuddered in apprehension, and he patted her back. "Doesn't seem like I'll talk you into going in one of those any time soon."

"Stars fall before I go up in one of those," she said. "Is all this why you built the city in a crater? As a way to defend it?"

"It's a sink hole. We founded the city on top of a reserve and proceeded to draw too much substrate out of the ground."

She looked at him in fear. "The city fell?"

"It can't drop any farther. We're on bedrock now. Had to build on the rubble, though. The oil market wouldn't wait for us to relocate."

She looked at him, speechless, and he shrugged.

"That's from seventy years ago. Don't worry. We're safe here."

"The cannons. There's steam coming out from them. They were fired recently."

Arthur leaned in close to see where Reiki indicated, but after a moment he shook his head. "I can't see what you see, but there are no flags hanging on the Namika's castle."

"The death of an important figure?" asked Reiki.

"I fear it's the leader himself," replied Arthur.

"You're sure?"

The train had reached the station where crowds of expectant people waited. Among them, Reiki spied out three torchbearers whose cloaks bore the House Galenden symbol. With their hoods drawn up and tall brass poles that burned on one end, they stood out from the crowd.

"They're waiting for me," said Arthur. "Looks like I get to start the evening in a meeting with my mother."

CHAPTER 7

GED II

After making sure Mallen would be able to accompany Reiki to a guestroom, Arthur debarked the train and approached the lead torchbearer.

They bowed to him at the waist in high formality.

Arthur addressed the middle one. "An honour guard?"

"Please, this way, milord."

At Arthur's signal, the leader set off. Arthur followed, with the remainder straggling behind.

The torchbearers led Arthur up a stonework path in the direction of the Namika's castle. That much made sense, since a welcome committee was more pomp and circumstance than he was used to.

The castle was a strange sight to behold, with a base of crumbled, poorly-aligned stone that was the remains of the original collapsed fortress. The new castle was mostly cylindrical, thrown together as simply and as quickly as possible, for Ged had been in dire need of a military outpost after the disaster.

They passed one of the cannons on the way through the front doors. Two servants cleaned it with wash-cloths they dipped in buckets. Reiki's guess was correct. There had been a firing today. But there was no sign of attack Arthur could see. Grave portent indeed.

Mothers held their children close instead of letting them play in city streets as usual. Guards were high in number and brandished their weapons in a show of strength. Many of the guards wore scars from various battles that they had yet to get healed. That meant double-shifts for them. Exhaustion and fear. Not a good combination.

The torchbearers led Arthur into the castle and made for the throne room. That meant his mother would be in audience with the Namika. Good thing Arthur had taken the final leg of the train ride in formal robes.

The doors to the throne room were closed, and the normal assembly of attendants and courtiers stood outside. That would be the sign of some private deliberation. But with whom? If their leader had passed away, who would have stepped up to plate? All seven of the Namika's sons had been killed in the last twenty years by the various wars and internal struggles. His only surviving daughter, Wendiah, was too weak an electrokinetic to claim the throne for herself. It would have to be someone of the remaining ruling elite.

Arthur's cousin, Hendry, stood among the attendants, reading from the pages of a ring-bound tome. Normally, Hendry would be overseeing House relations from his office in the castle. Arthur considered slipping off to speak with him, but the guards were already opening the doors to the throne room. Getting the full story on what was happening would have to wait.

Guards and torchbearers remained behind as Arthur entered. With a thunderous boom, the doors shut behind him, and he waited a moment for his eyes to adjust to the new lighting. No sign of the Namika or his retainers. Instead, the five leaders of the Great Houses stood before the throne. Patricia Galenden, Arthur's mother, stood one spot to the left, wearing her dress in the House colours of royal purple and a tapered red hat.

Accountants were gathered to one half of the throne room, going through chests of gold and other valuables and making notes on a ledger. Guards were in the process of bringing in more chests and bolting closed others that had been already sorted.

"Arthur Galenden," said Lord Muldret, who occupied the middle position of the line of high family patriarchs.

"I stand as named." He drew up before them and bowed.

"Be advised that the Great Houses, at the bequest of the people of Ged, have asked the Namika to step down from office."

Ah, all this pomp and ceremony makes sense now. Where could the Namika be now? Arthur couldn't imagine him going quietly. He would have found himself a defensible nook to hide in and refused to concede power, knowing that old goat.

Muldret pressed on. "As you are the eldest scion of Galenden, it is my pleasure to recommend you for the rank of Consular in the name of the new order."

Arthur took a moment to ponder it. Permanent rankings meant Muldret was setting up shop for keeps. That would be a lot of effort to defend since Ged would become a target for unnamed Lightnings looking for open turf to claim. This reminded him of the outgoing leader.

"The Namika?" asked Arthur.

"Deceased," said Muldret. "He garrisoned himself in a tower, and we flooded it with fluorine gas. All his trusted retainers went with him. We have his telepaths in holding."

"Well planned," said Arthur in genuine approval. It meant lead-lined holding cells prepared in advance without any thoughts of it leaking. A perfectly executed political coup.

"And so, you accept the title?"

Arthur made a show of looking about the room, buying himself time to look at his mother. She gave slight rounding of the lower lip. A no? That would explain the presence of his cousin. She wanted Hendry to take the position instead of Arthur.

"Respectfully, I must decline. As second of the household, may I nominate my cousin, Hendry Galenden, in my place?"

"Have him sent for," said Muldret.

Arthur thought Hendry took longer than was necessary to show, but perhaps it was to make it seem like he wasn't waiting around for the summons. He bounded through the doors as if thirty minutes late for his own wedding and bowed as he swept off his cap.

"I, Hendry Galenden, stand as named, and accept any duty to serve the people of Ged."

The ceremony was short, with Hendry signing the parchment in the specially prepared pigments that the archivist guild claimed sole rights to make. Muldret's assistants passed him the ceremonial sword of the Consular. Should Patricia Galenden be unable to stand for council, Hendry would now be her political successor.

Muldret adjourned council for a two hour break. This

was for expedience sake, for all the Houses had affairs to see after on such a chaotic evening. Arthur rushed to catch up with his mother who slipped off towards a side door.

"Mum, so happy to see you again," he said to her back.

His mother turned to eye him briefly before moving on. "I said in my note to come at once. I didn't mean to dawdle."

"I concluded my business in Hillvale. You should be proud."

He held the door for her and followed her into the hall.

"I've never seen so much lying and backstabbing going on in all my fifty years," said Patricia. "Expect a few of the new heads of state to shuffle through replacements in the next week."

"Is that why you wanted Hendry as the house political representative? He has that ability to give long-winded responses that make you forget the question."

"No. He's Consular because you're too smart for politics."

"Oh," said Arthur.

"You'll see over the family business. The oil market is too complex for me to train up someone new. And do me a favour and pop in on Wendiah tonight."

They reached the end of the hall, where guards admitted them to the tunnel that led to the Galenden's estate. Like all the high family living areas, the Galenden house was burrowed into the same cliff face as the Namika's castle. They buffered it against the encroachment of the rest of the city. And, ever since the revolts many years past, served as protection for an old, embattled Namika. These tunnels ran directly from the castle to each of their estates.

Arthur recognized the guards and caught a twinkle of

excitement in their eyes. There would be very little security in place tonight once the revelry got going.

He continued on after his mother. "Wendiah? That was a long time ago. What should I want with her?"

His mother eyed him with a look of exasperation. "Let the birds and the bees have their will. If you get her with child, we can pressure her into marrying Hendry."

Arthur considered the complexities. An electrokinetic son, should Wendiah be able to produce one, would stand a very good chance of declaring Namika one day. But... what would Reiki think of him if he took advantage of Wendiah like that?

He caught a reading look from his mother and nodded an assent he wasn't sure he felt.

"Know your duty," said Patricia. "If you'll excuse me, I must freshen up for tonight's Council."

Arthur allowed her to escape down a wide staircase to a downstairs den. All business, his mother. Not even a word of welcome for a returned son. That was what made her formidable in the courts, if a little cool on an interpersonal level.

The thought made Arthur grin. As long as Patricia Galenden was strong, the universe was running smoothly.

The same stairs that led to the den wound their way up to the guestrooms. Arthur took them two at a time. He would introduce Reiki to his mother in the morning. Preferably after they'd all had some time to rest. For now, there was an entire city for Reiki to meet.

CHAPTER 8

FIREWORKS

After Arthur was swept away from her side, Reiki followed Mallen into the Galenden estate. The architecture was unassuming, though tall and riddled in spires. The interior was a maze of polished stone and foreign decor beautiful enough to make up the difference.

Fourteen flights of stairs followed, of which a glass-walled lift covered half. That took her to a guestroom as sumptuous as any hotel, where she realized she had nothing to unpack.

There was a standing invitation to explore while the Galenden staff looked after their duties, so Reiki wandered the magnificent halls until she came to the music room.

It was a large, marble-floored hall of which a concert grand piano formed the centrepiece. Tall windows gave way to the deep blue of late-afternoon sky that peeked through trellises that would be covered in leaves by summer. Along the only wall that didn't have windows, various woodwind and stringed instruments hung on pegs, along with books of sheet music that lay stacked on brass stands.

Reiki went to the windows and looked out. The drop

was a dizzying eighteen storeys to the city streets. And there was a dead rat on the window sill, behind the curtains.

"Ew!" She drew back apprehensively, then tiptoed back to peek again.

There was a paper sachet of pink crystals that the rat had bitten into. Poison, no doubt. It must have happened recently, for there was no odour, and the servants had yet to find it.

Reiki backpedalled to the piano and forced herself to breathe deeply.

Calm down. It's dead. Don't get all worked up.

Still, she decided to sit at the piano instead of returning to the window.

The piano looked like it hailed from another century. The ivory keys were starting to yellow, but the cracks were free of dust. Reiki tested middle C. Perfectly in tune.

I hope there's no rule against playing this thing. Reiki doubted it. No one would keep it in tune if it wasn't meant to be played. She walked through a rendition of *Chopsticks* but hesitated at the end.

"I think I know the harmony part of this." She took a moment to think, then began to play in earnest.

At first it was the chords. Then, Reiki added harmony with her other hand. She replayed a few times, distractedly, allowing her mind to catch up with her hands before adding a flowery rhythm on top of it.

A human-sized furtive movement caught Reiki's eye, so she stopped. From the doorway, a large heat pattern indicated someone hidden in the hallway. She decided to address the person.

"Yes? Come in, why don't you?"

"Bravo," said a man who entered. He clapped for her as if *Chopsticks* was some masterpiece of musical score. "Hendry Galenden. I don't believe I've had a chance to meet you."

He wore a white shirt, a vest, and really tight leggings. He was Arthur's rival in looks, though his hair was long and clasped in a ponytail. A brother or a cousin? Either way, he was breath-taking. She could happily watch him all day.

Reiki knew she was blushing despite herself and started trying to think of some excuse to escape. "Thank you. I was just playing around, but my hands are a bit too sore to keep going."

"Here, let me see." Hendry swept up and fell to his knees before her. He took her two hands in his and jerked back in surprise. "Shades, your hands are freezing!"

"Sorry. It's just that you startled me just now."

"Perhaps," said Hendry, as he looked deep into her eyes. "You really are a demoness come to drain our innocent souls."

Reiki rolled her eyes. Why did every Gedanese male seem to recite that line? Her look of consternation seemed to set Hendry to laughing.

That laugh is as beautiful as Arthur's. And they look so much alike.

Reiki shook her head. *Keep your head on, girl. Don't multiply your problems.*

In a flurry of motion, Hendry had her on her feet. He held her by the waist and twirled them so Reiki was sitting against the side of the piano.

"You are stunning and beautiful," he whispered in her ear. "Tell me you're single. Say yes right now, and we'll sneak into my room. I must have you."

Her head emptied of coherent thought, and she struggled to explain herself. "What? No, I'm... I'm here with Arthur. I mean I'm– here as his... guest."

Her protests were cut short, for Hendry set a hand to the side of her face. Those eyes. And the slender curl to his lips. Did that trait run in the family? Reiki wanted to melt.

"He's not going to know. Say yes, my lady. We were destined to be."

He had Reiki in a ridiculous bind. She decided to say so politely.

"I can't. I don't know you."

"Do you really know Arthur?"

"I do. Arthur wouldn't be like this in a million years."

"Your words tell me how little you know of him."

"Unhand me, sir. This is inappropriate." Reiki twisted in his grasp and was horrified to see another heat-line from the hall. An eavesdropper. This entire house must be full of spies. Imagine if word got to Arthur that she was flirting with Hendry. He'd probably cast her out on the spot.

"Kiss me, evil one," said Hendry.

Reiki threw her arms up against her chest to keep their bodies apart and turned her head away so he could only kiss the side of her neck. He did so. It wasn't long–a fluttering of the lips. Then he pressed a metallic object in her hand and whisked from the room.

Stunned, Reiki plopped herself down on the bench. The cube Hendry had left her with had nine faces on each side with different colours painted on them. She rotated the facets and realized they were meant to be turned until all colours of the same type matched. It was some kind of puzzle.

Xandri walked into the room, carrying a blue evening gown on a hanger. Reiki sighed upon seeing her.

"I guess you heard everything."

Xandri winked and joined Reiki on the bench. "It's no surprise. He used some of the same lines on me about ten minutes ago."

Reiki pursed her lips. She wanted to be sick.

A white line on the horizon caught her attention. It was a rocket going up. They were in sight of the launchpad for the space project.

Xandri followed Reiki's gaze as the rocket carved a tiny line of fire into the deepening sky.

"You seem fascinated by it," said Xandri.

"I feel like I know enough to be on that rocket."

"It was all over the papers back home."

They watched together for several minutes even after the rocket had vanished from sight. Excited yelling noises from street level echoed to the windows.

"That'll be people getting ready for tonight's festivities," said Xandri. "Go get changed. I picked out your dress for you."

"What? I'm not going anywhere."

"Don't be silly. Arthur will be on his way up to fetch you soon. Or did you think the eldest son of House Galenden would just show up home and not have a welcome-back dinner?"

She was right. And Reiki had limited time to get ready. She'd be lucky to even change in time. Getting her hair done was out of the question.

"Thank you, Xandri. I'm in your debt. I'll repay you one day."

"You already have."

"Huh?"

"I did a lot of thinking last night, and I realized I got the chance to be a professional harpist because you tilted Arthur's internal compass."

"Oh, I didn't do that. You must be mistaken."

"Oi, can you deny that while you get ready? Come, I'll help you with your hair."

Together, they hustled to the bathroom.

It took some time to get ready. No sooner had Xandri gotten Reiki's hair combed to satisfaction did Vincent turn up to ask after her one last time. Reiki followed him down while fretting about her overall appearance, but one look at Arthur's face and she knew Xandri had done impressive work.

"I didn't know you could straighten your hair," was all he could manage.

"That's just because it's damp. In about an hour or two, it'll be a ball of frizz."

"I guess we'd better hurry, then," said Arthur with a laugh.

About twenty minutes later, he guided her into a free spot beside Mallen and his wife at a table for six.

Dizzying, she thought. Travel was best reserved for people who could remember home. For her, both Hillvale and Ged were foreign destinations. She felt the longing for a place she could call familiar.

The restaurant, a free-standing building, occupied the corner of what appeared to be a major crossroads between the various Houses. The interior, large and spacious, its tall ceilings seemed to absorb the noise of the two dozen guests.

In the corner near the door, a grey-haired man sat beside a waterfall where he plucked at the stings of a large cello. A cluster of men in top hats were filling up the front area as Reiki watched. At this rate, the restaurant would be packed within the hour.

"Oh, here comes Hendry now," said Mallen with a tilt of the head to the door.

Hendry, looking dressed up and unruffled, stepped out of the group with his arm looped through that of a woman in a pale blue dress. They made their way to Arthur's table.

"Hendry," said Arthur, rising as the couple drew closer. He shook hands with the man and kissed his date's hand. "And you would be Ellen, right?"

"Enchanted," said Ellen with a half-curtsy.

"Arthur, Arthur," said Hendry. "You've been holding out on us. Who's the lovely lady you have here?"

"This is Reiki from Hillvale," said Arthur as she rose to allow Hendry to kiss her hand as if they'd never met.

"Your demesne must be sad indeed to have lost its most beautiful citizen," said Hendry over her hand, which earned Reiki a caustic glare from Ellen.

"Thank you," said Reiki. She had to tug a little to free herself. Luckily, the waiter arrived with menus to rescue her from any further faux pas in the eyes of Ellen.

"You can read in Standard," said Arthur, sounding impressed when Reiki glanced over the laminated card that served as a menu.

"I can," she said. "But there's not much here to read."

Two choices of entrées. Steak and potatoes or poultry

and greens. She supposed an expensive restaurant could afford to skimp out on selection.

Her complaint drew a round of polite laughter from around the table.

"You're quite right. But the steak here is renowned across several lands. Do give it a try, won't you?" Hendry made it sound like the restaurant was doing her a favour.

"I will," said Reiki in an agreement she almost recanted on when the waiter refused to accept an order for well-done.

"One hundred percent sorry, milady. Our kitchen can prepare your entrée in rare and medium-rare."

"Ew, I don't want to eat it raw," said Reiki with a grimace. That did not sound appetizing at all.

Arthur stepped in on the exchange. "See if they'll at least go to medium, would you? Tell them it's a Galenden special request."

"Hmm," said the waiter, seeming unimpressed by the name drop. He swept up her menu and departed without another word.

"Medium steak is way over-done," said Hendry. "It's a way of killing the meat."

Ellen chimed in on his statement. "Where were you from again? Are there any famous chefs there?"

"Hillvale," said Reiki. She left out the fact that she was unsure.

"Oh." Ellen gave a wide-eyed look. "That hovel. You poor thing."

"Now, now," said Hendry. "Hillvale is the second biggest manufacturing hub on the continent. They're anything but poor there."

"Except in chefs," said Reiki, provoking more chuckles.

She smiled. Let them laugh at her expense; it wasn't like she needed to court their respect.

Hendry brought up the topic of his appointment to Consular and soon he, Arthur, and Mallen were chatting excitedly. Reiki sat back, absorbed what she could, and sipped at the red wine the waiter brought them.

Before the meals arrived, the crackle of fireworks reached her ears. Reiki blinked in surprise, and Arthur put a reassuring arm about her. It was a reflex reaction on his part; he didn't even notice her interest in the sound. Reiki had to poke him to get his attention.

"The fireworks," she said.

"People celebrating the death of the Namika," said Arthur. "He was not well loved."

Reiki hesitated on telling him they reminded her of something important, for she saw that the meals were on their way. Instead she excused herself for a trip to the bathroom.

"Hurry back," said Arthur absently. "Your steak will cool and turn into leather."

She lost him there. Buried into a conversation about which house could press the best advantage in the chaos. But that might be for the best. Arthur had tried to help her, but Reiki knew she needed to make an advance on her own.

Thus, feigning the need to wash her hands, Reiki snuck outside.

The streets were packed with celebrators. It reminded Reiki of the parade in Hillvale. And it made her sad. According to her memories, her life had officially started three days ago. She was, in many ways, a newborn.

Overhead, brilliant phosphorescent flowers exploded in

reds and yellows that wowed the cheering multitudes. Reiki stared at them, not knowing how to identify the thoughts and feelings that came to her. It was like the dancing embers above were trying to remind her of something.

A memory! Reiki shut her eyes, fell to her knees, and clamped her hands over her ears to reduce all outside input as best she could.

She was young. Possibly five years old, holding her father's hand (oh, but his face was clouded to her mind!) and staring at a sky alive in fire. How little she understood of them at the time. Little dying stars, she thought they were.

"Daddy, why are those stars exploding?" she asked, pulling the hand she grasped.

"Those aren't stars, hun. People made them."

"Is it a power?"

"No, dear. It's science."

Science. It was something that had turned into a life goal for her. From that young age Reiki had wanted to be smart enough to make fire. That meant she –

"Reiki! Are you alright?"

A pair of hands hauled Reiki to her feet and turned her around. She opened her eyes to see Hendry holding her.

"I'm fine," she said. "Let me go. I need to concentrate."

"Snap out of it, girl. Why are you kneeling on the dirty ground? Are you having a stroke? I'll send for the bios."

"Let me go, please," she begged.

"Water!" cried Hendry as he ushered her to the door.

Reiki tried to free herself, but more people came to help. Before she knew it, she was inside the restaurant and being set down in a chair. Arthur was there at her right, but Hendry still held her left hand.

With all the hubbub, her concentration had broken. The chain of memories no longer came. Lost. Possibly forever. Reiki buried her face in her hands and began to sob.

"Everyone get away," said Arthur. "You're all crowding her."

"What?" asked Hendry. "This woman needs medical help and that's your solution?"

"Trust me," said Arthur. "I know what I'm saying."

They began to argue overtop her, and suddenly everyone was yelling or moving about.

"Back off, everyone."

"I will not abandon this maiden in her time of need."

"Boys, our dinner is getting cold."

"Stop, stop," said Reiki. "Please. All of you."

That got everyone staring at her in surprise. Arthur was the first to recover.

"Come, Reiki. I'll walk you."

Hand in hand, they walked outside.

CHAPTER 9
FIREWORKS II

Arthur actually held Reiki's hand as they left the restaurant. Not an arm-to-wrist grip as was proper, but a lover's-style grasp. It was both electrifying and disconcerting because she knew people would talk. And so, reluctantly, Reiki pulled away.

"What happened back there?" Arthur took up her arm in a more appropriate fashion.

"The fireworks," said Reiki. "They brought back a memory."

"Then, we should go see more."

"I can see them from here." She pointed over Old Man's eyebrow. "But I don't think it'll work twice. Part of what jogged my memory was the surprise. I've lost it now."

"We'll keep them in sight, just in case."

They took a lonely stone walkway that zigzagged around the bowl of the city. The guards that patrolled it seemed to recognize Arthur, for they let him by without question. The only other people Reiki saw were in high family dress and seemingly eager to get to the festivities below.

"The change-over was a long time in coming," said

Arthur. "It's symbolic, really, since we, the five Houses, have been quietly running the show for years, but the happiness is still tangible, isn't it?"

"The Namika fell into disfavour with the people?"

"Yes, and you must understand, money controls Ged. Not Lightnings, not telepaths. We understand gold, both yellow and black. No one will ever be Lord of Ged by any other measure."

Reiki raised an eyebrow. How was it that she could think of a million sayings about gold and its inability to bring happiness, but still fail to recall her parents' faces?

"Penny for your thoughts," said Arthur.

"Oh, I'm still chasing memories, don't mind me. It'd be so nice to have parents again."

"I'm sure you'll meet them again. They're alive somewhere."

Reiki stopped walking near the edge of a promontory and turned to face him. "Arthur, you've never mentioned your father. Will you tell me about him?"

"He was..." Arthur stared off at the streamers of fire for a moment. "Strong. Strong and tireless. But he was a late bloomer. Had me when he was forty."

"Goodness. And your mother?"

"She was fifteen years younger than him. Theirs was an arranged marriage, like most high family pairings are."

"Mmmk."

This was that moment where Reiki would get to hug him if she was his girlfriend. He was a striking image with the street lights playing off his smooth features. Maybe if she pretended to be afraid of the fireworks, she'd score a quick embrace.

"Hey, at least the fireworks didn't scare your socks off," said Arthur.

Stars and shades, he'd unwittingly outplayed her by eradicating her one excuse to hug him. Reiki was going to have to think faster if she was going to get a chance at bat.

"Come, let's move on."

They walked to the end of the overpass and descended a flight of narrow stairs to reach the street level. It was a bit chaotic there, since the streets were uneven and filled with puddles and revellers. But very much alive with the voice of Ged.

At one point, a man juggling flaming clubs almost set Reiki's hair on fire, but Arthur smoothly swept her out of the way. He held her close, after that, and told her stories of his childhood in Ged, while Reiki yearned to be able to share her own stories in return.

At one point, Reiki spotted a woman with long black hair staring at her. The woman's aura burned fire-white, and her eyes flashed as she grinned in a devilish sneer. Something tugged at the back of Reiki's mind as she watched the woman's shoulders shake in a laugh that she was too far to hear. The crowd swallowed the woman before Reiki could make a conclusion.

They walked on while Reiki learned of the challenges of growing up in a highly competitive environment. She would have thought high family kids had it easy, but there was always the fear that Arthur's cohort would best him and take over to become heir. That could just as easily been Hendry, he explained.

The thought of that made Reiki shudder.

"Ah, here we are," said Arthur.

"Here where?" Reiki looked about, but all she saw were stone buildings, half-drunk staggering people, and the glass doors of a warren. Then, she clued in and shook her head. "No, I don't need healing. I'm fine."

Arthur ran a knuckle down her cheek gently. "You had some memories come back. Now's the time for healing, and Ged's biopaths should be better than those in your homeland."

"Tomorrow, please. I don't want to be poked and prodded at."

He raised an eyebrow in curiosity. "Why, Reiki? What are you afraid of?"

Reiki thought a moment. He was right. She didn't want to go in there because she was afraid. Might as well say so. "The warrens have been useless so far. I don't want to get my hopes up and have them dashed. I need time."

"Really?"

"I just want to not be a curious experiment for a bit. I might even heal on my own."

"Something happened to you in a warren in the past, didn't it?"

A younger Reiki lay on a table, body burning as if she were being drizzled in hot oil. It felt like the scoring of a thousand knives that chiselled at her bones. The pain was unbearable; it had her mind almost lost in shock. But her body was changing. And darkness welled up–

"Shades! Reiki! Talk to me. Are you okay?"

"Wha–?" she was back on the street in Ged, and Arthur gripped her by the shoulders.

"You have to go get healing."

She twisted free of his grasp. "I agreed. Just let me do it in my own time."

"Now, Reiki. While the memories are coming back. We shouldn't waste time."

Like she wanted more memories of burning. She pushed Arthur away before he could gather her back into his embrace.

"Really. I'm fine. Leave me alone."

She walked past him, intending to return to the overpass, but was surprised to find her path blocked by guards. Had they been following the entire time? What a cruel trick to play on her.

"Please, Reiki?" asked Arthur.

He's trying to trick me into thinking I have any choice, the bastard.

She whirled around and found him right behind her, invading her space. That's when Reiki slapped him. She regretted the loss of control the moment she did it, but he deserved it.

Having just drawn the line in the sand, Reiki decided to go with her limited options. She put her head up and marched into the warren.

CHAPTER 10

SEDUCTION

Arthur crossed his arms as he watched Reiki enter the warren. Eric hadn't mentioned any problems getting her looked after back in her demesne. What, by all the stars, made her suddenly so skittish about healing? Was it the frozen water show from her last night in Hillvale? He remembered Reiki denying the event in the train as if she truly didn't remember it. Perhaps there was something undiscovered awakening in her.

He turned to the guard captain behind him. "I commend you for being thorough, but the muscle show wasn't necessary. I'd have talked her into it eventually."

"My apologies. Orders of Hendry Galenden."

"I might have known. One of you follow her and make sure the warren knows she's with my House. See to it that she's escorted back to her suites if they discharge her tonight. If I'm needed, I'll be in my study."

"At once, milord."

Arthur retraced his steps home.

He found a small celebration going on in the manor.

Mostly extended family and a smattering of their friends gathered for a wine and cheese.

He came to the doorway of the hall and watched them. They would have to start fitting the guards into shock armour and installing a city-wide anti-lightning field, complete with broadcast tower, if they wanted to guarantee this peace. If a new Lightning came along to claim Ged, almost every one of these people would wind up dead or in prison. Protecting themselves would be tantamount.

"Arthur, come in, already." Hendry emerged from the crowd bearing a goblet of wine, which he passed over. "Shades, man. You look like you're carrying the weight of the world on your shoulders. Loosen up a bit, would ya?"

"The guards you sent after Reiki. That was a little over the top, don't you think?"

"Ged takes care of her guests." Hendry lowered his voice a little. "Especially nubile young virgins."

"Oh? And how would you know this?"

"Easy. If you were sexing her, you'd not have brought her here. Weren't you the one who told me never mix business and pleasure?"

Arthur guffawed, for Hendry was indeed correct in his quote. Come to think of it, Arthur realized he was in the middle of a very long dry spell. When had he even last had sex? He couldn't easily remember. How shameful.

"You're right, Hendry. I've had too much on my mind lately."

"That's the spirit. Come, let me refill your wine."

"Oh, I'm good, thank you." Arthur drained the goblet and passed it back. "I need to get out of these traveller's clothes. I've been on the road for days."

"Don't tarry. The rolling stone and all that nonsense."

Arthur slipped away from the get-together and took the stairs for his room. He really wanted to be back with Reiki, but under the circumstances it was better to wait until she cooled down. He was lost deep in musing to the point where the tread of someone coming down the winding steps escaped his attention until the voice addressed him.

"Hullo, Mr Galenden."

It was Wendiah, all done up in a pink dress. Her brown hair with its golden highlights was gathered up in a pair of corns in party-style. But the look of sadness on her face spoke funeral sombre.

Arthur peered at her, unsure what to say at first. He decided to state the obvious. Direct tact was one of his better skills when he needed to measure people. Especially when dealing with the local version of Iliara.

"I was always Arthur to you until now, Wendiah."

"Until... well, until our fortunes reversed," she said. She folded her hands together nervously, where just last meeting she had thrust one out imperiously for a parting kiss.

Arthur sighed and reached out to take one of those gloved hands for the kiss she wanted. It should be easy to lead her upstairs and fulfill his mother's wishes right now. Had he not done so quite willingly three weeks ago? Why was this so awkward now?

He decided to bail and take time to think things through. "I'm so sorry to bump into you and run off, milady, but I'm exhausted from my journey and need to crawl into bed."

"Stars keep you, milord," said Wendiah.

"And you," said Arthur.

He felt her eyes on his back as he fled up the stairs.

No doubt her bedroom door would be unlocked tonight. It made Arthur realize that Wendiah was quite aware of what machinations were going on around her. She was even attempting to influence the outcome in whatever direction she thought most favourable. Commendable. Even Xandri would be impressed.

The stairs to his room in one of the spires seemed so much longer now. Arthur remembered counting them as a boy. Two hundred and six steps from the ground floor unless you took some of the servant's corridors where the steps were higher and therefore less numerous. Tonight, it felt like a thousand.

Finally, he reached his room and found a light coming out from under the crack in the door. His luggage from the train waited outside his door, so that was probably Vincent inside laying out his clothes. With a grin of relief, Arthur flung open his door.

And found three women inside, sitting on his bed.

They wore their blonde hair long and loose, and wore the green dresses and coarse fabric of the Rionite mountaineer women which had the shoelace-style ties upfront that pushed up the ladies' assets. One woman on the end held a bottle by the neck, and the entire room gave off the odour of fancy liqueur.

"Hi, Artur," slurred the woman with the bottle. "We're loss."

"Lost, she means," corrected the middle one, who held out her arms to him. "Will Arthur help us find ourselves?"

"Any part will do," said the third, who had her index finger between her lips.

"Sorry, ladies. They sent you to the wrong room," said

Arthur. "You want one flight down and two rooms to the left. Room of Hendry Galenden, High Consular."

"You noht Artur?" asked the woman holding the bottle.

Her pronunciation made Arthur wonder if she had just gotten off the boat as it were. Any other time, he'd have kept them around for some entertainment, but he really wanted solitude, so he kept up the charade.

"I'm Peter Galenden. Third cousin, five times removed. You'll give Hendry my regards?"

They made a slow show of leaving, laughing and giggling almost to the point where Arthur feared they might vomit on his floor. But eventually he got them all herded out of his room and down the stairs.

Satisfied that he would have peace, Arthur dimmed the lights and locked the door. He pulled a chair up to the window where he could see down to the street and wait to make sure Reiki got back safely.

CHAPTER 11

OSSINGTON

"Milord? Have you not slept?"

It was Vincent's voice that stirred Arthur out of his dreams. He raised his head from the window sill, in tune to the protest of sore muscles.

Outside, the sky had lightened to early morning grey. A lone predatory bird circled overhead, looking poised for a deadly strike.

"I must have dozed off. Did Reiki come back?"

"Word just arrived from the warren that she's to return in an hour. They weren't able to treat her. I thought you would want to know."

"Thank you, Vincent. And you are right, that's important, though disappointing news."

"Shall I inform Yolanda that you'll be early to breakfast?"

"Kindly. And would you set out a traveling jacket for me? I'll head out to inspect the Ossington site today."

"At once, milord."

Arthur rose and went to wash up.

Reiki ended up taking two hours instead of one, so

Arthur put off his trip until afternoon and busied himself in the pile of newspapers awaiting him in the den.

High in the news, the League of Lightnings to the south was planning its third general election. Since the League was thirty demesnes strong, the outcome of a new administration would determine oil prices for the next four years. Oil prices would guide gold-to-credit rates and lay a guiding finger on all other parts of the economy for the entire continent. It made Hillvale's little rocket project look like child's play in comparison.

Arthur moved onto the speculation columns. Since the League was the only region in the world to select its leaders by democratic contest, these elections could be tricky to predict. He was still at it when Eric walked in carrying a brown paper bag.

"Sorry to be late," said Eric as he set the bag down on the coffee table beside Arthur. "We lost her medicine on the way. Rolled down the window and cast it into a chasm, the little minx did."

"She must really hate medicine," said Arthur. "Where is she now?"

"Yolanda accosted her on the way up. I left her in the front entry dining room. Took her medicine with me so it wouldn't have any more accidents."

"I see," said Arthur. He folded the paper up and rose to leave, but Eric stood in the way.

"You'll want to exercise patience with her today," added Eric. "She's in a trying mood."

"I'd noticed last night she was far from receptive to trained healing. Some new development?"

"Oh, she's mad at something. Stars wishing it's not you."

Arthur left Eric behind in the den and made his way to the indicated chamber. The front dining room ran along the street-side wall of the manor, with tall windows framed by green-painted lattice-work grills. It served no other purpose than for company to wine in while other rooms of the manor were in use. If Arthur had a choice, he'd have the wall knocked down and extend the hallway through it.

Reiki was in the room, as Eric had promised, sitting near the windows so the rays of sun made her cheeks glow. Arthur stopped in the doorway to watch for a moment, suddenly reluctant to break the tranquility.

A tea set lay spread out before Reiki, who sat in a leather chair that looked like a burgundy hand trying to swallow her. She regarded Arthur levelly as she sipped from a cup held in both hands. No trace of what she thought crossed her face. It would be up to him to make the first venture.

"The warren was unable to help, I hear."

"They did not, though they were very thorough in their investigation of me," said Reiki. She became interested in the window as Arthur approached.

"I hope you've forgiven me for forcing your hand back there. You gotta try all your options, right?"

"Of course, I've forgiven you. It is not my place to hold a grudge."

Upon that pronouncement, Reiki became so entranced with the window that Arthur realized he was anything but forgiven.

"Reiki, please," said Arthur. He reached for her chin to turn her to face him, but she peered at him through the corner of her eye, and the temperature in the room

185

dropped perceptibly. He decided to rethink coming into contact with her.

Meanwhile Reiki turned her teacup over the table, and a lump of frozen tea clattered out. She refilled her teacup, added a spoonful of cream, and swirled the cup in her hands instead of bothering to stir it.

Arthur mulled over his options and tried a different tact. "Reiki, I..."

"Yes, milord?" She regarded him cooly. As one might a stranger.

She plays the game well, he thought to himself. Any other time Arthur would call this an interesting challenge. But there was the topic of his mother to cover. Reiki would have to meet her eventually... best she not go in unprepared. Maybe he could take her out to the Ossington site and explain on the way.

"There's a lot to do today, Miss Reiki," said Arthur at his most formal.

"I'll promise to stay out of the way," she replied. "I really should go seek employment, so I should be busy most of the day."

"Employment?" repeated Arthur in surprise. "Don't you think you're a little bit too sick to be working?"

"I'm quite healthy, thank you. I don't remember certain important things. But I do remember that I mustn't impose upon your generosity."

Arthur couldn't help himself. He started to laugh. It drew a frown from Reiki.

"All is well, milord?"

Arthur bowed to her. "Why yes, milady. Now kindly

rise and have breakfast. Seeking work can wait. I have an amazing day in store for you."

The ride to Ossington took forty minutes, and it seemed to flash by since Arthur, Mallen, and Niobus discussed trade all the way there. Reiki sat beside Arthur and mostly tuned it out while she tried to solve the puzzle-cube.

There had to be a way to turn the segments so all six faces would show the same colours. But no matter how she rotated them, she could only get one or two correct. Very annoying. She was being outsmarted by a child's toy.

By the time they reached Ossington Castle, Reiki was about ready to hurl the puzzle out the window like that foul-tasting medicine the bios had given her. Arthur broke from the conversation to address her.

"Those things can't be solved once you mix them up, you know."

"It must be possible," said Reiki. "It got like that somehow."

"You're missing the scenery. And you'll give yourself a migraine. Who gave you that thing anyway?"

"Hendry. Up in the music room."

"Ah. What a cruel joke for him to play on you. Good thing we've arrived."

The Lansdale pulled up at the front doors of the castle and parked. As Reiki studied it, the building looked more like a fortified manor than a castle, for it had first floor windows and normal house-like doors.

Horse-sized spikes littered the sunny fields around the

castle, and the guard beside the only cannon bore a rifle. An open carriage awaited them near the doors. It was one of those door-less horse-drawn types that sported a canopy to keep the elements away.

The others climbed out of the Lansdale and mingled with the castle attendants. After Arthur helped Reiki out, he took her arm and led her to the front of the group for a round of introductions to the on-site staff.

Reiki plunked the puzzle-cube into her purse in order to get through the introductions. When they all boarded the carriage, she tried to work on it a little more, but Arthur interceded.

"Ahem. Give me the toy."

"But– But–"

He waggled his fingers adamantly, so Reiki relinquished it. She had it memorized anyway. She would work on it in her head.

Arthur passed the puzzle to Eric who exchanged it for a parasol. Reiki accepted the parasol and looked it over. White with blue frills along the ribs. How dull.

"It'll be hot today until the storm blows in," said Arthur. "I don't want you to add sunburn to your agenda."

"Good thinking," said Reiki, though her mind was on the twirling facets of the puzzle-cube.

If Arthur intended to comment further, Reiki was unsure, for the carriage started into motion, and the site-tour began.

CHAPTER 12

EYE OF THE STORM

They visited the Ossington site which was situated about one and a half kilometres from the castle, right on the border of the Planenn Badlands. The half-desert half-scrub, whose name came from the foolish Lightning who had once tried to claim it, formed a safe region for Ged, for few were the armies who would try to cross it.

In case of the worst, Ossington Castle stood within sight of the border. But it had never come under attack in Arthur's lifetime. That's why he toured the site with only his staff as guards.

Mallen and Niobus asked most of the questions, and the site foreman was doing all the explaining. They went over the basics as Arthur ambled along in the background.

"You already had an outside hydrokinetic in to have a look at it?" asked Mallen.

"Two, now, just in case the first was mistaken. We got an inexplicable level drop in the well," said the foreman.

They all looked up at the pumpjack, which was off for maintenance and refitting. They would probably have it disassembled so they could drop pilot lines for testing.

Arthur glanced back at Reiki. She had elected to remain in the shade of a copse of trees where the driver had parked the carriage. A pond had formed there from run-off rain water. The horses sipped at the water and nibbled at the grass. Reiki studied the ripples from tossed pebbles beside them.

The look of concentration on her face couldn't possibly be from a few tossed stones. Arthur bet himself that Reiki was still working on that starforsaken puzzle-cube in her head. He'd let Hendry have it for doing that to her.

As if called, Reiki glanced up. She dropped her handful of rocks and started around the pond to reach the group. Arthur lagged behind to allow her to catch up and smiled as he took her arm. Yep. Definitely distracted.

Seeing his stare, Reiki grinned. "You can take the toy from the girl, but it's not so easy solving the riddle of the woman."

Arthur laughed. "Where in the world did you get that line?"

"One day, when you're done being my foster mother, I'll tell you."

He chuckled again. This saucy version of Reiki was too much for him. He would have to take his time to think of the comebacks for her barbs.

The tour moved on as the foreman led them around the inactive pumpjack. As Arthur listened in on the facts, he realized they really had no choice. They would have to run lateral drilling if they wanted any more life out of Ossington. It meant they'd be down to the two other sites to maintain their cash flow for at least a year. If one more well went down, House Galenden would be operating in the negatives for the foreseeable future.

"It's not all bleak," said Mallen who must have read something of Arthur's thoughts on his face. "The scrubbers for the rocket will make up the difference and then some."

"What worries me is the possibility of foul play," said Arthur.

"From another House?" Niobus sounded incredulous. "Who could find a way to stop up an oil well?"

"Someone with an interest in making sure they control the local market?" suggested Arthur.

Reiki suddenly spoke up. "A seismometer would tell you. To block up a well, a shaped charge could be planted using *power*. It would register if you monitor for earthquakes."

"We don't," said Mallen. "Ged's just not prone to them."

"We could send someone down the well with an electric light to check for visual evidence," said Niobus. "Mallen's the thinner type. I bet he would fit."

"Ha," scoffed Mallen. "There's no way you're stuffing me down a one metre wide tube full of oil and toxic fumes."

"I'd recommend a P-wave scan," said Reiki. "Look for damage at 35.137318 N latitude by 84.711986 W longitude. I suspect you'll find a cave-in there that's choking the oil supply."

She paused and blinked at them in consternation since they'd all fallen quiet.

"What?"

Arthur was first to recover from his surprise. "Reiki. That's amazing. You're sure of all this?"

"I had a peek at the charts back in the carriage. And

the ground there is still glowing from a heat exchange. It makes sense."

"Mallen, can all the equipment be assembled today?" asked Arthur.

"If you'll lend me the Lansdale, I could have it all here in an hour."

"Done," said Arthur. He eyed the dark clouds on the horizon. They'd have a big storm by late afternoon or early evening. Hopefully they could get the studies done before that.

"Wait," said Reiki before Mallen could leave. "Eric has the cube."

"Oh, right," said Arthur. "You better go get it or who knows what will become of the thing."

Arthur watched Reiki walk off with Mallen, then sought out a rail he could sit on to wait.

Reiki collected her cube from Eric and deliberately avoided the well when she returned. She passed about three hundred metres around where all the men were sitting, so the roll of the hills was just high enough to keep her out of sight, and came to a vast, empty plain.

Let them wonder where I got to. Serves Arthur right for treating me like a kid.

The castle was still visible above the chest-high grass. She peered at it and decided it would be best to keep it in sight. Up ahead, there was a single tree and a pond. That would make a good place to sit and work on the cube. She headed for it.

Out here, the grass went drier and grew more sparsely than at the pumpjack. When Reiki peered into the far distance, the horizon went pale yellow, then blue under shifting heat waves. Trees were rare. She wondered if the fields turned into desert farther out.

A little green snake crossed over Reiki's foot as she waded through the grass.

I hope I'm not supposed to be afraid of snakes, she thought to herself as it slithered away.

Reiki walked over to her oasis and sat down against the tree trunk. She glanced back to make sure the castle was still in sight before settling in. Satisfied that she was safe, she worked on her puzzle-cube as the breeze carried warm air across the plains.

Reiki stirred from a light doze, surprised to find her face damp.

She clambered to her feet and stared a moment at a sky all grey and frothing with sinister clouds. It was raining, and the drops were heavy and cold. The tree had probably kept it off her until it was almost a downpour.

Where was Arthur? Why hadn't he come to wake her? Oh yeah. She had nipped his ankles all day. He was giving her room to assert herself. Why now of all times?

The parasol would have to serve as an umbrella. Reiki opened it and raced off in the direction of the castle. As if in response to her dash, the rain thickened into a hard-hitting torrent. She was drenched in a moment despite the parasol.

She was also lost. The castle had vanished in the distance as the rain cut visibility. Reiki would have to stumble forward blindly in the hopes of chancing on it. If she was lucky, she'd find the trampled grass of her arrival and be able to follow her trail back.

A clap of thunder right overhead startled Reiki, and she froze in her tracks. Caught in a lightning storm in an open field? Popular wisdom said she should lie down. But the castle wasn't that far. Perhaps she could make it.

Just then, a gale hit and turned the parasol inside out. Reiki fought it for a moment, but the winds tore the lining away and left her with a wiry skeleton attached to tufts of fabric. Her dress flapped about her. It snapped like a large, wet tent flap and threatened to pull her off balance. For a moment Reiki almost lost the battle to stay on her feet as cold rain slathered down her neck.

I'm not going to get very far like this. I better go back.

Reiki dropped the remains of the parasol and gathered her dress into a bunch so she could jog back to the tree by the pond. She made it and wrapped her arms around the trunk. Probably not the best of ideas during a storm, but blowing away sounded far worse than the off chance of getting hit by lightning.

Minutes ticked by, and Reiki stood there with water trickling off her shoulders. One good thing was that she couldn't possibly get any more soaked. All she had to do was wait out the brunt of the storm.

Another gale hit, bringing with it cascades of white rain water. For a minute Reiki could only see an arm span of distance. And the roar of thunder echoed not far off. She saw flashes of lightning strike very close. Just over the hill where she would probably be if she was stumbling about in the rain. Then the thunder drowned all sound and thought.

At first Reiki thought her eyes were playing tricks on

her, but no, those were headlights approaching. Once the gale passed and rain returned to a more reasonable torrential downpour, Reiki realized the Lansdale was here.

It moved slowly. Slower than she would even walk. Reiki imagined it wasn't very good at off-roading. She was shocked to see it at all.

Maybe I'm imagining this, thought Reiki. *Maybe if I tap my heels together I'll wake up at home and have a good laugh at this nightmare.*

The Lansdale rolled to a stop not far from her. The engine went into idle as rain splattered on its windshield with such ferocity it sounded like hail.

For a moment Reiki stood there staring at it. She supposed that if she didn't move, Arthur would eventually drive on with out her. He was giving her an option to take the rescue even now.

She released her death grip on the tree and hustled to the car. The door opened for her, and she climbed inside to sit beside Arthur.

Silence reigned as soon as Reiki shut the door. The Lansdale changed gears and lurched off as she fought to think of something to say.

"You didn't have to come," she said at last. "I didn't deserve it."

"Don't undersell yourself," said Arthur. He steepled his fingers and watched her with a bit of mirth in the slight curve of his lip.

"Thank you, anyway. Twice over I owe you. Very bad karma."

"Since your idea will get me my well back, I'd say we're even."

K. Hippolite

"It worked?"

"Found the fissure. Right where you predicted. We have a number of ways of dealing with it from here. But it's all thanks to you."

Reiki found herself smiling despite the shudders that ran through her from the water dripping out of her hair and down her back. At least one good thing would come of the day.

Arthur gave Reiki lodging in a guestroom in the castle, a pile of towels, and a dry dress to change into.

She gratefully peeled off the old dress, wrung it and set it to dry on a wooden hanger in front of a window. Her hair took over an hour to tend to. Reiki beat it into submission with a comb and liberal applications of conditioner she found in the washroom.

The storm abated to a steady rain, and Arthur announced that the roads were too muddy to travel. He would spend the night in the castle and set out in the morning.

Somehow, that announcement translated into the entire staff of the pumping station assembled in main living room. They pulled all the sofas and loveseats into a ring and sat in them while Mallen played the fiddle for laughing people who danced in fours.

Power normally came from the castle's old electric generator, but the lines were down, and Arthur stopped the servants from forming a team to go outside and drag it into the basement. They had an antiquated fluorine power core in the castle, but the fuel tanks were empty when the servants checked. Fluorine had gone extinct as a power source in Ged far too long ago to make starting it viable.

196

"We will use lanterns tonight," he said. "It'll be like ancient times. Come, someone find coal or kerosone and we'll roast corn and drink wine."

Before long there was corn and quail, not to mention generous helpings of red wine, though Reiki limited herself to a single glass. And she danced as much as anyone, since partners seemed to be interchangeable on the fly, just as much as the dance step itself.

Arthur danced with her whenever the opportunity presented itself. She chatted with whoever was also not dancing and often took a minute to glance over the puzzle-cube. When Arthur eyed askance of the cube, she stuck her tongue out at him.

Laughing, Arthur joined her on the loveseat after his dance. Reiki moved her wineglass aside so he wouldn't kick it over. She continued to roll the cube in her left hand, still struggling to come up with a solution.

"I can't believe Hendry thought of giving you that thing," said Arthur. "He must have become a really good reader of people."

"Apple doesn't fall far from the tree," said Reiki.

"Ha, at least I do it the proper way. I bet Hendry had to search your purse and see the protractor before he thought of that."

Reiki stopped and glared at him. "He didn't. Don't be a creepo."

Just to be sure, she checked her purse to see if anything was missing. That proved futile as it was too dark. Someone needed to invent a purse light or something for women in theatres and situations like this.

"Hey, I'm not the one who figured out such a great idea in a few hours. It's him you should be calling the creep."

Memories of the music room came to mind. Reiki returned her gaze to the cube and asked as nonchalantly as she could, "Hendry's married, right? To Ellen from the restaurant?"

"Ah no. He's only dating her. She's a Muldret, and our two houses don't much get along. I think Mum promotes the coupling to use it as a political wedge."

"That's mean of her."

"Ah, don't worry. She'll break them up when it serves her purposes."

"That's terrible," said Reiki. "And I have to meet her?"

"The storm bought you an extra day, so don't sweat it."

"Thank you, but I will anyway."

"Oh, heads up," said Arthur.

"What?"

Arthur Galenden was on his feet. He took Reiki by the hand for another turn at dancing.

CHAPTER 13

CHEMILUMINESCENSE

Noon of the next day saw Reiki back in Ged, shopping for parts. Armed with seventeen gold borrowed from Arthur and three of her own, she needed components to build the purse lights she'd thought of.

Reiki envisioned a chemical reaction in a polymer tube, much like a glowstick. To make it work repeatedly, she needed a way to stop the reaction, and here, the monofilament tubes used in the rocket's engine would help.

The tubes would help extract unused substances from the glowing mixture, thereby saving some for the next use. A given light might work a thousand times this way–more than worth the replacement cost of the light. The trick was making the mesh in the first place.

Arthur had dedicated her a room in the basement for a laboratory. Reiki would rather have rented facilities, but with her seed money about to go into machinery, she saw the advantage of going cheap for now.

Reiki would be filling that entire lab. The big one was the stamping wheel which would be taller than her and work like a metal windmill to iron out the mesh pads. She would need a crankshaft to turn it and an engine of some sort to drive it. Many of those parts she'd have to make herself. So far, smiths in Ged seemed reluctant to do business with her once they saw the complexity of the design sketches.

When Reiki got back, near dinnertime, she found Arthur waiting anxiously to see if she'd found everything she needed. She showed him her shopping list where she had all the raw materials checked off. Five gold remained to spare.

"What in the world are these chemicals?" asked Arthur. "What's this chloro-thing?"

"One-chloro-nine, ten-bis-phenylethynyl-anthracene," said Reiki. "It's a bit of a mouthful, but that's the molecule that will release the light energy. It's a polarized molecule, so I'll be able to extract it from the mixture using paramagnetics."

Arthur handed the list back to her. Wonder filled his eyes. Reiki hoped it wasn't with a mix of disbelief, because she knew her idea looked like magic.

"All this chemistry will break your head," said Arthur. "We could play chess after dinner if you wanted. That would get your mind off puzzle-cubes and this chemiluminescence stuff you're on about."

"Sure. I'd love that."

Reiki ended up beating Arthur at chess. She tried to throw the game for him, but he saw through her, so she was forced to win. They played again, and Reiki took a less aggressive strategy, but she managed to corner his Namika and almost force an accidental draw. He only held three of her soldiers and one material piece.

"I was very good at chess until a moment ago," Arthur complained.

"Night, night, Arthur. Thank you for going easy on me."

"But–But –"

Reiki got up, walked around the table and, in a fit of daring she was unaccustomed to, kissed Arthur on the cheek. He barely registered since his attention was still on the game. She decided to leave rather than stay and press her luck with him.

Besides, a lot of designing awaited her in the morning.

By dawn, Reiki was in her lab getting her test tubes and other chemical extraction equipment set up. Parts for the stamping wheel started arriving by noon, and she got her conveyor set up. The lab became a jungle of cogs by the end of the day, but she got the wheel turning. She spent several hours aligning it.

Vincent came to call on Reiki as she was trying to get the conveyor's timing belt to work properly. The lab still smelled of pine tree resin since she had some shells warm-air-baking on an aluminum tray. Lines of beakers littered every table space clear of moving cogs and belts. Vincent had to dodge around it all to reach her.

"Milady, Yolanda would have you know you're late for supper."

Reiki glanced up in surprise. She'd been too busy to notice lunch go by.

"Thank you, Vincent. Tell her I'll be right up."

On the way through the main foyer, Reiki noticed the heat glow of someone hidden around the corner to the stairs. She pondered going a different direction, but then pressed forward. If it was Hendry waiting to surprise her, she'd be happy to get a hand-shaped print of machine oil on his clean white shirt.

However, Reiki's surprise guest turned out to be Patricia Galenden.

"Reiki, so nice to meet you," said Lady Galenden, who had timed it to walk forward as if this was a chance encounter.

"Ms. Galenden. Pleased to meet you." Reiki stopped in her tracks, mind reeling. With her hands covered in grease, she could hardly curtsy or kiss a hand. And she dared not call attention to them or even clasp them behind her back, for they would leave tracks on the small of her back.

Patricia Galenden drew to a halt and crossed her arms disapprovingly. Reiki had no choice.

She did the half-curtsy and managed not to wince at the destruction of her upper hem.

"Come," said Ms. Galenden. She walked in the direction of the stairs to the dining hall, and Reiki hastened to catch up. "I hear you play piano with measurable skill."

"Yes, milady. I can play."

"And apparently you're quite the builder."

"Not normally, milady. Just hammering out an idea."

They reached the base of the stairs and stopped.

Patricia Galenden was striking to behold. Fair hair, filled in heavily in white, so that Reiki was unsure if it was greying or just a very light blonde. Her dark eyes were fierce coals. The type of eyes that missed little and gave even less. Her heat aura was constant–Reiki saw no sign of energy or excitement.

Overall, she's possibly the most intimidating person on the planet.

"You have no name, Reiki."

"Not that I know, milady." Wouldn't it be funny if she was high family this whole time? But the letter had no surname listed, so it was a fair bet she was either a commoner or a serf. Most likely the former, given her advanced scientific knowledge.

They started up the carpeted spiral stairs.

"My son could use a smart woman at his side, but he also needs a strong political tie. What sets you above the obvious choices?"

"Milady, I would never presume to pursue him."

That was a lie. Reiki would pursue him if she could. It wasn't just his looks or the fact that he was being nice to her in her time of need. There was just something about him that suggested he liked her more than that.

"Never think to pursue him? What you're telling me is you have zero ambition."

Trapped by her own words. Reiki could see no way to talk herself out of it. She settled on an aggressive stance.

"My ambition is to make something of myself."

Lady Galenden smiled, though her aura remained flat. They climbed the last of the steps to the second floor.

"This has been enlightening. See that you follow through with this goal. You have two weeks to make yourself useful."

She whisked off without another word. Reiki had no chance to even say goodbye. She stood there trembling for a moment. She was so nervous, she even forgot and put a finger to her lips.

And so Reiki's first meeting with Patricia Galenden

ended with the bitter taste of oil in her mouth. It left her feeling anxious, and she ate dinner in a distracted state. After dinner, she went up to the music room to play and relax her nerves.

Musical score was sitting on the stand when Reiki arrived. A simple concerto in D. She flipped through it, memorized it, then did what she thought was a passable rendition of it. At the end, she was joined by Xandri who walked in, carrying her harp.

"I came to rescue that song from you," said Xandri. "You're killing it."

"What? I thought I did okay."

Xandri shook her head and smiled as she teased back. "You're sucking the life out of it. Don't you live inside? Or is your musical heart made of ice?"

"Oh, don't exaggerate. I wasn't that bad."

Xandri sat on the bench beside Reiki and angled herself to be able to see the score.

"Try again," said Xandri. "I'll accompany you."

She and someone else, it seemed. As they played, a guitarist joined them from a curtained alcove.

Reiki glanced over as the first chords emerged from that part of the room. She could see the outline of heat from the guitarist through the curtains, but had no idea who he was. A servant perhaps? Whoever he was, he had the song memorized, for he never faltered as they played.

Xandri piped up about it first.

"Hey, back there. You gonna hide all day?"

When she got up to go investigate, the guitarist ran away. Reiki watched the heat lines get up and sneak out the window so that when Xandri parted the curtains, the alcove was empty.

"Hmm, no one there," said Xandri.

"He ran off. Maybe he was shy?"

"Bet he'll be back. The sheet music is probably his."

"Let him. I have a chess match to play. I hope Arthur's been practising."

"Oh, I have to see this."

Arthur had not been practising, Reiki discovered. Instead he had four of his family members assembled, who launched an animated in-game discussion about how to beat her. After an hour went by, and the game moved at a crawl, Reiki tried to help them.

"You know, boys, I'm leaning on my Naiskarin deliberately to distract you so I can hook you with the Lightning."

They misunderstood her and tried to pin down the Naiskarin, so she hooked them and captured a cannon.

"Argh, she's about to beat us all," moaned one of Arthur's cousins.

"That's just not possible."

"Let's take those moves back and try again."

Reiki interceded. "How's about this. We'll put the game on hold until tomorrow night so you can think of a strategy. How's that?"

They accepted the offer. Reiki and Xandri left them there arguing and devising strategies.

"They'll be up all night," said Xandri. "That was perfect."

Reiki giggled and took one of Xandri's hands. "What are you doing tonight? Would you like to hang out?"

Xandri's smile disappeared, and her eyes went a little hollow. She recovered after a moment, though Reiki thought her smile looked strained.

"What? Xandri, are you okay?"

"I... um... can't. Not tonight."

"It's late. Surely, you don't have a performance now."

"I... have a date."

Reiki hugged her. "Oh, Xandri. That's wonderful. Who is he? How did you meet? What does he look like?"

"In the shopping centre. We... um... meshed."

Xandri's eyes darted about as she spoke. Reiki was sure she was only going to get half the story on this romantic interest. Xandri wasn't normally the shy type, so Reiki realized the date was someone fantastic. He might not be a looker, but he had charmed Xandri's socks off. She was guarding it as a secret because she wasn't sure it would work out.

"Okay, Xandri. You go on your date. I'll wait up for you, so you can gush after."

"Oh no, please don't wait up. I might not be back early."

Xandri looked like she wanted to leave right away, so Reiki kissed her on the cheek.

"You take care of yourself, Xandri."

'Thank you. Bye, now."

Xandri took advantage of the opportunity to escape. Reiki smiled at her back.

I hope Xandri's date goes well. She's so sweet, she deserves it.

Reiki scaled the remainder of the steps to her room and burst through the door to check on her first light. She'd set it on her dresser to finish drying, and the amber-coloured orb was no longer sticky to the touch.

When Reiki squeezed, the orb burst into orange light, but it faded out right away. She needed to put more fuel in the next prototype.

Reiki set the light back down beside the only other item that adorned her dresser: that letter she'd first found in her purse. She picked it up and held it, the only confirmation she had of her name.

Arthur seemed to think she had something to do with the space program, but the letter didn't seem to suggest it. Reiki remembered seeing another rocket go up during dinner. She was certain she knew how to fly it, but not how she'd come across that knowledge.

So many clues that don't add up.

On a whim, Reiki tore up the letter. She had it memorized now, and seeing it only made her sad about the life of someone else. She cast the bits from the window and watched them flutter into the darkness.

The new Reiki was an inventor, and soon she'd have the lights ready for sale.

CHAPTER 14

CHECKMATE

Reiki had her second prototype ready by the end of the next day. It failed to stop glowing, but she saw where she'd gone wrong. The monofilaments weren't smooth enough to allow the matter to crawl through them. A few more tries and she'd have it.

Having ended her work half an hour before dinner, Reiki retreated to the music room to rest. The room boasted shelved books of sheet music, so Reiki selected one at random. It was a learner's song, but the exercise would do.

Near the end of the song, guitar strings joined her. Reiki peered into the curtained recesses of the music room and saw a figure sitting in a window.

Oh, you're back, are you?

The figure had one foot propped up on the sill, and looked to be wearing close-fitting leggings or tight pants. Decidedly male from the pose, though Reiki couldn't make out his features through the curtain.

She went back to the beginning of the song, and he followed her in. His playing was chaotic and furious. He treated the strings of his guitar more like six metal whips than something of musical value. Reiki found herself speeding up as a result. She switched to a 6/8 waltz on a whim.

The guitarist was onto her time-change. He rolled smoothly between the chord progressions after just two notes of confusion.

Such adaptation. Who is that playing there?

He changed keys on her this time, going up two steps and switching to a gentler rhythm. Reiki struggled to catch the new key, failed, and struck three wrong notes in succession.

Reiki stopped playing and rose to her feet. She strode to the alcove and pulled back the curtain, but the guitarist was gone before she could see him. Out the window, and gone through the trellises by the time she ran over to look out.

Reiki frowned. Add one more mystery to the list.

Arthur spent that day looking after the final touches on the reactors and getting them shipped. He laughed to think that both he and Reiki were tinkering at the same time, even if he was only paying people to tinker for him.

When they met for chess that night, Reiki looked distracted. Probably working her designs in her head. That was perfect. The more distracted, the better. It made for a shocker when his cousins showed up, for they came with a servant bearing the dress they'd agreed on the night before.

"What's that?" asked Reiki as the servant hung the dress on a nail by the mantel.

"It's for you to wear if you lose," said Arthur.

The dress was very short–suitable for boudoir night in a club. If Reiki were wearing it, the hem would brush her fingertips.

"You want me to wear that?"

"Only if you lose."

"That's not happening."

"No problem. We'll drop the dress requirement. But you can't get out of finishing the game."

"Wouldn't dream of it," said Reiki. She corrected the position of some pieces that Arthur's cousins must have moved around during the day, and the game continued.

Arthur was unashamed about pressing his psychological advantage. He looked Reiki deep in the eyes while she was trying to think. When she noticed him, he glanced at the dress so she'd not forget it.

Reiki flushed. If she was picturing herself in the dress, that was a bit less concentration she'd have on the game. Arthur fought not to grin.

Finally after half an hour of that, Reiki made an error, and Arthur took her best piece. Spontaneous applause broke out, and even Reiki had to laugh.

"Hold on, do-over," she said.

"Can't. You let go of the piece," said a cousin.

"I gave you guys do-overs."

"Doesn't count."

Arthur smirked as he listened to them argue. He was almost tempted to intervene, but if he let Reiki have her piece back, she'd destroy them. This might be his only chance to win a game.

"You keep your win," said Reiki, echoing Arthur's thoughts. "This game's not over."

She proceeded to trounce them. No amount of eye contact distracted her. It was a pure blood-letting, and soon Arthur's team had to admit she was a few moves from a checkmate.

When Arthur laid down his Namika in resignation, Reiki slinked out of her seat and leaned across the table.

She batted her eyelashes as she spoke. "Next game that has conditions, I'll choose the outfits."

The gathered family applauded as she walked out.

CHAPTER 15

INDECENT PROPOSAL

For ten days, Reiki worked on perfecting her design.

She played chess against Arthur almost every night, often playing simultaneous games against others who wanted a try at her, though they were smart enough not to lay down any more winning conditions.

One night Arthur and Reiki read ghost stories to each other under candlelight in his private library. Reiki enjoyed that so much, the evening was over in a blink. Arthur walked her back to her room and kissed her on the forehead. She decided not to wash her face for a week.

The next day, Reiki asked Arthur for a clue about her mystery duet partner.

"Arthur, does anyone here play guitar? I think I heard someone playing, but there's no guitar in the music room."

"Hendry plays guitar. I know he's serenaded no end of women."

"Oh?"

"There's a latticework of wires outside the music room under the trellises for hanging vines. We used to climb them when we were younger to watch the girls' music lessons.

There are a zillion ways to climb out. It was very hard to catch us."

"Oh, you guys," said Reiki in exasperation. She should have known Hendry would still be trying to come on to her. First the puzzle-cube and now this. She vowed to beat him at something.

The final prototype of the handbag light was ready in time for a gala, so Reiki got dolled up and went with Arthur. They piled into the back of the Lansdale with Hendry and Ellen Muldret. Reiki resisted glaring at Hendry since she didn't want Ellen to get upset. He sure had a lot of nerve skulking around the music room when no one was looking, then showing up looking all innocent.

"What is that?" asked Ellen when Reiki opened her purse, and the golden light streamed out.

"Oh, sorry. Just testing my new light. I think I made this one too strong. It looks like I've got a lantern hidden in here."

"How does it work?"

"When it feels the pressure of my purse opening, it lights up. It fades after a minute of not being squeezed."

"I want one."

"Oh, there's only one as of yet. I can make you one when we get back."

Ellen shook her head and pointed. "I want that one. How much?"

"How much? Well I–uh." Reiki hadn't worked out a price as yet. She was thinking a gold coin each. That was double her projected material costs.

"Will one hundred suffice?"

Reiki blinked. If she sold for that, she'd be able to repay

the loan from Arthur and keep a healthy return. It was an astronomical amount of money.

Ellen fetched the money from her purse. Ten platinum coins in cash. Reiki accepted the trade. Forget showing off the prototype. She'd cut and run with the money.

Arthur chuckled and patted her hand reassuringly. Reiki smiled for him and wished she was curled up in his arms reading stories instead, now that she no longer had a reason to attend the gala.

Later, Reiki was glad she went through with attending. Other high family women, seeing Ellen proudly displaying her light, begged Reiki to make lights for them. She left the gala with ten more orders.

One thousand gold. That was more money than she knew what to do with. Reiki sat at the piano the next day, trying to express her feelings in music.

Streams of afternoon sunlight caressed the varnished surface of the piano as Reiki coaxed melodies out of it. Three songs in, she was joined by the guitarist from the window.

Reiki smiled. Hendry must have heard the music and rushed up here. Now was her chance to show him.

She shifted to a classical melody that had a number of hard key changes. He took the bait and followed her in. He matched her seamlessly through the first two key changes. It was like he knew the song.

Bastard. He's figured out which songs I know and practised the hard ones in advance.

Unable to throw him, Reiki ended the song early. She carried the last chord progression into an interlude, and he took over with a new, unfamiliar song. It was simple enough to catch; a very basic G-D-C song as a base. With a few instrumental flourishes on the C.

It was the strange shift he did to a reverse variant that made Reiki shudder. The way he tapped the strings and threw in a D-minor-A-minor roll. It was a song she had played before, back in school during band practice.

Reiki's hands knew which keys to hit. A strange sensation, for her mind was in another place. She was lost in a room of her peers, where the same evening sun glittered through half-drawn metal blinds. There was Francesca, playing her viola. And off to the side was Sanny pecking away at the xylophone. All while Reiki played the school piano and –

She snapped to reality. Hendry had figured out this song from her past. He was playing this on purpose to jog her memory.

Arthur was right: Hendry was a sly one. He had researched her and figured this all out. The puzzle-cube... it wasn't an accident. She must have had one before whatever changed her.

With a crashing final chord, Reiki ended the song mid-verse. She swept off the bench and hurried to the alcove, but Hendry was a step ahead of her. He was gone from the window just like the last time.

"Wait, please!" she called. But it was too late. Reiki ran to the window and saw his heat prints running up the trellises. Too dangerous to follow, though she considered it. Besides, he'd know his way around the upper parapets. She might lose the trail while climbing.

Bereft of an important chain of memories, she fell to the sill and began to cry. The outpouring of tears ran its course, and no servants came to check, which was a boon. The last thing Reiki wanted was a rumour that she'd lost what was left of her marbles.

Hendry. She had to find him. Find him and talk reason into him. If he knew her past, why withhold it from her? Whatever the reason, she would get to the bottom of it and get the answer from him. Her universe depended on it.

Reiki took the lift down to the main floor and asked around for Hendry.

The Galenden doorman offered some advice. "You should try the den downstairs. I saw him come in and head down there not long ago."

Coming in from a lengthy climb, no doubt.

"Was he holding a guitar by any chance?"

"Why no, I'm afraid. Why do you ask?"

"Nothing. Thank you," said Reiki. "I'll check downstairs."

The stairs to the downstairs den formed a twisty passage like a worm's home. Reiki knew Mallen's offices were down here, but little else past her lab.

Hendry sat inside an office labelled "Consular", seated at a desk, where he penned a document with a quill pen. He glanced up when Reiki came to stand in the doorway, finished the word he was writing, and set the pen back in the well.

"Good evening, Reiki. It cheers my heart to see you." He dusted the letter and set it aside carefully before leaning back in his chair. "You are a welcome sight on eyes too used to the confines of office."

"You know my past," she blurted. So much for the

diplomatic approach. "You played that song. I recognized it. I need to know more. Please tell me."

Hendry raised an eyebrow. "Do tell."

"On the guitar. In the alcove in the music room. That was you, was it not?"

"The music room, is it? I'm not sure what you mean."

Reiki clenched her fists. "Don't lie to me. It's like you knew I'd be addicted to that puzzle-cube. I need to know, Hendry. You can't play me like this."

Overcome, she turned to face the hall. Hendry pushed back his chair and rose to his feet. While he approached, Reiki wiped her face with a sleeve. This wasn't going at all like she'd planned.

"Reiki, Reiki," said Hendry. "I know a lot of people. Like archivists in Ged. People whose power it is to trace a lineage. And I had a hair sample you carelessly left me that night in the restaurant."

"You had my parents tracked down?" She whirled to face him, no longer caring if he saw her reddened eyes. "Tell me, please. Tell me everything."

"Ah, but..."

"But what? Tell, me, Hendry."

"All this information did not come cheap."

"I'll pay you back what you spent. Only tell me and end this suspense."

Hendry smiled and ran a finger along her jaw. "Oh, I was thinking about an entirely different form of payment."

A cold icicle of fear ran down Reiki's spine. "I can't give you what you want. Take the money and have done with."

"Can't? Or won't? What price is too high for you, my dear?"

Reiki opened her mouth to reply, but no words came forth. She backed up a step, which put her in the hall. As coherent response fled her mind, she turned to leave.

Hendry spoke behind her. "You know where my room is if you change your mind tonight."

And what could Reiki hope to do, other than meet his demands? She left the basement, head up and eyes dry. Meanwhile, her stomach churned.

CHAPTER 16

I NEED YOU
TO KISS ME

Reiki sat in her room for almost an hour, staring at the smokestacks of Old Man in the waning sunlight. Her brain bounced from topic to topic without forming a complete thought. Should she take Hendry's bait in trade for her life back? Should she report him to Arthur and risk setting the cousins against each other? If she reported him, what would stop Hendry from murdering her to cover things up? It's not like anyone but Arthur would really miss her right now. And there was Patricia Galenden to worry about if Reiki tarnished the reputation of her political heir.

Only one thing to do. Put her body on the line for the greater good. The shame would wash off eventually. Years from now she would probably laugh about this. *Remember the time I had sex with a stranger in exchange for my memories? What a riot.*

So hilarious, Reiki felt her eyes watering. But her mind clicked too much to finish crying it out. Instead, she went out to catch some of the boutiques before they closed for the evening.

Arthur was back by the time Reiki returned. She knew this because she saw Eric inside, talking to the doorman. She avoided them all and went right to her room with her two paper bags. There was so much to do, she couldn't afford any distraction.

Right after she'd bathed, Vincent came to call on her.

"Good evening, Miss Reiki. Arthur sent me to remind you he was winning his first game last night when you left off, and he would like to continue."

"Thank you, Vincent. Kindly tell him I cannot play tonight. I'm feeling under the weather and might go to bed early."

"I shall, milady."

A white lie, really. Reiki would drop by to see him that very night. But first to get ready.

Now that she owned a safety-razor, Reiki did her legs. She worked carefully, and managed to nick herself only once. Then, an hour on her hair, the same on her nails and eyes, and she was ready for the final touch-ups.

What kind of lipstick does Hendry prefer? Reiki put three shades of red in her purse just in case. She set her purse down on her bed and shoved her new bottle of spermicidal gel into it. The label claimed ninety percent effectiveness. Hendry wouldn't even have to see her use it if she timed things properly.

It was late evening by now. They would normally be still up playing chess, but Arthur would likely retire early without her. Reiki got up and walked out of her suite. She left her purse on her bed. For this first errand, she wouldn't need the lipstick or the gel.

Arthur was in his room, as Reiki had guessed. He answered her knock, and his eyebrows went up when he saw her.

"Reiki? Is that you?"

"Of course, it's me. Let me in."

His room was neat and organized, with a new suit laid out for him on his bed, and a folded towel and soap at the foot. He had a desk and writing papers under an electric lamp. Covering the papers was that *Sinister Storm* book. He had probably been trying to read until Reiki arrived.

"What happened to you?" asked Arthur. "Why are you all dressed up? That is a new dress, isn't it? Is it silk? Did more memories come?"

"Arthur," said Reiki. "I need you to kiss me."

"Wait, what?"

"Kiss me, you bastard. It's extremely important."

He blinked back surprise and smiled. "I do enjoy filling requests."

Arthur put his hands on Reiki's hips and leaned forward. She straightened out to catch him on the lips, but he drew back and got on his toes in order to plant the kiss on her temple.

"There, you go, little lady."

"That wasn't a kiss at all," she cried.

"My lips touched your face. I'd call that a kiss."

"Oh, you stupid boy. Do you want me to spell this out for you? I need you to fuck me."

"Wha– Reiki?"

She shrugged her shoulders out of the gown so it fluttered to the floor around her feet. Arthur just stared at the black lace and crotchless straps. Both in shock and in undisguised lust. It was all the encouragement Reiki needed to jump into his embrace.

They flailed a moment, for Reiki wrapped her legs around Arthur's hips. He stumbled and managed to topple over the foot of his bed. They rolled off, and Reiki landed first, with Arthur using his hands to break their fall. Their momentum carried Arthur to his back, and Reiki managed to find his mouth during the chaos. She scored that kiss she wanted, even if Arthur broke off.

"Hey, we can't do this," he said as he tried to pry himself free.

Unfortunately for him, the bulge in his pants rubbed up between her legs. Reiki sighed and squeezed tighter.

"Ohh, she likes that," Reiki informed him. She thought that noise might be her body purring.

"What in this corner of the universe is wrong with you tonight?" Arthur sounded exasperated. So much so that Reiki stopped wriggling and looked him deep in the eyes.

"I think I'm in love with you," she told him. "But after tonight, I can never have you."

"Wow– wait, say what?" Arthur managed surprise, relief and confusion all in one stuttering question.

Reiki tried to lock lips with him again, but drew back when he reached out and used the bed to pull them up. Reiki allowed him to collect her hands and cup them within his. Unable to bear the thought of him escaping, she kept her legs wrapped about him.

They just stared while Reiki wondered how long he

was going to keep that lump hidden in his pants. Arthur gently set a finger on her lower lip. He traced a line down her chin, along her throat, and down to the lace of her bra. Every inch of that touch burned her skin. But that's where the contact ended. Arthur withdrew his hand, looking as if he was horrified at what he'd done.

"What? Why'd you stop?"

"Listen. I just want to check that you're sure about this."

"I'm wearing next to nothing and I'm sitting in your lap. Do I need to go downstairs and build you a flashing neon sign?"

"But—"

Arthur stopped when Reiki set a finger over his lips. He was going to talk her out of this if she let him. She took his arms at the elbows and guided them around her sides so his hands rested on her bra. Instead of doing the honours, Arthur leaned forward and kissed the base of her neck.

Finally! Progress.

She tilted her head to give him room to work. Her pulse went up and down as he kissed along her collarbone and out to the other shoulder. It was like a roller coaster for her heart. And when it ended, she wanted it to start again.

Instead of repeating the motion, Arthur set his hands on Reiki's hips and rocked her backward so he could get to his feet. He laid her on the edge of the bed, leaned over, and kissed her with such passion she had to break off as a diver surfacing.

Arthur's hand slid along her side, so Reiki arched her back to give him room to reach the clasp of her bra. After that, she had a moment to inhale raw air before his lips closed around hers.

A distant bell sounded the third hour of the morning as Reiki disentangled herself from Arthur's embrace. She dressed while he snored. Well, half dressed–she wouldn't need underwear for the next part of her plan.

Good thing all our rooms are in the upper floors, she thought as she returned to her suite to collect her purse. It meant no skulking around and waking people up. And it meant she could keep her rangy sex-hair. Hendry didn't deserve to see her dolled up.

Just to spite him all the more, Reiki coated her lips in black with two carefree strokes that would leave traces on her cheeks. Let him think she'd lost her mind too. After what she was about to give up, maybe that would happen for real.

Hendry's door was closed, of course. But when Reiki pressed her ear against it, she heard moaning and the press of bodies. She'd have to wait her turn. That almost broke her resolve right there, but she willed her feet to stay put.

Whoever was in there with him moaned louder. Hendry must be really good at his game to elicit that kind of reaction. Nowhere near as good as Arthur, she thought with a trace of satisfaction. After her night, no one, not even Hendry, would be able to make her feel a thing.

What makes you think Hendry's even telling the truth?

"I'm here to get my life back," she said aloud. It sounded hollow and unconvincing.

This will never wash off. You will allow him to use you, and he'll have forgotten you by morning.

"Good. I don't want him to remember me."

And Arthur will never, ever kiss you again.

She mulled that over. She would live the rest of her life unable to face him and reliving this one baleful night.

It was too much. Reiki fled.

CHAPTER 17

UNFORTUNATE CHOICES

Reiki bit her lip in anger and frustration all the way back to her room. Why wasn't she strong enough to go through with it? If she spent the rest of her life a husk of a person, she'd have only herself to blame.

Foolish girl. How did Hendry trace your roots? Copy him.

That wouldn't work. Hendry had high family connections. Nothing Reiki could accomplish in a decade would emulate Hendry's research.

Tears blurred her vision as she stumbled her way into her room. She dumped her purse on the dresser and curled up on the floor to weep. That lasted only a minute before her ticking mind informed her that Arthur's bed was not yet off-limits. Hendry could wait for another night. For now, Reiki could again taste happiness.

Reiki grabbed a dinner napkin from her night table and tiptoed back to Arthur's room as she cleaned the black lipstick from her face. She found him sleeping still, with his arm draped over the empty spot. She watched his face while she slipped out of her dress. Happy, she would hazard. Having dreams of them together. Dreams she'd just been on the verge of shattering.

Gingerly, so as not to wake him, Reiki lifted his arm and crawled back into bed with him. He seemed to sense it, for the arm tightened around her back and pressed her to him. She failed to suppress a shudder that woke him.

Reiki felt a stirring. Apparently Arthur had managed to recharge while she was gone. Goose bumps covered Reiki's skin as he roused to full awareness and began to caress her side.

"Your hands are freezing," said Arthur.

The look of concern that clouded his face made Reiki tremble with desire. She looped an arm about his neck and drew in for a kiss. She wanted to freeze every moment of this in her mind in case of the worst, but soon after, Arthur's hands got busy and broke her concentration.

Golden morning sun bathed Reiki's sleeping form. Arthur knew she was really tired because she failed to wake, even when he ran his fingers through the delicate curls of her hair.

A pity he'd have to disrupt this tranquil moment. She needed to sneak back to her room before she got seen here and the servants got to talking.

As if in response to his thoughts, Reiki wrapped her arms around his chest and snuggled in closer. He managed to hold still despite the iciness of her hands and feet. He'd either have to get used to that or make her wear socks to bed.

A knock at the door told Arthur Reiki was too late to sneak out. He'd have to use one of his auxiliary plans. Hide her in a closet until the coast was clear. Unless it was Vincent–he was used to seeing women sneaking out of Arthur's room and knew how to be discreet. For anyone else, Arthur couldn't be sure that word wouldn't reach social circles. Such news would cast a pall over his mother's political schemes, which would complicate life for everyone.

The rap at the door sounded again. It sounded insistent. Arthur ruled out Vincent, as he disentangled himself and climbed out of bed. Vincent was allowed in Arthur's suites. If it was important, the boy would let himself in and awaken Arthur personally.

Arthur leaned over Reiki as he buttoned up his nightshirt. He kissed her on the cheek and whispered in her ear.

"Here's to a thousand more sunrises together, sweetie."

Reiki mumbled and turned into a bundle of sheets. Arthur smiled and made his way to the door as he finished dressing. This would be bad news, of course. Something gone horribly wrong at the Ossington oil rig. Today would prove very trying.

When Arthur threw the door open, he was surprised to meet a wall of men that rushed him. It was a mix of the city guard and some sort of constabulary he didn't recognize. They shoved Arthur back, and he fell, but rolled and came back to a knee.

The head constable, with his navy blue jacket and tall hat, led the men into Arthur's suites. He pointed a gloved hand at the bedroom.

"She's in there. Take her."

Arthur tried to beat them to the doorway, but there were too many of them. They grabbed him around the waist and pulled him clear of the door.

Reiki managed to roll out of bed before they caught her. She took a running leap at the window, but the constables snagged her mid-stride. They hauled her to the bed, and one held up a sheet to cover her while a second wrestled handcuffs onto her.

Meanwhile Arthur tried to get to Reiki, but six men formed a wall and pushed him back.

"What is the meaning of this? Release her at once!" yelled Arthur.

"No can do, milord," said the head constable. He pulled a sheet of paper from his breast pocket which he unfolded and handed to Arthur.

Arthur snatched it from him, as Reiki's yelp of pain tore at his heart. The paper was an arrest warrant signed by the five heads of the Gedanese government. His own mother's signature was there, and it was dated yesterday. That meant his mother had deliberately omitted to warn him.

They had Reiki on her feet, and the way they were handling her body made Arthur want to go fetch his sword and go on a rampage, but he forced himself to try to think clearly and read the rest of the warrant.

'...for failure to honour contract terms,' said the bottom line.

"What contract term is this?" he demanded.

"She never told you? She signed a contract when she joined the Academy of the Stars that she would report if someone ahead of her had to bow out. She failed to report, so now she's under arrest for dereliction of duty."

"Wait," cried Reiki. "I have amnesia. I don't remember anything about a report or a contract."

"We staff an internal biopath team. We'll have them verify your story."

"No! They'll just deny it."

Arthur jumped in. "Wait, we have a letter. It sounded like a rejection. There was nothing in it about having to report."

"Show me," said the head constable.

But Reiki put on a look of horror. "It's... gone. I tore it up. I didn't think I'd need it."

The constable shook his head. "Get her down to the cars, boys."

Reiki put up a good fight, even made some of them yelp in pain and retreat to deal with sudden frostbite. But they were too numerous. They got her down, managed to cuff her ankles together, and dragged her out of the room in a wall of jostling arms and elbows.

"Arthur!"

He heard Reiki's desperate cry as the other men held him back from reaching her. It happened so fast, his mind was still reeling when the last constable left the room.

"Milord?" Vincent came up to him and set a hand on Arthur's shoulder when he collapsed against a wall.

"Vincent. Tell Eric to warm up the Lansdale. They're not getting away that easily."

After doing the walk of shame through the Galenden household clad in cuffs and a bed sheet, Reiki found herself stowed in the back of a sedan and whisked along the narrow Gedanese roads.

She complained to the two men in the front seat. "Could we have at least stopped for me to get dressed?"

The driver ignored her, leaving it up to the man in the passenger seat to reply.

"Every second counts. The rocket leaves in four days."

"Wait, rocket?"

"Of course. You signed on to go to the moon."

"What?"

"We've used up the two people ahead of you, and there's no one else left who's trained for the job."

"Used up? What do you mean by that?"

"They all died during practice missions. Like I said. You're all that's left. Either you go up, or the rocket's grounded for eighteen months."

A knot of terror took hold in Reiki's chest. She decided not to ask any more questions for the rest of the trip. Not if the answers were going to be that dreadful.

"Stars save me," she said.

And in the distance, the rocket awaited.

CHAPTER 18

FETTERED CHAINS AND CHOCOLATES

It was a frustrating day for Arthur. He drove to the launch site on the far edge of Gedanese territory and tried to find Reiki, but every legal avenue he took met with insurmountable hurdles.

Many of those hurdles had the guiding hand of his mother behind them.

The first problem was that Reiki's situation was classified, so almost everyone he asked in the space program's administrative channels denied any knowledge of her. The Academy behind the program had special diplomatic status in Ged. For him to compel them to relinquish her, he needed authorization from at least three council members. And with his own mother dragging her feet on it, Arthur had to admit the odds were slim.

He cornered her on it that evening. Lady Galenden was in an upstairs library, as was her wont in that final hour before bed. He walked in and started without preamble.

"Mum, you're hatching some sort of plan to force Reiki onto that rocket. It's like you have it in for her."

"I'm afraid I don't. Cheese?"

"No, thank you." Arthur declined the offered platter and sat down in a facing easy chair. "Everyone at Mission Control's been giving me the cold shoulder when I even ask to talk to Reiki."

"Speaking of the ladies in your life, how's Wendiah?"

Arthur smiled and narrowed his eyes. "You know well how Wendiah's doing. You and the council never let her out of your sight. I bet you could tell me the colour of her underwear right now."

"Red. Could you hurry things up with her before one of the other houses sneaks in?"

"You're dodging the topic."

"I hear your little peasant girl can play chess."

"Peasant? Maybe she's a high merchant guilder now." That reminded Arthur he needed to hire people to finish producing the ten orders Reiki had promised to make. That was way too much money and exposure to pass on.

"If you like them mind-wiped and pliable, I can find a few Muldrets for you."

Arthur sighed. It was like they were having two separate conversations.

"A truce. Assign Reiki a legal scholar to represent her. In trade, I'll take Wendiah out to the next ball."

"Reiki's out of my hands," said Patricia. She popped a bit of cheese in her mouth and became interested in her book. A smile of glee teased the edges of her lips as she chewed.

Arthur decided to offer a suggestion. "You can push a motion to council."

"The Academy is paying a princely sum to launch the rocket from our lands. What now shall we do to change the flight plan with three days' notice?"

Arthur gritted his teeth. She was right—council would barely have time to approve any motion in such a small time frame.

"There's a launch party the night before liftoff. You should go. Take Wendiah, maybe."

Arthur strode to the door and paused while he tried to think of a parting retort.

"I mean it, Arthur. It'll be a chance to say goodbye to your peasant girl."

"Don't write her off yet, mum. If anyone can get to the moon and back, it's Reiki."

The next day, Arthur had his staff seek out a crew of five to man her lab. He ended up with a pair of chemists and three textile workers. He remembered from talking to Reiki that the lights themselves were nothing fancy—it was the wheel that created the monofilament mesh to stop the reaction that was new. This meant it was safe to show the chemists Reiki's production notes. He had her designs for the wheel burned, certain Reiki would be able to recall them if needed.

The chemists were able to puzzle out Reiki's notes and make statements that Arthur found convincing about their ability to produce the lights. Arthur hired them and moved the lab out to a rented building, so his mother wouldn't be able to come up with a claim on Reiki's profits.

Once everything was established and production was on the go, Arthur made known that he was seeking someone to become operational manager in Reiki's stead. The first applicant who showed was a bit of a surprise.

"Why so shocked?" asked Xandri. "I'm the best choice you could get."

"I don't know... I was hoping for a Süffite merchant-prince. You know how good they are with money."

"I understand how high family works just as well as he would. If anything, I spend more time among potential customers than he ever will."

Xandri had some good points, but Arthur wanted someone who understood business, too. He quizzed her on it.

"What do you know about things like supply and demand? Production and freight? He can give me all that."

"He's a man. How is he going to sell a purse?"

"What do you mean? Of course, men can sell purses."

"Really?" Xandri batted her eyelashes, but Arthur put his foot down.

"Yes, really. There's nothing to it."

"A dare, then."

"What?"

"Carry my purse. If you can last twenty-four hours, I'll agree that your merchant guy can do the job better than me."

An hour later, Arthur handed back the purse and named Xandri operational manager of the new microguild.

Xandri was rarely seen for the next two days. When Arthur managed to find her, she mumbled something about organizing a fashion show in the League capital. He left her to it and went to the launch party by himself.

Mission Control was a squat tower thrown up on top of a small castle near Ged's airstrip. A hundred forty-four buildings lay nestled in close to it like a small town of brick lean-to's. Dwarfing this village was the rocket that three years of blood had created.

The rocket's star-shaped wing pattern made it look like a brown eggplant balanced on the larger end. The colour came from the ablative material that would protect it during re-entry. From what Arthur knew, that coating would burn off as the rocket plunged back into the atmosphere.

The launch cradle was a mass of gears and pulleys. It would extend during the launch and help the heavy rocket get off the ground like a giant crossbow. It was almost a kilometre in length—a giant man-made sword of steel beams thrust into the soil.

People had come from the world over for the event. When Arthur disembarked from the Lansdale, he saw foreign outfits and heard chatter in unfamiliar languages among the members of the crowd who waited outside the castle.

Four metal legs ran from the corners of the castle's outside walls and met in a conflagration of steel bars that supported Mission Control. Two glass-tube elevators gave access to it, and those vanished into the bowels of the castle. Already, strains of music drifted down from the open balconies and windows. The celebration of mankind's greatest design was well underway.

The door guards recognized Arthur and let him by. He took the short flight of interior stairs two at a time and drew puzzled glances as he attained the throne room that was now the epicentre of the festivities.

Eight members of the flight crew were present. The women wore matching white gowns that bordered on high family Naming wear. The men wore tuxedos and carnations. All posed for a swarm of photographers, while the world's elite milled about in a complex game of posturing.

Arthur approached the nearest Academy official he could find and asked after his quarry.

"Excuse me, sir. I was told the whole crew would be here. Do you know of one called Reiki?"

"They're all about the castle doing their photo-ops," said the man. "Nigh on fifteen of them, you know. I don't know them all by name, but I'm sure everyone's present."

"Young woman. Tall. Long curly red hair."

"Oh, her. Yes. She's thataways."

The man pointed up to the second row of balconies. Arthur thanked him and took to the stairs.

He found Reiki outside, standing on a balcony that gave view of the rocket. Like her colleagues, she wore a white, strapless gown and carried a bouquet of roses. So tranquil was the scene, that Arthur felt like he was intruding.

Reiki turned to look at him and spoke one word as she dropped her bouquet.

"Arthur..."

She got no further, for Arthur was at her side. He gathered her into a hug and felt her tremble. Her hair smelled of olives instead of the summer meadow it had the night they'd coupled. But it was her. At last, he had her back.

"Where have you been?" he asked when Reiki drew back to speak. "I searched all over for you."

"They tested me for amnesia. No surprise, the Academy's in-house bios found nothing wrong with me, so I've been cleared for launch."

"But you don't want to go. Quit. I'll have the best legal representation in the lands back your case."

"The Academy has all the witnesses and written proof they need to verify I was a student there. And they showed me the contract I signed. The signature is mine. It matches the one I thought I invented a few weeks ago."

"We'll fight it, Reiki."

"It's twenty-five years in prison for dereliction of duty. They said it's to discourage us from deserting. The case is pretty iron clad. And who knows how many years I'll spend in jail while fighting the conviction."

She was right on that matter. Arthur knew his mother would be only too glad to lock Reiki up for ten years before even considering a hearing. Legal scholars would eventually get her out, but with all the obstacles in place, she was guaranteed jail for a third of her life.

"So, you're going up," he said. He paused to swallow because his voice wavered and threatened to crack. "All's the better, because it buys you freedom in thirty days instead of thirty years."

Reiki giggled. "Such an optimist. What if we blow up like the other rockets?"

"You'll eject and tumble from space, and I'll be waiting here to catch you."

"I hope you have a very large net."

They stared at each other a long, timeless moment

before Reiki threw her arms around him and squeezed. Arthur kissed her long and hard. He couldn't get enough of her... couldn't taste her enough. Let the moon cease to turn, he would still be here holding her.

Reiki disentangled herself. Arthur tilted her chin up.

"Come. The music has started. Let's go teach those prissies how to dance."

Reiki gave him a crestfallen look. "Arthur, I can't dance right now."

"What? Of course, you can. You were very good that time–"

She lifted her dress so Arthur could see the fettered chains and blinking black box bound to her ankles.

"It's a low-powered explosive. If I try to get farther than broadcast range of the castle, it'll blow my leg off. They'll still send me up with one leg, too. They were quite clear on the matter."

Arthur fought down a surge of anger. Where did they think Reiki might run in a desert?

Reiki hugged him while he collected himself.

"Could you sneak me a few things?" she asked into his cheek.

"A hacksaw and pliers?"

"Chocolate."

"What?" Arthur held Reiki away to look in her eyes and see if she was joking.

"We're on special diets to reduce waste when we launch. I'm starving and there's a huge table of Selanese chocolates in there that the guards won't let me near."

"I will if you'll agree to dance."

"Dance? But how?"

"Just here. Use little steps you can manage in the chains. Yep, just like that."

Arms folded about each other, they swayed to the chords of the music coming through the entryway. Their dance ran several songs as the moon burst from occlusion over the rocket that was destined to one day meet it.

"What if I die up there, Arthur?"

"If you don't come back, you leave behind the man who loves you a million times over."

Wrong choice of words. The veneer of control Reiki had in place shattered into a fit of tears. It took him a few minutes to calm her down.

"There, there. You're coming back. Don't be like that."

"Foolish boy. Get me out of here," said Reiki between gritted teeth.

"B-but the bomb on your leg–"

"I don't give a flying spark about my leg if I'm going to die in space. Get me out of here and I'll spend my life legless but happy."

"Oh, Reiki."

"I mean it. I'll get crutches. If I have to choose between you and a leg, I can't do it."

"Shhh, now. It'll be alright. Let's just enjoy the dance."

They got one more song in while Reiki dried her eyes. When the song ended, two constables turned up.

"Orders are for crew to retire for the night," said one. "Launch is tomorrow, and there's no room for tired astronauts."

"Please, two more songs," said Reiki.

The constables exchanged a glance. "You can sleep naturally or by injection. Doesn't matter to us either way."

Slowly, reluctantly, Reiki released Arthur. Her eyes said it all.

I've changed my mind. I don't want to go up because I'm not coming back.

"You'll come back to me, Reiki. You'll see."

"Good-bye, Arthur."

She marched off in little steps, paused in the doorway, and blew Arthur a kiss before the constables swept her away.

Arthur stared after her, as an uncaring moon made the side of the rocket glisten.

CHAPTER 19

JOURNEY

The launch day was partially overcast, so the sun peeked out occasionally from between thick clusters of cloud.

Arthur stood among the members of the crowd on that warm Gedanese spring day, separated from the ramp to the lift by a row of guards and a rail.

Many were the bleary eyes around him. Few had managed to get to bed at a reasonable hour, save the astronauts and Mission Control staff. From the grins and sidelong glances, Arthur was willing to bet a number of people were yet to get a wink of sleep.

He'd arrived an hour and a half early, but it looked like they were going to wait until the last second to launch. The countdown was at nine hundred before the doors to the staging area even opened to allow the crew onto the ramp.

Out they came in single file. Led by Captain Spacerman, with whom Arthur had shaken hands last night. "Spacerman" was an assumed name, Arthur knew. Awarded for demonstration of valour in a previous spaceflight. It was a little consoling to know that the captain of the ship at least had experience with emergency situations. The Academy had such a poor track record at bringing its astronauts back alive, the crew would need every boon it could get.

Reiki was fifth in line, being the lowest ranking member of the bridge crew. If Arthur understood correctly, she would hold position of Store—a kind of repository of data since there was no room on board to bring a computer and a library of storage cartridges.

Each crew member wore a silvery spacesuit and carried a helmet. The scene looked surreal out here in the desert. The moon seemed an impossible destination—a storybook trip. Arthur pinched himself to make sure he wasn't hallucinating.

Spectators cheered and waved as the crew marched by. Reiki spotted Arthur in the crowd and slowed, but someone bumped into her from behind, so she stepped out of line to wave.

Arthur pulled out the puzzle-cube she had yet to solve. Reiki had left it behind along with the rest of her belongings, but Arthur thought she would have taken it if she could.

He threw the cube to Reiki. She caught it and blew him a kiss. Cheering from the crowd broke the sombre decorum, but Spacerman barked an order and pointed at the clock. In a moment, he had them all lined up and marching forward again.

Reiki glanced back and grinned at Arthur one more time. He wondered if that would be the last time he saw that smile.

The guards herded everyone back to a chainlink fence as the crew reached the transport vehicle that would scoot them across the tarmac. Earlier that morning, crews had lowered the rocket so it now rested on the launch cradle at a sixty degree angle. It took several minutes to get everything organized, and by then the crew had vanished inside. The announcer declared two hundred over the loud speaker.

At one hundred, the first of the three thrusters burst into a cone of red flame. The other two came on at ninety and eighty. By twenty, the crowd was chanting along with the loudspeaker. All engines kicked into yellow flame on one.

With a deep, ground-shaking roar, the rocket took off. It ejected from the launch cradle and carved a lazy curving line into the clouds.

People cheered and screamed all around him, as a stream of exhaust formed a line pointed at the heavens. Here, man said to the stars, "We're coming to meet you." Here, the fate of the universe might change.

But Arthur stuck his hands in his pockets and watched.

Iliara approached Kajo's fortress in a dark and foul mood.

Three weeks. Almost a month of being shuttled about having to play diplomat as punishment for a crime they couldn't pin on her.

Once that bitch Reiki had passed out, word had gotten to Iliara that Kajo was on his way to her suites. She'd had plenty of time to have Reiki's half-conscious body dumped in the streets—by all accounts Iliara had proven her innocence. Kajo was such a despot, he'd still blamed Iliara for Reiki's fingerprints showing up on her table. That wasn't proof of anything. What a travesty of justice. It was so unfair.

Apparently, Iliara's word was worthless to the guys in charge, for they'd agreed to punish her with diplomatic duty. Hours of boring meetings with old men who just wanted to look down her top. She'd been lucky to survive the ordeal. One day she'd show them all. They'd regret trifling with her.

A ground-based spotlight blew out, giving Iliara a bit of a scare.

Easy, there, girlie. No more electrokinetic surges and no more broken lights. People got pissy when she melted out wiring.

She reached the front entrance and gestured for the guards to open for her. As they did so, she heard Doli's unmistakable chuckle and the whine of an electric weapon charging.

Reaction came before thought, and Iliara latched onto the nearest guard with her powers. She reached across the attraction part of the telekinetic spectrum and pulled him off balance so he fell across the opening.

The gunshot that killed him was muffled under some sort of silencer. He gave a single groan as his arms splayed and his head snapped back. As the body fell, Iliara saw Doli and the hitman she must have hired, electrorifle in hand and aimed for the door.

"Shades," said Doli, who turned to flee.

The hitman tried to charge for another shot, but Iliara held up an open palm in their direction and willed all the energy in the vicinity to pool at her feet. In a moment, she had enough collected that it crawled up her body, leapt from her hand, and exploded on the pair, killing the hitman outright. Doli careened into a heap of fabric and limbs.

Iliara folded her arms across her stomach and fought to get her powers under control. She was probably tenth place in the land at bolts, but the refined things like holding back were not in her range. Doli almost had time to recover her footing and escape before Iliara felt collected enough to move forward.

Sparks danced off Iliara's shoulders and splashed on the scorched walls as she approached Doli. That bolt had probably measured over a hundred thousand volts. Any other time, Iliara would stop to admire her own handiwork. Maybe she would yet. After dealing with the traitor.

"Mistress, no!" Doli threw her hands over her head as Iliara came upon her and took up a fistful of her hair.

"And what was that about? Thought to do away with me?"

"Of course not. That guy made me do it."

"How stupid do I look?" Iliara charged up a little bolt so her hand glowed menacingly.

It had the desired effect. Doli began to sob.

"Mercy, milady. This one meant you no harm."

"Beg."

When Iliara released her, Doli scrambled to her knees and kissed Iliara's shoes as required. Satisfied, Iliara beckoned Doli follow and led the way to the front stairs. More guards were rushing in to investigate the racket, and she'd soon have to think of some excuse to rescue Doli's worthless skin.

Once they reached the steps, Iliara turned to Doli. "Did you do as I instructed while I was gone?"

"I did, mistress. I followed them to Ged, and Reiki doesn't seem to know about the ledger. She's started a microguild to sell fashion accessories." Doli lowered her voice, for a band of guards drew near. "And I think she's dating Arthur."

"Miladies, can you tell us anything about the altercation?" The lead guard saluted as he drew to a halt.

"That hitman sought to take my life," said Iliara.

"The guard at the door reported hearing a woman's scream."

"That was Doli, here. She takes fright easily. Thank your lucky stars neither of us were hurt during that lapse of security."

"Y-Yes, milady. We'll find and punish all the guards who allowed this to happen."

The guards marched off to deal with the body of the hitman and reassign watches. Meanwhile, Doli dared to hug Iliara.

"Thank you, mistress. For not reporting me."

Iliara frowned at Doli rubbing her disgusting lips on her cheek, but managed to resist the urge to pull away. Having Doli owe her a debt of gratitude was worth getting slimed.

"I need you to return to Ged, Doli. Destroy her guild. Even if she finds some way to survive the moon project, I want to completely break her."

"The moon project?"

"Yes. Before I left, I took steps to ensure she goes up. I doubt she'll be coming back, but just in case."

"I'll grind her fledgling guild to dust."

As Doli stalked off, Iliara almost felt sorry for Reiki.

"You just picked the wrong woman to mess with," she said. "Next time you'll choose men who aren't already claimed."

There was more to do during a spaceflight than Reiki first thought. One of the harder tasks was the regular shifts getting the frozen propulsion fuel out and separated for engineering. She knew she would find herself "voluntold" into that role more often than the others since the freezing temperatures in the lockers didn't bother her.

Reiki was the only crew member who didn't fit in. The others had been prepping for the flight together for several weeks. She'd spent the entire time away from them in Ged. It meant when she floated into the mess hall to join them for that first post-launch celebration, the conversations fell silent and grew awkward.

She didn't mind a bit of ostracization. She decided to enjoy the quiet theatre of her head, and recall fond memories of Arthur.

Thinking about Arthur made her warm and tingly inside. And everything seemed to make her think of him. Even the puzzle-cube she was working on while she sat on the ceiling and waited for a tray of fructose bricks to thaw.

Ossington Castle came back to mind, where Reiki spun in Arthur's arms to mad fiddling and clapping. Reiki pushed herself off the ceiling and used the freezer doors to launch herself into a twirl in the middle of the room. A phantasmal apparition of Arthur linked arms with her, and, for a moment, she was back home.

"Oi, Reiki what are you doing here?"

It was Ferra, fully suited up—minus the helmet, who had come to join her. Ferra had been eyeing daggers of Reiki during the meet-up in the mess hall. Reiki was certain she must have run afoul of her during the training everyone claimed she had had with them.

Now how to explain that terrible attempt at a dance?

"I'm... uh... trying to stay warm."

Ferra joined Reiki as she retook her perch on the ceiling.

"Trying to stay warm? I can't blame you. How can you stand this? The temperature here is two degrees."

"Dunno. Seems okay to me."

"You're being sent outside to work the blast-coating at the end of your shift. Better suit up."

"Mmmk."

The chore of spraying extra layers of protective sealant was never-ending since the atmosphere had stripped away much of what the ship had to start with.

"What is that toy you keep playing with, anyway?"

"A puzzle-cube. Here." Reiki tossed it to Ferra who grasped it and gave it a few exploratory twists. "You have to get the colours to match up. I've never been able to solve it."

"Yes, I see," said Ferra, sounding distracted and confused.

Ferra spent a few minutes twisting it and staring at it, and Reiki thought she was about to give up. All at once, Ferra's hands flew into action, turning the segments of the cube so hard it clicked and protested. It was awesome and terrifying to watch, and Reiki had no idea what Ferra thought she was doing.

Under Ferra's hands, the facets of the cube lined up into patterns of fours and fives. A few more twists, and she had it fully solved. Ferra released the solved puzzle to float between them.

"Needs more subdivisions," said Ferra. "Like this, is not so challenging. Even a little child can solve it."

Reiki knew she was blushing as she collected the cube.

Little child indeed. She'd spent weeks breaking her head on it. But now she knew how to solve it at least. Provided she could figure out the patterns to Ferra's hand and eye-motions.

Using her outside duties as an excuse, Reiki escaped the locker room, suited up, and cycled through the airlock. She had to bail back inside to redo her seals because once the pressure dropped, she heard that telltale hiss of a loose fitting. The second time worked, fortunately. A lucky thing the captain didn't see that; he'd ream her out for being inattentive.

The enormity of the blackness of the sky from the belly of the ship would never cease to take her breath away. Reiki carried the spray canister and nozzle along with her as she traversed the ship's wing and took in the sights. Many things made her want to cry. That strange way the stars held a steady beam on her. The blue disk that was the cradle of civilization. Even the field of brown ooze that was the ship's ablative coating, for it formed an undulating lake of melted, rippling chocolate waves under the blinding rays of the sun.

Like a fondue swimming pool with Arthur at the end. Oops!

She'd almost lost her footing and stepped into the mixture. Her magnetic boots would find no purchase there, so an error like that would send Reiki floating off into the depths of space. What a hideous way to go.

Reiki found a patch that looked a little thick and stopped to spray it with relaxant from the canister. She stared at Home again and sighed. It would be afternoon right now in Ged. The inevitable thought came to mind.

Where is Arthur right now? What's he thinking?

CHAPTER 20

BAD APPLE

It was on a glorious spring afternoon that Arthur stood on the roof of one of the towers, staring into the deep blue sky. Up here, near the top of the city, he was almost ground level. He could sightsee in solitude that echoed how alone he felt.

The tower was flat-roofed, with a ramp-shaped wedge for the door to the stairs and a box containing lift gears for the elevator. There were no safety rails up here–a minor slip would send Arthur tumbling to his death.

Arthur heard hard-soled shoes coming up the stairs behind him long before Xandri opened the door and joined him. She bravely got up to the edge with him.

They stared at the city together. Old Man puffed away, as oil made its way through the system, and the various Houses became richer. Ged bustled on, not seeming to care that Reiki was leagues above her in the sky. It felt so empty and alone.

"It's been a week," said Xandri. "She must be almost to the moon by now."

Arthur nodded. "That's so impossibly far away. I can't even visualize the gulf between us."

He reached his hand toward the sky and pictured Reiki in a derelict spaceship, floating away from him. She was banging at a portal, screaming to him to throw a rope. But he was too far. Too far for even the longest rope to pull her back.

He tried to shake himself out of those thoughts. Business would distract him. The oil market was booming, and the League's elections were about to take place. An expansionist party was in line to take power there. Soon, all oil this half of the continent would be drawn into their vortex of consumption. Prices would skyrocket.

It reminded Arthur that Reiki had business to ask after.

"How's the guild going?"

"We have our first retail merchant on board. Wants to export five hundred lights overseas. I can't find anywhere near the number of people I need to make that many lights."

"Maybe we can import people."

"We could move the guild to Hillvale. There's a manufacturing workforce there I could tap. No one in Ged wants to work for reasonable wages."

"That's the oil market for you," said Arthur. "How hard would it be to move?"

"Maybe two weeks. The hard part would be dismounting Reiki's stamping wheel without damaging it."

"Two weeks? By then, Reiki should be back to take over."

"Hopefully. If that wheel breaks down while she's gone, no one here can repair it."

"Don't worry. Nothing could go wrong."

They stared at the city for a moment longer before Xandri spoke.

"I hear you and Wendiah were a bit of an item in the past."

Arthur looked at Xandri sharply. "Where'd you hear that?"

"Around. I hear lots of stuff. Besides, she's here now."

"What?"

"I saw her arrive earlier. Maybe she's sneaking up on you right now."

Arthur glanced over his shoulder, which set Xandri to laughing.

"So! There's unfanned passion left between you and Wendiah."

"While we're on the topic of passion, maybe we can talk about where you were for the Orionite New Year? I heard you were gone all night."

"Lies."

Arthur smirked. "I heard it. Around. I hear lots of stuff."

Xandri crossed her arms and returned to the view. A strong, sandy wind blew across them, and Arthur realized his guess might have struck closer to the truth than Xandri wanted to let on.

"Wait. Xandri. You didn't..."

"Don't judge me."

Arthur sighed. He'd been certain Xandri would lift herself out of her previous life.

I suppose you can take the girl out of the country...

"I'm going to have them fit you for a chastity belt," said Arthur. "I'll be holding onto the key. I'll give it back to you when you graduate from the conservatory of music. Think of the time without sex as a motivation tool."

Xandri dug up a sharp nail file from her purse and brandished it at him. "Do you value your life?"

It was a fight that could wait for another day. Arthur had bigger fish to fry. Namely, Wendiah and his mother. Arthur turned and led the way to the door, which was still slightly ajar, and heard someone else coming up.

He opened the door in time to see Wendiah turning to make the last flight of stairs. She wore a low-cut dress with a generous view of her bosom from his angle. When she caught him looking, her eyes twinkled in mischief.

Great. Of all the people to meet. She must have been looking for me since she arrived.

Still, Arthur managed to smile instead of grimacing. He greeted her when she reached the top. "Wendiah. Hi."

"Arthur. Your mother invited me over for tea. I was hoping I'd be able to find you alone."

"I'm not, actually. I– ah–"

Xandri had contrived to silently disappear. Probably hidden around back of the riser for the stairs. A very impressive feat for someone wearing hard-soled shoes on a gravelly surface. Xandri had likely done her share of sneaking out of windows during her career.

"Arthur, kiss me."

Wendiah threw her arms around him and tried to plant a kiss on Arthur's lips. He barely avoided it, getting the kiss on his neck instead. She was the daughter of a Lightning, along with the many benefits that entailed. She had the telekinetic grip of ten men as she hugged his arms to his sides. Arthur struggled to breathe.

"Stop, Wendiah. I can't."

"Your mother told me all about Reiki. Don't worry. I accept. But she's not going to know about us."

"What?"

"Come."

Wendiah leapt from the roof, carrying Arthur with her. They landed on a more secluded rooftop some twenty-five metres away, and slid down to where the shingles brushed the side of the cliff-face. They wrestled there, while Wendiah laboured to plant kisses on Arthur's cheeks.

Kinda funny. Before I met Reiki, I'd have been in heaven scoring play on the side like this.

The old Arthur would already have his pants around his ankles. He'd been worse than Hendry in many ways. That someone of Reiki's integrity loved him was such amazing luck. A rare thing to happen to a player like him. The thought of his old ways made Arthur want to be sick.

"Your mind is far from here, isn't it?" asked Wendiah.

"Eh, I can't stop thinking about Reiki."

"Having a girlfriend's never stopped you before. Is something wrong with you?"

Arthur could only laugh at Wendiah repeating his own self-assessment.

"Now that I have Reiki, there can be no other."

Wendiah blinked in surprise. "How do I count as another when I know I'm on the side?"

She allowed Arthur sit up, which he did, gratefully. He thought carefully before trying to explain.

"Look, Wend, it's like this. Reiki's a part of my soul. Even if I have sex with you and she never finds out, I'd have to go through the rest of my life with knowing I'd failed her."

"But you agree she wouldn't know."

"A part of me that is her would shrivel up and die."

Wendiah smiled and put a finger to the side of her chin. "Oh, I see."

"Y-you do?"

"Oh, yes. It's a very pure love. The kind I'm not allowed to have. That's probably why I throw myself at you."

"Wait, there's been someone you love?"

"Who's recently single. But the council will never let it happen, so I can only watch from afar."

Arthur got to his knees and took her hands. "Wendiah, that's terrible. Tell me who it is and I will change the council. They will listen to me if I have enough time to knock heads together."

She closed her eyes, unable to hold his gaze, and shook her head. "Everyone would laugh. Please don't ask this of me."

"Wendiah. I would never laugh at you. Only tell me the name, and I will do everything in my power to make it happen."

Wendiah's countenance changed to a look of wrath and she suddenly pushed past Arthur to reach the edge of the roof. At first, Arthur thought it was something he'd said, until he realized she was glaring at the street. He crawled up beside her.

"What? What do you see?"

"There's that freaky woman again. I keep seeing her lurking about."

Wendiah pointed out a woman standing in the street on the narrow sidewalk. The woman wore her hair long and dark, and a devilish grin to go with the hearty shake to her shoulders.

A name bubbled to the surface of Arthur's memory. Doli Stanton, friend of Iliara Välenus. No good could come from her skulking around the streets of Ged.

"She's a Lightning," said Wendiah. "I sense from here that her powers lean into pyrokinesis. Her aura glows like a fire dragon, all twisted and pained."

"Wendiah?"

She turned to look at him, eyes narrowed in anger.

"Stay here, Arthur. I'll protect you."

With that, Wendiah was over the edge. Arthur scrambled after her and found her leaping from parapet to parapet, headed for Doli.

Wendiah was a kinetic-type Lightning. She might be about to get herself in over her head against someone like Doli, who could launch sheets of fire. Arthur had to intervene before Wendiah got hurt.

Hurriedly, he sought out an open window to climb through.

By the time Arthur made it to the street, both Doli and Wendiah were gone. The guards asked passers-by and took up pursuit, accompanied by Arthur.

The guards were eight in number. Four bore plain rifles, and four carried electrorifles. The electrorifle was slow to fire because it needed a moment to charge up, but the shot would penetrate the natural protective field of a lower-order Lightning like Doli.

It took two hours to find them because Doli and

Wendiah kept moving about, but Arthur finally cornered them on a stone bridge overlooking a water-filled chasm.

They were poised to fight, with their arms extended, as if stalking prey. As Arthur directed the guards to spread out and take cover in the nearby buildings, Doli and Wendiah circled each other. He nodded to his one guard with a shield and backpack bolt-absorption capacitor before moving forward.

Doli took in the sight of him approaching as she circled with Wendiah. The darkness of nightfall did little to extinguish the glow of her eyes or the gleam of energies that danced on her fingertips. Wendiah carried no outward signs of power. It was all in the lithe, feline motions she took as she stepped. Such power to each of them. The fight would be determined by magic or brawn, and the victory would be decisive.

"You shouldn't have come, Arthur," said Doli. "This could get dangerous."

Preceded by his shield man, Arthur approached the bridge along the centre of the road. The only sound was the whir of the grinding station that laboured to haul water from the chasm to the surface.

Doli addressed him again. "I could kill you know. Imagine Reiki's horror to find you dead."

"I will kill you first," said Wendiah, who feinted an attack and got Doli to retreat a step.

Arthur watched them circle again, though Doli changed patterns to keep her back away from Arthur's side of the bridge.

Doli's here to pursue Reiki, according to what she said. Arthur dared not release her back into the city. Who knew what mischief she'd get into? He'd be lucky to even separate her from Wendiah without one of them getting hurt.

Arthur held up a hand, and the sounds of electrorifles charging arose. He waited a moment while Doli's eyes darted about–waited for her to realize she was surrounded by guards bearing the one physical weapon that could kill her. She might be able to block using concentrated power, but would she be able to block from all those directions? Arthur doubted it.

"So many," said Doli as the smile faded from her face. "How did you get them all?"

"In Ged, you can buy anything if you have enough money."

"I see."

"My men have orders to fire if you so much as make an aggressive act towards me. And I can assure you, they're very good shots. We toppled our Namika, who was a much stronger Lightning than you."

They faced each other for a timeless moment, during which Arthur assumed Doli was assessing her options.

"What now?" she asked.

"We're going to walk you to the train station. You will board the next departure for Hillvale and not return."

"And if I do?"

"After tonight, wanted posters are going up. It'll be open season for any bounty hunters who want a piece of you."

Doli began to laugh. It was a confident laugh that made Arthur second guess himself. The electrorifles could only hold a charge so long before burning out the core. His men would have to power down if they didn't fire soon. Perhaps Doli was trying to wait him out?

A difficult decision lay before him. He needed to order the men to shoot but not to kill. A cruel move, but it might spare her life.

Wendiah made the choice for all of them by diving for Doli. For a moment, the universe seemed to hold its breath, catching Doli with a look of horror at a fist aimed for her nose. Tendrils of fire crawled along Doli's fingertips, and Wendiah's dress flapped and rippled like a flag underwater.

With an angry flash, time resumed its normal pace. Wendiah was rolling across the bridge and Doli was running for the edge.

Gunshots sounded as Doli dived. She cried out in pain, but completed her jump and vanished over the edge in a rustle of cloth. Arthur dashed to the rail and looked over in time to see Doli's form at the bottom of the chasm slipping into the man-sized spout of a pipe that expelled polluted water from Old Man.

His guards ran up to join him, and the captain cried out.

"She won the exchange with Wendiah, but we scored a hit, milord. 'Got her in the leg when she jumped. She won't be getting far."

"She's gone in the refinery," said Arthur. "Put three men here with orders to kill her if they see her. One of you stay here and tend after Wendiah."

Wendiah struggled to rise as they spoke. Her hair and clothing were singed with Doli's fire, but she would live. It was close to the best outcome Arthur could have hoped for.

The guard captain completed the assignments, then turned to Arthur. "Shoot to kill, is it, milord?"

"Yes. Three of you will have no chance of containing her. We'll get more firepower, enter the front doors, and try to take her from inside without bloodshed."

"As you wish."

CHAPTER 21

FLOATING

Arthur's familiarity with the layout of the refinery helped, as he led the guards through the maze of corridors and pipes. After scrounging for more guards, he had three with electrorifles and another ten with plain rifles. The shield guard was running point. He would be able to take a single bolt in the fifty kilovolt range, depending on Doli's power-level. It wasn't much. Doli would likely be able to bolt them four or five times before exhausting herself. If she proved that dangerous, they would have to end the fight forcefully.

Workers yelled at them as they passed, but acquiesced when they saw Arthur among the guards. Military presence within the refinery was unwelcome because it could disrupt Old Man's round-the-clock production. Doli had picked the one place to hide that demanded Arthur flush her out quickly.

They came to several intersections, and Arthur pointed out which way to head from his position in the middle of the group. The captain of the guard queried him on it.

"Milord, how do we know where she'll be in this maze?"

"Think like an injured fox. You have a bullet in your leg.

You're in an unfamiliar forest and the hunters are on you. The forest makes loud clinking and grinding noises. Where are you going to go?"

"Scramble anywhere, I'd think."

"Somewhere quiet. Even if that quiet place is strategically unsound. You just want to hide."

He led them to the stage-one separation chambers. Here, crude oil sat in large tanks while temperatures equalized before moving over to the boiling tanks. It was the quietest part of the refinery that was in easy reach of the pipe Doli would have taken.

"Target ahead," called the point man when he reached a bend.

The group took to tactical movement to get around the bend and into a large chamber of three-storey-tall metal tanks. The floor was a thin layer of sheet metal on a substrate of spaghetti-like pipes. Some of those pipes made waist-high runs for certain lengths. A blood-trail ran to one of those mounds of pipes. That would be Doli's hiding spot.

The men fanned out and sought cover as Arthur walked up to the shield guard. His options for saving Doli were getting slimmer. The biggest problem was that there was no way to contain her short of asking her to cooperate.

"Doli," he called out. "We have you surrounded, and you can't crawl back out the pipe. So, here's the plan. We're going to take you in for healing, then put you on the train for home. No one gets hurt, we all live happily ever after."

There was no reply from the hiding spot. The guards all looked at each other nervously, but Arthur held out his hands for calm. If they started charging up to fire, Doli would hear the noise and panic.

"Okay, Doli. I'm going to come around there on a count of five. I'll help you over to the guards and we'll see you to a warren. Ready?"

Against all logic and common sense, Doli tried to bolt them.

The stream of fire arced from her hand when she poked her head over the barrier. It was too weak to reach them, and landed on the delicate pipes instead. The reaction was immediate, with pipes bursting all over that portion of the floor to release thick black smoke into the chamber.

Klaxons sounded, and Old Man trembled beneath Arthur's feet. Guards ran back for the corridor as the distant yells of workers arose.

Arthur allowed the guard with the shield to flee past him as he prepared to charge forward, but the captain of the guard stopped him.

"Milord, where are you going? We have to evacuate the room before fire control seals us in."

"Not without her."

The guard stared in shock as Arthur shook himself free.

"Run," said Arthur. "Hold the doors."

He took a few deep breaths before charging into the voluminous black smoke. On the other side, he ran around the mound of pipes to find Doli sitting with her back against the metal bulwark, injured leg relaxed on the floor.

She looked at him with a sickly appearance to her face. Blood-loss had sapped her strength. Or perhaps, adrenaline could no longer keep her going.

Arthur knelt beside her and noted how little resistance she put up against being picked up. The pain in the leg would have to be excruciating. It was remarkable of her not to cry out as he got to his feet.

Smoke had already filled the chamber to the point of forming an artificial ceiling Arthur could reach up and touch if he wanted. He tried not to think of what poisonous carbon-laced soup he was breathing as he charged for the door.

Arthur discovered that the door was closed when he burst out of the smoke. It must have shut automatically, though the guards had a rifle butt underneath and were trying to pry it open.

Arthur's knees gave out when he reached the door. He collapsed there with Doli, as light-headedness took him. She hit the ground harder than he would have liked, but he could do nothing else. It felt like he was underwater and in slow-motion.

I feel like I'm floating.

Blackness licked at the edges of Arthur's vision. He closed his eyes and prepared to welcome it. As sleep started to take hold, and the door shuddered behind him, Arthur's last thought went to the woman he loved.

Floating away. I wonder if this is what Reiki feels like right now...

Ferra obliged with the countdown. "Moon landing in five, four, three, two, one."

Reiki felt the slightest of bumps as they set down. She was strapped in at her station on the bridge with her spacesuit on, but basically twiddling her fingers. She had little to do. Somehow, despite her anxiety, she kept herself from moving more than her fingers.

Captain Spacerman had an elevated chair that towered over them. He had access to helm controls from there, as well as fold out displays. Ferra, Verifier and navigator, stared at the radar screen.

"Perfect landing," said Spacerman. "Ferra, the landing gear reports solid contact?"

"Numbers three and four indicate elevation loss on the range of zero point zero one millimetres per second. It's too early to accurately project, but I give it a constant second derivative of twenty-five micrometres per hour per hour. We won't sink far."

"Reiki?" asked Spacerman.

"Ferra's measurement falls within one standard deviation of Nerat's Law based on our current mass of forty-six tons," she said as she recalled the charts. Which chart to use exactly depended on that important second derivative Ferra had estimated. If Ferra was off by ten or fifteen millimetres, they risked toppling, which would scuttle any attempt at lift-off.

"Mission control online, captain," said Ferra.

"Put them on loudspeaker, please."

The crackle of radio was all Reiki heard for a moment. When the voice rang out, it was full of static and tended to cut in and out.

"Mission control to Moon... et. We got you....touchdown. Position stable..... Copy?"

"We copy, Mission Control," said Captain Spacerman. "Landing has occurred, and all hands reported."

More static followed his statement, Reiki thought it sounded distinctly like cheering. After a moment, the voice of Mission Control came back. "That's great to hear, Spaceman. Deploy rover...."

Captain Spaceman took over once the connection to Mission Control faded out. "Ferra, you have the bridge. I'll go check on Janan and the boys downstairs."

The captain left the bridge, which officially put Ferra in charge since she was tenth in order of rank. Reiki had no commission. If everyone in the crew died but her, she still wouldn't be captain.

There was also nothing for the Store to do during the rover part. Reiki would be expected to man her station on the bridge for the next four hours, then take a four hour break. After that, she would have rotating twelve-hour shifts with Ferra so that there would always be someone on hand to listen for updates from Mission Control.

Reiki sighed and went to work on her puzzle-cube. She was determined to learn to solve it like Ferra had. It was the fact that Ferra called it a child's toy and had beaten it in minutes of even attempting it. If she couldn't solve it now, Reiki knew she'd mentally concede she was as stupid as Ferra claimed.

Things were quiet in the bridge for the next forty-five minutes. By assent among the executive command, Spaceman would be first to disembark, thereby becoming the first man on the moon. Accompanied by one of the guys from engineering, he would encircle the equator in the moon rover. During that time, the rest of the crew would go out on short excursions. Then, they would all pack up and launch for Home.

Ah, Home, thought Reiki. She had mixed feelings about the Academy's recently chosen name for mankind's planet, the third world from the sun. Other suggestions were just as zany, such as "Rock", "Earthball", or "Waterdrop". Home was the only name everyone could agree upon in a hurry, as there was a rush to name the remainder of the celestial bodies.

"Aie, Reiki. Look at this." Ferra swivelled her screen so Reiki could see the monochrome green lines twirling in it. It took a moment, but an unexpected seismic pattern traced itself and vanished.

"What in the world was that?" she asked.

"It doesn't stay long enough to be traced in detail, but it's come up three times in the same area. If it were Home, I'd say a buried cable rattling. Here, I'd have to guess we're sitting on some kind of rocky shelf."

"You're saying we could sink?"

"You better go tell the captain."

Reiki was unsure how it ended up falling to her to deliver the news. Worse, Captain Spaceman was disinclined to agree when he heard the report.

"Are you sure it exists? Mission Control said nothing of this."

Reiki turned over her hands in a gesture of futility. "They wouldn't have any seismic data except for what we'll broadcast in our next report."

She didn't need to add that there would be no changing of the landing site. They only had enough fuel for one lift-off—that of their return trip Home.

"Have Miss Ferra keep an eye on it. Anything happens, clear it through me before you talk to Mission Control."

In other words, ignore it and hope it goes away since Captain Spaceman would not likely take any action that might deprive him of his moon walk. Somehow this was going to end up in a stand-off between the ship's Verifier and her command crew.

Reiki returned to the bridge to report the news. Ferra addressed her concerns before she was even through the door.

"He said monitor it, didn't he?"

"You got it."

"Of course, he did." Ferra smiled grimly. "I imagine he'll conveniently omit to check with me before going outside."

They had a video feed from Main Hold, since the ship's first officer had a camera. The picture went blank, as the first officer cycled out of the airlock with the captain, then resumed once he got it attached to the external connector.

"They need to invent a way to compress a video signal enough to broadcast it by radio," said Ferra. "All those tapes we've been making take up more mass than they should."

Captain Spacerman chatted back and forth with Mission Control as he took that first step onto the moon. Back planet-side, they would be making their own tapes of this event to be sent to every demesne in the world who cared to air it on local radio. When the ship returned, the video footage would go straight to theatres.

Other crew members came into view as they worked to disengage the moon rover from its fasteners. Some planted sampler tubes, others walked out to drop landing markers. It looked like a party, where the dress code was an obscene silver suit.

The screen went blank again. The first officer had disconnected. He would continue to record during the rover part of the mission.

"Those guys left cables and suit-casings everywhere," said Janan by radio from Main Hold.

Reiki chuckled. "Janan, they were in a hurry to get out. I'll come help you store it away."

"Thanks. If I have to deal with all this myself, I'll just open the door and push it out to space."

"Aie, don't be a litter bug," said Ferra as Reiki got up and left.

Ferra was still chatting with Janan when Reiki arrived in Main Hold. He was right. The room looked like a tornado had whipped all the fasteners off the walls. Most of the crew had cycled outside by now, so there were scant few hands remaining to deal with the mess. She pitched in, starting from the airlock.

After ten minutes, Janan got called back to engineering to attend to the injection chambers. Since they were almost done, Reiki waved him off and set to finishing it by herself.

The job was almost complete when screaming squawked over the radio.

"Aie, Captain, what was that?" came Ferra's voice a few seconds after the screams. There was no response.

Reiki went to the airlock and peered out. Through the small aperture of the double doors, she saw the moon rover lying on its side.

"No response from anyone," said Janan. "Can either of you see them?"

"Reiki, go outside and check," said Ferra.

"Me? I'm not trained on emergency procedures." *Or even fully trained on my own job*, she mentally added.

"You're closest to the airlock, and you're our spare hand right now."

Translation: expendable. But Reiki complied and picked up a helmet that she latched into place once she'd tied her hair back.

After a procedural leak-test / pressure-test, Reiki cycled out of the airlock and took to the stairs. No textbook nor captain's speech could have prepared her for the feeling when the lunar panorama stared back at her. Alien soil, alien sky. Nothing in between, not even the glimmer of blurred horizon.

Bodies littered the area from the base of the stairs to the rover. The ground was trodden down from around the landing gear to the farthest person. Most parts of the moon still looked untouched. Like fresh snow. Reiki had a strong temptation to go push her boot in it... to scrawl her name in the dust, where it might sit for the next thousand years.

The crackle of the suit radio broke the perfect tranquillity. "What are you doing, Reiki? Daydreaming?"

"Sorry. It's very beautiful."

"Can you report on the status of the crew?"

"All passed out, I think." Reiki climbed down the stairs to approach the nearest person. She turned him over and was shocked to find his helmet and suit broken up. Little ice-blue shards poked out from the ground in the spot he had covered. They looked sharp enough to have punctured his suit.

"What do you see?" asked Ferra.

"There's damage to his suit. Some kind of crystals. Maybe a meteor shower peppered them."

"I don't think so. No high-velocity particles registered as striking the ship."

Janan chipped in an idea. "Can you fetch the camera? The footage might give us a clue."

"Sure." Something didn't feel right as Reiki looked around, but she shrugged it off since the ground felt sturdy enough. Behind her, the door closed. "Wait. Why is the airlock closing?"

"I closed it. We need to limit the amount of lunar particles that can enter the ship. You know regulations."

"Hmmm," said Reiki. She couldn't recall any regulation like that. And she was certain she knew more regs than Ferra did.

"Be fast, now. You're wasting time."

Reiki bounded to the moon rover and found the first officer with the camera still fastened to his hand. She peeled it off and looked it over. Smashed by those crystals. Probably beyond repair. Reiki ejected the tape and dropped the camera.

The rover looked clear of crystals, which registered as odd in Reiki's mind. At least one surface should have the crystals on it if they had rained on the crew. That's when she connected that odd feeling from earlier. The crystals showed neither sign nor spread of precipitation.

Whatever this was, it had come from underground, not above.

Likewise, whatever it was that had killed the crew, Reiki was standing in the middle of it.

CHAPTER 22

I FORGIVE YOU

Iliara entered her suites, carrying a candle on a stand and a stack of written declarations to sign. She swore as she stumbled over furniture in the poor lighting. Apparently, they had yet to repair the wiring in her room from one of her tantrums, so it was going to be open flame for lighting for the foreseeable future.

It was crucial that Iliara get these documents filled out with the new bank account numbers. In just a few weeks, she'd have managed to transfer all her monies out of the compromised ledger accounts. With all the accounts closed, she'd be clear of any tendril of blame.

This time, Iliara had been very careful instead of allowing greed to rule her. Each account had been created by a different commoner whose corpse now littered the bottom of the canal. Zero chance of leaving an ugly paper trail. She only needed to get the funds all moved about in small transactions that would pass below the radar.

Iliara walked past Booboo's perch and noticed someone's reflection in the stand-up mirror as she made her way to the bed. She whirled in surprise, dropping everything she was carrying except the candle, and sighed in relief when she saw it was Doli.

"Doli, you scared me half to death. Why are you back so soon?"

Doli looked on in silence instead of giving her customary laugh. Iliara glanced around the room, trying to figure out where the reflection was coming from, but realized, with a shudder, that Doli's reflection had no physical source.

Now that Iliara had a moment to look closely, Doli's face looked a little blue, and her lips were puffy and blackened. Her eyes were red and unblinking under tangled hair riddled in burnt patches.

"Doli? What kind of trick is this? Where are you hiding?"

"Iliara."

The voice came from right over her shoulder. Startled, Iliara whirled to see Doli standing in a room that had been empty a moment ago.

Like the reflection in the mirror, Doli looked dishevelled and listless. She advanced upon Iliara who dropped the candle and ceded place.

"Doli?"

"We didn't make it."

"We? What?"

"The chamber filled with toxic smoke, and I couldn't run because of my leg. Arthur came back for me, but it was too late. The doors sealed us in."

"Chamber? What chamber? Speak, girl."

With a sigh that sounded like the whispering of the afterlife, Doli shimmered and paled. "There'll be no more picnics where you complain about the food."

"Doli, no." Iliara reached out to her, but drew her hand back in fear. "You can't be dead."

No trace of emotion crossed Doli's haggard face. "We'll never meet again this side of life. You should have been nicer to me growing up."

"Wait, Doli. Don't go. I..." Iliara searched for the words, to explain her whirling thoughts. Despite trying to kill her not long ago, Doli was the only person in the world Iliara had ever trusted. What was a minor assassination attempt between lifelong friends? Doli couldn't actually be dead. This was some sort of a trick to wring a confession out of her. A successful trick, too, because Iliara couldn't imagine life without Doli there to pick on.

Iliara swallowed hard.

"Okay, Doli. You win. I need you. Lay off the magic tricks, come out of hiding, and I'll make it up to you for all the bad things I've done to you."

Doli shook her head. "Should have learned how to love from Arthur, Iliara. He's the only one who would have come back to try to save me."

"Doli?" Iliara rushed forward when Doli turned translucent. She reached out a tentative hand, but Doli turned into wisps and vanished.

"He's the only one who would have cared, Iliara."

"I care, Doli. Don't go."

...the only one who would have cared...

"Doli, get back here this instant!"

There was no response. The ghastly apparition in the mirror was the last remnant of Doli to fade away.

In growing up, Iliara had mastered bringing up tears on demand as a negotiation technique, so it surprised her to find her eyes watering unbidden. She plunked herself down on the floor, righted the candle, and wept loudly for the loss.

[*** Reiki ***]

I need to get back to the ship.

Easy thoughts for someone cowering on the side of an overturned moon rover.

A handful of crystal shards glistened from Reiki's bootprints where she'd stood a moment ago. When she bent her foot back to check, there was scoring on the sole of her boot. Another minute or so and those shards would probably have formed into crystals and punctured her suit.

Death had come within a narrow margin right there.

Stupid, stupid. I should have stayed on the ship and tested the ground first. Now, how am I supposed to get back?

The ship looked impossibly far away. Almost as far as Home, which glowed invitingly above.

If I jump really hard, will I drift all the way home? Will Arthur be there waiting to catch me like he promised?

She shook the silly thought from her head. It would take her decades to coast home from a jump, even if she could hit lunar escape velocity. There were no backup moon rovers to rescue her. Getting back to Arthur was going to be up to Reiki alone.

Reiki leapt from the rover and bounded for the ship as fast as she could. About halfway there, a patch of crystals suddenly protruded ahead of her. Reiki had to land with her feet really far apart to avoid it.

That almost seemed like an intelligent decision on the part of the crystals.

Impossible.

Hopefully.

Three more jumps to the ladder. Reiki took her next hop diagonally left and was pleased to foil the crystals that popped up where she should normally have landed. That got her wondering what surface area the crystals were capable of covering.

Two leaps remained. Belatedly, Reiki realized she should have varied her stride-length on the way rather than pick the longest possible jump. The crystals only needed to form an arc of radius equal to her steps to catch her.

The next landing put Reiki right at the edge of a patch of crystals, and she saw the crew members bodies twitching.

Yes, this is it. All the crystals are retracting so they can converge on me.

Sure enough, as Reiki came in for the final landing, the crystals appeared all spread out, covering an area too wide to avoid. She made a snap decision in the air and threw the video tape down to make a miniature landing pad.

Reiki landed with one foot and sprung forward. Impossible for her to do that under planet-side gravity. Here on the moon, she managed to make the ladder.

That's where Reiki stopped to catch her breath. She crawled up two more steps just in case the crystals found a way to reach her. As she stared in horror, the video tape shattered and unspooled like a volcano of ribbon.

Living moon crystals. And Reiki had just used the only evidence as a springboard. She'd catch it when Mission Control found out.

With shaking hands, Reiki reached up and tapped the

airlock's open-door button. When it failed to respond, she tapped it again a few times.

"Ferra," said Reiki. "The crew's been eaten by some kind of crystals. Don't laugh, but I think those crystals are alive."

One of the bodies sank into the ground. It went down hip-first so that the legs bent up unnaturally to brush the back of the helmet. Watching this, Reiki decided her position on the metal ladder was unsafe. She jammed her fingers on the open-door button a few more times.

"Ferra? The airlock seems to be jammed. Can anyone come open it? Janan? Somebody?"

Reiki tapped the side of her helmet. She wondered if her suit radio was dead.

"Hello? Anybody copy?"

"Reiki." Ferra's voice was a welcome sound.

"Ferra. I can't get in. Can you come open the door?"

"That's on purpose, Reiki."

"What?"

"I know this is a terrible way to say goodbye, but from here our roads must separate."

"Ferra? You can't be serious," said Reiki. She banged her fist on the window. "Janan? Reiki to Janan."

"He can't respond right now. I took care of that."

"Ferra, don't be silly. Open the door."

"I have to go now, Reiki. It's time to start the launch sequence. I suppose you could say it's been a blast."

Ferra chuckled at her own joke, and the line went dead. Reiki collapsed to her knees and stared at the closed door.

No windows to engineering that Reiki might throw rocks at because the engines were deep in the bowels of the ship under the many layers of protective coating. That's if Janan was even in engineering. He might be tied up or something.

Face it, Reiki. You're going to be incinerated here.

"No!" Reiki launched herself at the airlock and beat at the door. "Please, Ferra. I just met the man that I love, and he's waiting for me at home. I'm begging you."

No response, and dust was starting to stir around the base of the rocket as the engines warmed up. Reiki was running out of time to decide how she wanted to die.

The engines looked blazing hot to her acute thermovoyance, and they had yet to even fire. Reiki imagined it would be decidedly unpleasant to roast to death as the rocket launched. In fact, the fire might not even kill her. Maybe she'd lay around for a few minutes, all baked like a potato within her suit.

No, if she was going to die, it was going to have to be quick. She would let the crystals get her. Let them break her helmet and expose her to the harshness of space. Death would be a long time coming that way. She'd probably suffer for six to ten seconds before passing out. But it was better than getting half-cooked.

"Ferra, before you launch, I need a final favour," said Reiki. She unzipped a pocket and got out the trusty puzzle-cube, which she set on the top step. "I'm leaving my puzzle-cube behind, and I'm going to jump into the crystals. I'd like this delivered to Arthur Galenden if you could."

The radio was silent, but Reiki thought Ferra might be listening. The ship's schematics included no power-off system for the radio. The designers hadn't thought it necessary. At best, Ferra could turn the volume to a murmur or disable it by damaging the system and hope to repair it before landing.

"I know you're doing this for your reasons, Ferra. I wouldn't agree with them if I knew what they were, but that choice is out of my hands. Tell Arthur I love him. Tell him I'll be waiting for him on the other side."

Reiki climbed to the bottom rung of the ladder and stared at the lunar surface. The last remnants of the other astronauts were still being drawn under the soil. Beneath her feet, the sand pulsated, as if something underground sensed her closeness and was getting ready to welcome her.

This is it. Is there anything else I can possibly tie up before I go?

Yes. There was one more thing.

"Ferra, I'd also like to say that I forgive you. I know that sounds a little weird, but maybe I can make your life a little better by saying it. I hold nothing against you. I –"

"Reiki, you're mad."

"Ferra?"

There were a few moments of heavy breathing. Was Ferra holding back sobs?

"Why would you say such things? Why forgive someone who's about to do such a hideous thing to you?"

"I don't think I did anything to make you want to kill me, Ferra. Am I right?" Reiki took the following silence as confirmation, so she continued. "Someone must be making you do this. I want you to know I don't blame you. Or, I blame you, but I forgive you. Does that make sense?"

"Truly mad. I just cannot believe..."

Reiki eyed the thrusters which continued to warm up.

She had a very short time left before she'd be turned into a crisp. No shame in a little creative begging here.

"Listen, Ferra. If you're undecided and all, you should know that I'll still forgive you if you open the door. I'm not just saying this because the ship's thrusters are about to kill me, but because you're a part of my past, and I wouldn't mind getting to know you."

Reiki licked dry lips and glanced at the thrusters again.

"And yes, I admit that I'd really, really like to live to see Arthur again."

The airlock cycled smoothly open.

Reiki gathered up the puzzle-cube and boarded the rocket.

CHAPTER 23

NEVER FORGET YOU

The blue skies of Home loomed far below in the front windows, as Reiki stared at the controls and tried to make sense of all the input coming in.

"Mission Control to Miss Reiki. We've double-checked your approach angle. Everything is right on target."

Reiki grimaced and wondered if she'd know what to do if they told her she was off-course. Mission Control assured her that she had a hundred hours logged on the flight simulator, which would be a great help if she could get more than a vague recollection of how she'd fared.

Wisely, M.C. refused to tell her in plain language if she'd ever successfully landed a virtual rocket.

"Please report on the status of the prisoner," droned the voice on the radio.

"Ferra has not asked to leave her quarters. There haven't been any incidents."

There was no way to lock quarters from outside, and they'd agreed it was unwise to weld the door shut. Ferra was a bit of a voluntary prisoner for now. Reiki was in favour of having her on the bridge to handle the landing, but everyone had flat out refused.

Her argument that Janan and the engineers knew the controls better fell on deaf ears. They all had equal time on the simulators, and Janan was needed in an undermanned engineering department. They had no room for a drop in engine power, or the ship would fall too quickly and burn up. Reiki would have to play the role of the entire bridge crew by herself. No one else could be spared to help her.

"Initiate entry roll."

Reiki guided the thrusters until the swirling blue mists turned to black. With the nose of the ship pointed to space, they could now fire the engines to slow their descent. From here, the hard part went to Janan in making sure the engines never choked. Reiki's only task was to keep the ship pointed within a five degree arc of the vertical.

As flames began to lick at the portal, Reiki pictured what they must look like from outside. A large, clay pot hovering over an ocean of white. In the background would be this daunting black sky of piercing stars and a giant, boiling, primordial sun.

And somewhere in that morass of swirling clouds was Arthur waiting for her.

What if we blow up like the other rockets?

You'll eject and tumble from space. I'll be waiting here with a net to catch you.

Reiki smiled at that recollection and patted her suit helmet beside her. If anything did go wrong, she was going to take Arthur up on that offer.

The flames above grew stronger, and a deep, water-like roar joined them. Reiki turned her attention to the readouts as wind buffeted them and threatened to push them off-course. She was so busy with navigation that when she managed to glance back to the window, blue sky peeped at her between the tongues of fire.

Fifty thousand metres.

Still an ocean away. Reiki self-consciously patted at her hair. Space travel had been unkind to her scalp. She was going to need a week of conditioning to tame things. What would Arthur think when he saw that mess? If he dared to laugh she was so going to deck him.

Thirty thousand metres.

There was also the matter of his family to consider. Arthur's mother would not easily agree to a marriage between them. It reminded Reiki that she had lights to make if the orders still stood. If she could get some cashflow going, maybe Patricia would accept her. And making lights made her think about Hendry and his unholy offer to get her life back.

Ten thousand metres.

The kick of engines on full power made Reiki's stomach lurch. They had to get down from almost a thousand kph to zero in a very short window. One engine failure here, and they'd splatter on the ground so hard not even dental records would survive.

However, Janan's team showed their skill, and Reiki only felt a little bump as the roar of the engines died out. The sky was overcast and grey from this altitude. Rivulets of water beaded down the window.

M.C. came on the radio to the backdrop of cheering. "Landing."

Reiki burst from her chair and was at the portal before

tarmac operatives could even drive to meet them. Steam hissed from the baked pavement as raindrops splattered on it. Rather than melt her boots in an attempt to leave, Reiki decided to wait for the flatbed truck to arrive and ferry them to the control tower.

A green tarp formed a canopy for them to keep the rain off as the truck carried the crew to an opening barricaded by guards. Photographers where in the lead of the crowd, followed by jostling, cheering people. Reiki studied them, but there was no sign of Arthur in the crowd. She looked at Janan who smiled and waved for the photographs.

"Sit, Reiki. This is your moment. You brought the ship down by yourself."

"I can't. I'm too excited."

She was off the bed of the truck before it even rolled to a stop, stumbling at first, as her legs tried to remember how gravity worked, but then running into the ranks of spectators and journalists.

"Miss Reiki, wait!"

"Say 'Cheese'..." A photographer with a large pile of flash powder on his stand blinded Reiki momentarily, but she managed to escape them and get into the crowd. A sea of hands reached out to pat her shoulders or touch her hair. She ignored it and wiggled between extended arms as she could.

Where is he? Knowing Arthur, he'd be back from the press of the crowd. He'd have come with the Lansdale. Ah, there it was. And Eric beside it under a large, black umbrella. Reiki fought her way over.

When she burst out of the crowd, Reiki ran three steps while laughing until she noticed that the Lansdale was empty. The grin faded from her lips, and she found herself unable to move forward.

Where was Arthur? Only death would have kept him from being here–she was sure of it.

The sound of cheering faded away. Reiki might as well have been alone for all the attention she paid it. She fell to her knees as her heartbeat thundered in her ears, and her mind worked out the inconceivable.

Something terrible has happened to Arthur. Could he be dead? Terminally ill?

"Reiki!"

That voice. Could it be?

Arthur Galenden emerged from the crowd and stooped to pick her up. Reiki's face must have been a frozen mask of anxiety, for Arthur laughed as he swung her about.

"Arthur?" Her voice sounded like a hollow echo of its normal self.

He set her on her feet and caught her up in a hug. "You sound like you weren't expecting me."

"I hate you. Now, kiss me."

The crowd cheered as they kissed, and journalists rushed to get pictures.

"Why'd you have to scare me like that?" demanded Reiki when she broke off the kiss.

"You ran past me in the crowd. And I'm still recovering from an accident so–"

"Accident?"

"Big oil fire. The warren had to do some tissue regrowth on my lungs. I–"

Reiki kissed Arthur mid-sentence, but journalists interrupted.

"Miss Reiki, is this your significant other?"

Shades! What would Arthur's mother say if she saw Reiki on the front page kissing her son?

"Hey, come back," said Arthur, as Reiki released him.

She would have none of it and jogged away from him in search of the rest of the crew.

Just in time: Reiki found Ferra being marched away by a pair of constables.

"Ferra, wait!"

Reiki ran up to them and grabbed up a perplexed-looking Ferra in a hug. Cameras lit them up like a lightning storm, and people cheered even more.

"Reiki, you're so strange." Ferra was smiling and crying at the same time.

Reiki dug up the puzzle-cube from her pocket and pressed it into Ferra's hands.

"I want you to have this. I was never able to solve it, even after watching you do it. When you come back, I want you to teach me."

"Silly girl. They won't let me out for twenty years."

"I'll be here waiting for you. I'll never forget. I think you know this."

More cheering drowned them out, and the constables led Ferra away. When Reiki could hear again, she found more constables at her sides.

"Miss Reiki. You're needed for debriefing."

Academy brass was unamused with the antics of the crew when they heard the story in detail. They berated Reiki for not going over Spacerman's head and reporting the suspect seismic activity. When they learned that she'd destroyed the only video evidence of the crystals, they were furious. So much so, it made Ferra's attempt to kill her pale in comparison.

There was talk of a court martial, but it got squelched as Reiki was technically a civilian. Her lack of rank had saved her. They ended up releasing her after several hours with a warning that everything she'd seen was classified. There was to be no talk of 'moon monsters' until after Academy spin doctors had decided how to present the findings.

It was still drizzling when Reiki burst out the doors to discover that Arthur had waited around. All during the ride to the Galenden manor, they held hands and stole glances at each other while Reiki wished the windows of the Lansdale were tinted so she could wrap her legs around him.

"I've missed you like a kidney," she said.

"A lot happened while you were upstairs. Xandri's been running your growing microguild for you. Selling your lights. We've called it Reinergy."

"That's spectacular," she cried. But something in Arthur's face told her there was bad news. "What? What's wrong? Is it the accident?"

"A ghost from your past showed up. She passed away during the chaos. Pronounced dead on arrival. They said I was lucky to make it."

"Oh, Arthur."

"That's the worst of it. Something else I've not told you is I used to be sort of seeing Wendiah before I met you."

"Oh."

Arthur must think she knew who that was. Apparently it was meaningful enough that he needed to set her at ease on it. If he had strayed, Reiki was unsure what she'd say. She hadn't even considered the possibility. How foolish of her, given his stature. She cursed herself inwardly.

"Wend was at my bedside during my recovery," Arthur went on to say. "Nothing happened, but I wouldn't want you to hear that from someone else and think the worst."

What a relief. Reiki expelled a sigh and looked at him slyly.

"You've been naughty," she said. "Maybe you'll have to be spanked."

Arthur roared with laughter. "Oh dear, you're impossible tonight."

"I think you're blushing."

"You're one of a kind, Reiki."

Arthur was still blushing when they arrived at the manor, for Reiki blew on his ear a few times on the way and coaxed a physical reaction out of him. He had to remove her hands from his lap when the car rolled to a stop.

"Mother was agreeable to a welcome back banquet for you tonight. Seems your prestige brings a little honour to the house. Do be a nice guiding star and dress up for the occasion?"

"You mean spacer overalls are unpresentable? If you insist."

Reiki giggled as she released his hand. Eric opened her door and had an umbrella for her, which he used to shield her as she rushed inside. As Eric returned for Arthur, Reiki went on ahead of them to get ready.

She found her suite almost exactly as she'd left it. Even her purse was still sitting open from her aborted rendez-vous with Hendry. Reiki only paused briefly to take stock. She raced to get her hair combed into something presentable.

A deep blue dress awaited her in the closet beside her green one from Hillvale. The new dress had golden threads in X-patterns across the chest. A bit of a fashion nightmare, but there were marching shoes for it at least. Reiki dressed without thinking on it and found herself a ribbon in the top drawer to bind her hair.

A knock at the door made Reiki's heart race. She hoped it was Xandri here to help with her nails.

"Come in."

Patricia Galenden appeared with a servant who wheeled a tea tray in after her. Reiki caught her breath and hastened to give a formal curtsy.

"So pleased to see you well, milady."

"Yes," came the response. "You were more tardy than expected."

"I was held up late for a debriefing, milady."

Patricia Galenden drew to the centre of the room and put her hands together. The servant fetched a chair from a corner for Patricia to sit in. Once comfortable, Patricia took in the tray with a sweep of her hand.

"All the guests have eaten. Do enjoy some tea and a slice of cake."

"Thank you, milady. I would like that."

Reiki joined her, as the servant selected a table from the same corner and set it in front of Lady Galenden. The servant poured tea for two and set out a slice of cake for Reiki after seating her. He bowed and went to stand by the door.

Reiki noticed the cake had white frosting with little crystals of red powder on it. The crystals gave off a gassy-vapoury scent almost like mothballs. She tried to remember where she'd smelled that before.

"Do try the cake," said Ms. Galenden. "We ordered it just for you."

"Thank you, mistress."

The source of the red powder came back. Rat poison. She'd seen it in the music room near the dead rat on her first day at the Galendens.

"Go on. The cake isn't going to bite you."

Reiki decided to see if she could slide out of eating it. "Oh, Milady. It's just that I'm allergic to cake."

"Nonsense. Who's allergic to cake? There aren't any peanuts in it. Eat some. Or shall I have to face the master baker and tell him you didn't like his work."

The implication was clear. Reiki was not going to be able to get out of eating the cake.

She sighed and picked up a fork to break off a piece. When she transferred it to her mouth Reiki chewed only lightly and used her powers to freeze it. She swallowed it in a slushy state and felt the coolness in her stomach. With any luck, she'd be able to keep it frozen long enough...

"Do try some more. Come now, it's not that bad."

"Yes, milady."

Reiki repeated her actions with a second bite. She could feel her stomach fighting to digest the first piece. The effort of maintaining it in a frozen state under those conditions was taxing. She felt herself start to perspire.

"And some tea to wash it down."

How long can this torture go on? Reiki obliged with a few sips of tea and managed to smile.

At last, Patricia Galenden took to her feet.

"Excellent. I shall go downstairs, now. Stars keep you, Reiki."

"Stars keep you, milady."

Patricia stopped at the door as the servant collected the tray. She watched Reiki for a long, uncomfortable moment before leaving.

As soon as the door shut behind the servant, Reiki raced to the washroom and voided into a basin. She got both pieces of cake out, but not quite soon enough, for her insides churned painfully.

For a moment, all Reiki could do was lie on the washroom floor, arms clutched across her chest, as her insides constricted. The feeling passed after fifteen minutes. She had managed to dodge the worst of it. Had she eaten the cake straight out, she would now be dead.

Reiki crawled to her hands and knees, and only one thought crossed her mind.

Arthur.

She had to save him. Reiki clambered to her feet and raced from her suites.

CHAPTER 24

ENGAGED

Reiki found Arthur in a drawing room having tea with about two dozen family members. They reclined in sofas and love seats, listening to a poetry recital when Reiki arrived. Tea and cake had been set out. Arthur even held a saucer with a slice of it in his hand. Reiki had arrived in time to prevent him from eating his first bite.

Reiki hurried into the room as Arthur made to eat his cake. He looked up and saw her but that fork with its deadly cargo continued to trace its way to his mouth.

"Arthur, wait." Reiki gathered up her dress in order to make it to him in time and batted the cake from his fork. In his surprise, he dropped the plate, and it shattered on the floor.

Recital interrupted, the room fell into a hush. Reiki looked about and realized, by the empty plates, that she was too late. Everyone had eaten of the poisoned cake. In a moment, the death spasms would begin.

That's when Reiki realized their cake wasn't poisoned. How foolish of her. Why would Arthur's mother poison her own son?

Mercifully Lady Galenden was absent. Still, there were enough people present to ensure that word of this caper spread to all Arthur's social circles.

Yep. Right about now, I feel like the word "stupid" is stamped on my forehead.

Arthur got to his feet. "Sorry everyone, She has a cake-phobia. We'll be right back."

On that note, he guided Reiki out of the room.

Arthur shut them into a window-side servant's storeroom and turned to Reiki.

"What was that about?"

Reiki put her head up defiantly. "Your mother tried to poison me."

"What?"

"She gave me cake with poison in it."

"Poison." His voice went flat.

"Rat poison. It almost killed me."

"Reiki, my mother is many things, but a murderer is not one of them."

"She did. I'm not lying." Reiki put her back to Arthur and crossed her arms. She was unsurprised that Arthur doubted her. She'd have to take him to her room and show him the remains of her cake. If he still didn't believe, she'd get a lab rat and demonstrate.

"Reiki." Arthur set his hands on her hips and breathed her name in her hair.

All at once, Reiki's scalp began to tingle, and she remembered the long lonely nights in the rocket. As Arthur's hands encircled her, she closed her eyes and remembered the feel of his hands on her skin that night they'd made love.

Arthur hands reached her stomach and traced up to her ribs. Reiki arched her back and twisted her head to kiss him when her reached her breasts. It was a distracting position to kiss from, but he made it work by standing taller.

Perhaps frustrated with the lightness of the kiss, Arthur broke off, got Reiki turned around, and pressed her back against the door. From that position he kissed her properly while he squeezed the air out of her with hands pressed to her spine.

Arthur's lips were a song, and Reiki was lost in it. She threw her arms around his neck and ceased to be herself until he broke off.

"Hells, I've missed you," said Arthur.

Reiki's reply was buried under another heavy kiss. She threw out her arms and flailed in mock despair when he managed to get his sweet-smelling hair in her nose.

"Trying to sprout wings and get away?" Arthur sounded amused.

"We need to go back outside before people ask."

"They can wait."

Arthur started hiking up Reiki's dress, but she fought him.

"Silly boy. We can't lock the door to this cubbyhole."

Unperturbed, Arthur got Reiki's dress bunched up to her hips and lifted her so she was straddling him. He pressed her against the door to keep it closed, as she stifled a laugh. But the feel of his manhood on her precious area wiped all trace of humour from her throat.

Reiki pushed away from the door to get room for a few experimental bounces, shuddering in desire from the effect.

This would be a very interesting position, and she'd gone without for so very long.

Footsteps coming down the outside hall sent them scrambling to dress before anything further could develop. Reiki straightened her dress and fought not to burst out laughing. Getting caught like that on the heels of her cake fiasco would be the end of Arthur's reputation.

I have to be on good behaviour for now, or Lady Galenden is going to scuttle my chances of being with Arthur forever.

The footsteps receded into the distance. After some time, Arthur took Reiki's hand and led them out. Secure that no one remained to observe, they tiptoed to the nearest stairs.

"Come to my room," said Reiki. "I have the proof there that I was poisoned."

They snuck into the guestroom, and Reiki marched Arthur right to the washroom. The basin was empty. Residual fingerprints showed someone had been by recently. They had probably replaced it while she wasn't looking.

Arthur put on a thin smile. "Yes? This proof..."

"It was right here. It– They– hid the bits of cake–"

"My mother might not like you, but murder? Really, now."

Reiki sighed and pouted. Arthur gathered her into a hug.

"You okay? Seems like the flight's getting to you."

"I'm leaving," said Reiki. She turned away, and Arthur released her. He spoke from behind when she reached the dresser.

"What? Why?"

"You think I'm staying here so your mother can put a dagger in my chest? I'm getting myself a nice, safe hotel room, with no rat poison and no guillotines to cut my head off while I sleep."

"You don't have to." Arthur walked up and put his hands on her shoulders. "You're safe with me. Stay, would you?"

"Not in a million years."

"Please don't leave me."

Reiki lowered her head. Staying would be of the utmost stupidity. Why was it that she desperately wanted to? Resolutely, she set her hands on the dresser, which tipped her purse over. The bottle of spermicidal gel rolled out. That, and her black lipstick were the last two items she'd placed in it before getting sent up. They both spun clear of her grasping hands, and the bottle shattered on the floor.

Shades! I should have thrown that thing out.

Arthur reached down and picked up the bits of glass the label clung to. Reiki covered her face with her hands while he read it. Why had she kept that bottle? How would she explain this?

Arthur frowned as he looked back up.

"Reiki, I think we'd better sit down and talk."

Arthur left Reiki's room a short time later and stalked towards Hendry's suites. Reiki grabbed his arm and tried to hold him back.

"Arthur, please. Don't get mad."

He looked at her, and she made a choked noise before releasing him. Arthur kissed her hand, and guided her back inside. He closed the door gently. With any luck she wouldn't follow.

So help me if Hendry doesn't die this evening.

Arthur made his way to Hendry's suites and stood

before the door to give himself time to calm down. Inner peace failed to come. He settled for burning rage instead. Arthur gritted his teeth, then kicked the door open and set foot inside.

A woman with long black hair stared at him in horror. Hendry lay on his back, and she knelt between his knees delivering ministrations to his manhood.

"Leave," said Arthur.

She gathered up her clothes and hustled out the door. Hendry clambered to his feet while struggling to do up his pants.

"Arthur, Arthur," said Hendry. He got no further because he had to duck under Arthur's fist. "Hey, that's no way to greet a cousin."

Arthur leapt for him and grabbed him by the neck. He shoved Hendry all the way to the window, and they rammed into it hard.

"Calm, man. Have you gone mad?"

"Give me the information you collected on Reiki," said Arthur.

"Information? Oh, that. Hrrk"

Arthur eased his stranglehold. He didn't want Hendry to die until after he'd given up the details.

"Out with it, Hendry."

"I didn't collect any information. I just made all that up to get her to sleep with me."

"You what?"

"You should be proud of me for thinking of such a scheme. What's happened to you, man?"

"A puzzle-cube happened. I don't trust you."

"That was your mum's idea. You were the one who told

her how smart Reiki was. She gave me the cube, and I passed it along. It's how we do things, guy."

Arthur relaxed his grip even more. Hendry was right. Before meeting Reiki, he would have been the one to go along with any scheme to get a little play. And the puzzle-cube idea was far above Hendry's normal *modus operandi* of scoring the maximum interest from women with the least amount of thought.

"You're not the mystery guitarist," muttered Arthur. But if not Hendry, who else could it be? It just *had* to be him.

"You think I'd trifle with matching notes against a skilled pianist? Come on. That's way too hard a way to impress a woman."

Exactly what Arthur was just thinking. He hung his head. Hendry might actually be innocent.

Still, doubt clouded his mind. Arthur left, but paused at the door.

"For your sake, I hope you're telling the truth because I'm going to get to the bottom of this one way or another."

Sunrise brought Reiki fully awake without trace of sleepiness because her body was still on "world time" which went by the prime meridian. She tried not to move and awaken Arthur, but her slight stirring brought him out of slumber soon after. He reached a hand up to tickle her chin, and she mock-bit him which got him the rest of the way up.

"Morning, Arthur," said Reiki as she kissed him on the nose. "Feels like the choo-choo train is ready to carry more passengers to work."

"Woman, that train made three stops last night. The engineers are on vacation."

Reiki grinned at his use of her own metaphors to get out of an early morning performance. There was uncovered ground between them she decided to address right away.

"Arthur, I wanted to thank you."

He sat up, looking puzzled. "For what?"

"For talking to Hendry. Even if he said he's innocent."

"Claims he's innocent. I still doubt that."

They held each other for a long moment before Reiki spoke again.

"Is your mother ever going to accept me?"

"Yep. She doesn't see much of your new-found celebrity status, but your guild is going to turn a lot of coin."

"Not enough money to impress her."

"She's Gedanese, Reiki. Money will impress her."

Another comfortable pause fell between them.

"Arthur?"

"Yes?"

"Does this make me officially your girlfriend?"

"Wha-huh?"

His eyes showed he hadn't considered the possibility. Reiki made a pout as if miffed.

"Oh, I see how this is, Mr Galenden."

"Wait, wait. Hold on."

Arthur got out of bed and went to the dresser where a small pile of spare handkerchiefs sat folded. He was a moment fidgeting before he came back with a bit of thread torn from some unlucky piece of cloth. He rejoined Reiki between the sheets.

With solemn airs, Arthur tied the thread around Reiki's finger as he intoned the words.

"I, Arthur Galenden, hereby pledge my hand to the Rocket Girl if she will be my wife."

"The Rocket Girl says I do."

They had another quiet moment, but Reiki broke it by diving under the sheets.

"Hey, what are you doing?" cried Arthur.

"Vacation's over. Station's ordering the engineers to report."

They were at it for the rest of the morning.

It was several hours later that Reiki made her way to the music room and sat down to play. She knew she would move out today. Seeing Arthur could wait for evenings or when time allowed, but her safety was in jeopardy if she stayed. This might be her last chance to play such a magnificent old instrument.

"I'll miss you, dear piano," she said as she opened the lid.

Melodies came in fitful bursts for fifteen minutes as Reiki warmed up. Her playing attracted Xandri, who entered the room carrying her harp in her arms. Xandri selected a stool and added a harmony to Reiki's song.

Would Xandri be willing to be musician for a wedding? Reiki pictured herself in some sort of fancy blue dress carrying a bouquet of roses down the aisle. Arthur would be waiting at the front, flanked by his cousins, as strains of harp music filled the large hall, and sunlight danced overhead.

Reiki smiled to think of Arthur's eyes drinking in the sight of her. The betrothal rights would go by in a blur, so mesmerized in each other they would be.

The pronouncement and the cheer from the crowd

would follow. Reiki Galenden would lean forward and kiss the man she would grow old with and–

Guitar chords broke her reverie. Reiki's mouth turned to ash. Hendry. There could be no joy in her heart while he taunted her like this. She switched to a lugubrious C / F-Maj7 to G pattern, all slow and lumbering like a lonely elephant in search a final resting spot in an unforgiving wasteland.

The song was so melancholy that Xandri stopped playing. She stared at the hidden alcove in curiosity. Yet, Reiki and the guitarist played on.

Arthur came running to the doorway out of breath. Reiki bet Vincent had just told him Hendry was here.

Or, perhaps she was wrong, for Hendry also came running up behind Arthur. Between Xandri, Reiki, Arthur and Hendry, all four stared at each other.

And the music died out.

Arthur was the first to speak. "But if we're all here, who's that playing guitar?"

Reiki slid the bench back and stood up. As she approached the alcove, she noted that the guitarist stayed put instead of running away like the previous times. She drew back the curtain, and they all stared in shock.

It was a young man who slung the guitar over his shoulder and straightened his jacket. His smile was mysterious and attractive. Recognition popped up in Reiki's scrambling mind.

"I know you. You're the fellow who watched me in the train."

"Yes," said the man. "My name is Jude Tavenern, and I'm your fiancé."

CHAPTER 25

SOMETIMES DREAMS DIE

Reiki stared at Jude in shock while she tried to come up with a logical thing to say.

"I'm engaged? To you?" It was all she could sputter.

Jude bowed slightly, a move which cast an errant lock of hair across his face. "I proposed to you before a crowd of applauding witnesses."

"Engaged?" Arthur breathed the word with a note of sarcastic disbelief. He entered the alcove, followed by Hendry and Xandri.

"You know what happened to me?" Reiki sat beside Jude on the window sill. His eyes looked large and soft. Tender was a better word. He wore a high-collared jacket over a ruffle-pleated shirt, whose sleeves were deliberately too long. If he was telling the truth about being engaged, she certainly knew how to pick 'em.

"I know most of what happened to you. We were in my car in Hillvale when that cart rolled out in the street. You remember it, don't you?"

"I remember nothing," she breathed. "Tell me everything."

"I woke up. The car was totalled. And even worse, you were gone. For days, all I had was my memories of you. And this." Jude reached back into his guitar case and withdrew a fancy shoe.

It was a high heel shoe. Purple, and of medium height. Reiki recognized it as one of hers. It was like a tiny chunk of her past had wriggled into Jude's hands.

"May I?" asked Jude.

He got up from the window sill, knelt, and reached for her foot, but Reiki drew her leg back. A memory bubbled out of her still mind just then. She was sitting in a ritzy department store, and Jude was slipping this same shoe onto her foot.

Reiki caught her breath in her throat to choke back a sob. Jude must be telling the truth. Here knelt the man she had agreed to marry.

As the silence dragged out, Arthur finally intervened. "Now just a second there–" he started to say.

Hendry interrupted and charged past him. Jude was out the window and on the railings before Hendry even made it halfway across the room. Reiki put out a protective arm.

"Stop. I know this man." She collected the shoe from Jude and held it out so Arthur could inspect it.

"Reiki, I knew you'd come around." Jude tried to grasp two of her fingers, but Reiki jerked her hand out of reach.

"I believe you that you know me," she said. "But I don't remember you. Please understand that."

"Atta girl, Reiki," said Hendry.

Reiki drew her hand away from him before he could

take it. "And as for you, you scheming bastard, if you touch me again, I'll freeze your eyeballs into stones."

Actually, that might be playing too nice. She should freeze his testicles instead. That would serve him right.

Arthur studied the shoe carefully, as if Jude had contrived some means of falsifying footwear. Reiki wondered what he was thinking. If it was anything near what she was thinking, the list of questions would be long indeed.

Hendry pointed an arm across Reiki's field of view. "You, knave, have impersonated me."

Jude pretended to sniff at the air. "If I was mistaken for you, I must have turned ugly indeed."

Jude and Hendry were crowding her. Reiki scrambled to her feet and got herself out from between them. She took another step back, as Jude held his open embrace to her.

"No, I told you. I don't want to hug you."

"But, Reiki. I've missed you. What more can I say?"

"You can start by explaining why you've not come out of hiding sooner," said Arthur. "Why wait this long?"

"I tried, you know," said Jude. He climbed back into the room, inched toward Reiki, and pointed at Arthur. "This ruffian drew a gun on me when I tried to reach you. I feared for my life. Ask him."

"Liar. That was before she lost her memory," said Arthur.

"And he slept with the prostitute," said Jude.

"I am not a prostitute," cried Xandri, with a look of extreme vexation on her face.

Reiki looked back and forth between them. Something here didn't add up. She picked it out once she defined the problem. "Arthur. You knew I was engaged and you didn't tell me?"

He looked shocked at the question, for he drew breath and had to compose his answer. "We fought before you lost your memory. I promise. And he didn't seem genuine. He—"

Arthur stopped explaining as Reiki raised her hand. Her legs felt all rubbery, and she collapsed to her knees there on the music room floor.

She looked to Xandri. "Is it true? A prostitute?"

"Reiki, I.... I couldn't... I..." Xandri glanced back and forth between all, then buried her face in her hands and fled the room.

Staring after Xandri, Reiki tried to work saliva into her dry mouth, but failed.

Hendry tried to use me. This guy claims I was about to marry him. Arthur and Xandri have hidden things from me. Who shall I believe?

She could see only one logical course of action from here.

"Jude," said Reiki. "Please take me home. I want to meet my family."

Things got trickier from there instead of easier. The first problem was that all three men wanted to accompany Reiki to her room to get a chance to explain themselves. She walked down the hall, listening to them bicker and who did what and when. They ignored her pleas to be left alone, as they couldn't agree on who would be the first to leave her side.

Reiki appealed to Vincent to fetch the one person she could think of who could hold sway over all three.

"And what is going on here?" demanded Yolanda once Vincent returned with her.

"We're discussing a proper strategy for the handling of Miss Reiki's return to her hometown," Hendry informed her.

Yolanda planted her feet slightly apart and set her hands on her hips. "Well, gentlemen, the strategy just ended. The two of you are late for dinner, and you, stranger had best wash up and join them."

"Now's not the time–"

"He's hardly a guest–"

"I can't leave my beloved–"

Yolanda stomped her foot and seemed to inflate before Reiki's eyes. "Now. Or do you want to see me whip off this apron?"

Grumbling, the men stalked off.

"Reiki, I'll be at the train station tonight," called Jude.

"The faster you get ouf of my house, the better," growled Arthur.

"I'll even show you the door," said Hendry.

"Poor boys," said Reiki.

"Come, let's get you packed before they do something stupid," said Yolanda.

Arthur escorted Jude off the premises, and they faced each other in the road before the manor. It was easy to lord it over Jude who stood two fists shorter than himself, but Jude held his ground under steady eyes.

"Looks like she's going with you," said Arthur. "Seems you've won, for now."

"For now?" Jude gave a smile that bordered on a sneer as he flicked that errant lock out of his face. "I always win."

Arthur stared at Jude's back as he walked off. He willed himself to stop gritting his teeth and threw out a parting shot. "This is far from over, Jude."

"Any time you're ready, guy," came the light-hearted response. Jude even had the nerve to start whistling.

Enraged Arthur whirled and stormed into the manor. The nearest object he could lift turned out to be a decorative vase, which he heaved at the wall. The shattering noise did little to lighten his mood, but it brought a score of servants to investigate. The concern on their faces was enough to extinguish his wrath.

"Sorry, everyone. Not having the best of days," said Arthur. He left them there and went to the fencing room, where he took out his frustration on a wooden punching-pillar instead of a defenceless vase. He was at it for an hour before a voice interrupted him.

"Milord?"

It was Vincent who lingered in the doorway. Arthur left off with striking the post and sat down on the floor against it. Vincent joined him there and crossed his legs as he sat down.

"Why did Reiki leave?" asked Vincent. "Everyone was taking wagers you were going to marry her."

Arthur chuckled at the thought of his staff making bets on his amorous endeavours. He wondered which of them was citing the odds, and how much money they had down on it.

"She left because she promised to marry someone else, Vincent."

"I know that. It's just that... it seems unfair for her to have to leave. She only just came back, after all."

"Life's unfair that way. And now, since I need to give her a little space, would you do me the favour of running to the winery for a bottle of the 357 scotch?"

Minutes later, Arthur had the bottle in his hand and a large tumbler into which he'd poured himself two fingers. But though he swirled the golden fluid around in the glass, he'd taken just one sip.

He knew what the problem was: he didn't want to drink Reiki's memories away. He wanted each one as vivid for him as it was for her.

And so Arthur sat there with his eyes closed and meditated. Maybe if he focussed on every detail of Reiki, he'd never lose any part of her. If only he could trap the smell of her hair on his pillow, perhaps the longing would abate.

Eric eventually showed in the fencing room as Arthur sat there. He looked at the untouched scotch and blinked.

"I see you're making huge inroads into that bottle," said Eric.

"She's gone?" asked Arthur.

"An hour ago. Only took her a few minutes to pack."

"Ah, good." Arthur laid his head back against the post. "She should manage to catch the overnight northbound train. She should be in Hillvale by noon."

"You could see her off if you're done hiding. There might still be time."

"Hiding?"

"Where would you be now if Jude hadn't appeared but Reiki was going home?"

Arthur tilted his head. If not for Jude, he'd be at the

train station either wishing her well or going with her. He supposed that could be construed as hiding.

"If you don't see Reiki off, you'll be letting Jude have the final say."

"Fine," said Arthur.

"He'll go laughing all the way home while you cower here with your tail between–"

"Stop, stop," said Arthur.

"Hmm?"

"Go warm up the Lansdale. I'll be right out."

The overnight train for the north was already there and loaded when Arthur arrived. As he climbed out of the Lansdale, he checked the clock tower and realized it was ten minutes late. He had been saved by some fortunate last-minute engine work.

Arthur ran down the length of the train until he found Reiki's window. She leaned with her hair pinned to the glass, and Jude sat in the facing seat. The lines in her face, Arthur thought, might be a mix of fatigue and sorrow. But she looked beautiful nonetheless.

Reiki gave a start when she saw him, and her smile seemed to change the entire sky. She leapt from her seat and left Jude gaping, mid-sentence.

Arthur ran for the door and made it before Reiki. She arrived and ran off the stairs, soaring into Arthur's embrace.

Their lips came together, and the kiss was long and hard. Reiki drew back to speak, seemed to change her mind, and they kissed again in a desperate affair, full of raw need.

"You're the first man I ever loved, Arthur," said Reiki.

"I realized today," he replied. "That without you, my heart will never be complete."

The train gave a whistle, and some distant voice cried "All aboard!"

Arthur sighed. It seemed the stars had decided his time with Reiki was up.

"I can't leave you," said Reiki. "Take me home. I want to be your wife."

"No," he said. "First reclaim your life. When you need me, you'll know where to find me."

The train gave a final shrill whistle, so Arthur set Reiki down on the first step. She climbed down to reach for him, so he collected her in his arms, set her back on the steps, and walked along beside her.

Reiki searched her purse, but Arthur knew she carried no handkerchiefs to throw to him. He saw her eyes light up with an idea, noticed her wriggle, then saw the cloth fall around her ankles.

Panties. Reiki kicked them to her hand, balled them up, and threw them to Arthur. He caught them as the train picked up speed and formed an ocean of longing between them.

"I love you," he shouted.

"I love you," she called back. And then, faintly, she added, "And I need you."

Arthur watched the train roll past him until it transformed into a smudge of blinking lights down a stony track. He stared at it until the final light vanished over the crest of the sinkhole.

"I need you too, Reiki," he said. "Please come back to me."

Evening constellations glittered in an azure night as the rumble of the train announced loss, life and opportunity. Eric rounded the corner of the station and tipped his hat. Arthur reluctantly turned to follow.

CHAPTER 26

SAID I LOVED
YOU BUT I DIED

Reiki dozed through most of the ride, only waking whenever she drooped off balance. Frequently, she was lost and confused in those waking moments. Usually, it was about the man sitting across from her.

"What are you thinking?" asked Jude for the umpteenth time.

Reiki shrugged. She was thinking about Arthur, but Jude likely knew that. How could he not, when other passengers would stop by to wish her a speedy reunification with Arthur. It made her engagement to Jude seem a bit of a sham. An empty shell of her past that she was being forced to explore.

She wondered what her ring had looked like before the incident. The thieves who had stolen it off her fingers after her car accident must have sold it by now. Was it unique enough to find again and buy back? Now that Reiki had money, she could afford to think about things like that. She decided to ask about it.

"What did the ring look like?"

"What?"

"The engagement ring. Before the accident. Before it got stolen."

"Oh, it was gold, with a bunch of diamonds on it."

Reiki suppressed the urge to roll her eyes. "How many diamonds? Can you bring me back to the jeweller? I want to find it again. An engagement ring would stand out, I'd think. Unless they harvested it for diamonds already, but I'd think it would still be on the market."

Jude blinked in surprise at her questions. "Oh, the jeweller's dead. He... was old. Passed away shortly after making it."

"His store, then? They would have records."

"Out of business, sorry."

Reiki sighed in frustration. The ring would be very difficult to track down now. Perhaps she'd best let that go. Yet, more questions remained.

"What did I say when I saw the ring?"

"Huh? You said yes, of course."

"I want to know how I said yes. Did I go all gaga over the ring? Or did I have to think? Was I genuinely surprised?"

Jude shrugged. "You said yes. I got the ring on the cheap side. Really it was just a token ring. A symbol of a much greater love."

"Oh, okay," said Reiki.

Just a token *engagement* ring? Men. Just when she thought she understood them.

"Why are you asking me about a ring but nothing of your parents?"

"I don't want them to get all coloured through you.

I'll be meeting them for the first time. I want that first impression to be everything."

"Reiki, you continue to be an enigma."

That made her smile and think of the puzzle-cube. If she hadn't given it away, she'd be working on it right now, perhaps never to find the answer. Perhaps getting rid of it was her ultimate response to Hendry's advances.

They arrived in Credd, and Jude led Reiki out of the train station by the hand. In the parking lot, he tracked down a couple who seemed to recognize them. Between them, Reiki remembered the woman, but it was her partner who spoke first.

"You found her at last," said the man. He clapped hands with Jude, then came to kiss Reiki's wrist. "You look like you don't even remember me. My name is Lucius. I know you because of Jude."

"Good to have you back, Reiki." Sanny waved and gave a cute little hop.

"Hi." Reiki knew her response was pathetic, but she was a little overwhelmed. She gripped the paper bag of her belongings to her chest and looked from one face to the other, wishing she could remember something, but only the image of Sanny playing her xylophone during that one song came to mind.

"Well, let's get rolling," said Lucius.

They all piled into his car and drove off.

Hillvale was a bit of a surprise to Reiki, for a large mob had gathered downtown. Guards tried to enforce order, but it was clear they'd be lucky just to prevent a riot. Paper littered the ground as if street cleaners had gone on strike for a month. Traffic was at a near standstill for all the yelling and chaos.

"We're still on food rations," Jude explained. "All excess food is first-come-first-serve."

"That sounds terrible," said Reiki. "Are people starving?"

"No. There is plenty to eat if you like staples and starches. It's things like sugar and salt no one can seem to ship here in enough quantities."

Hillvale was very flat, compared to Ged. It took some getting used to. The buildings were quite tall, and every second block seemed to have a fluorine power core with its morass of gears all grinding away to provide electricity. The electric buses all ran on cables. Ged didn't have buses, but Reiki imagined they'd run on gasoline if it did.

Lucius drove them to a fifteen storey apartment building, and they all climbed out to meet on the sidewalk.

"Thanks for the lift, guy. I owe ya." Jude shook hands with Lucius, then they rubbed double fists.

"No prob, yo," said Lucius. "Anything for you and your hot-ass girlie."

"Lucius," said Sanny. "Might I remind you that your girlfriend's right here?"

"Oi, I remember bear-brain. You're my flavour of the week."

"Keep digging that hole." Sanny linked an arm with Lucius, and he kissed her on the cheek.

Reiki knew she was flushing to hear them so openly intimate, so she gave Jude an impatient look. Jude took the hint and started them for the apartments.

Sanny gave them a coquettish smile and swung her hips

like a shy schoolgirl. "Bye, Jude. Should have taken us up on that offer for a threesome while you had the chance."

Gross. Reiki felt her ears burning red at the thought. Sanny was worse than Hendry. What strange friends she had.

The doorman seemed to recognize Jude, for he let them in. The elevator ride and the walk down the hall were all a blur to Reiki. It was only when Jude knocked on the door that she realized the magnitude of what she was about to face.

"Jude, I can't do this."

Too late. The door flew open, and a woman threw herself on Reiki.

"My dearest, dearest Reiki."

My mother? The woman had long red hair and a slight build. The man who came to the door had dark brown hair and a stockier build. Neither of them had Reiki's freckle pattern, so she must have taken after a grandparent.

They got Reiki herded into a three-bedroom apartment she didn't recognize and sitting on the couch. On her lap, they dropped a photo album of strangers, and in her hand they deposited a cup of tea.

"We saw the news, hun," said her father. "They say you were first woman on the moon."

The words surprised Reiki. The moon project had been very much out of the news in Ged due to the bigger elections in the League and changes in the oil market. She was surprised to hear it popular over here.

"It made the paper?" she asked.

"Hold on, I think I have one."

He thought? Reiki would have imagined an event of

that magnitude to be worthy of having two dozen copies and one framed.

The newspaper was not to be found, though, and there were a great many more photographs to look at. Reiki dutifully made herself sit through them all, until three hours later, she reached the end of the ordeal. They had a late lunch, for afternoon light was already starting to wane.

After the meal, Reiki tried to make an escape.

"I'm sorry, everyone. This is all so strange to me. Would it be okay if I took a walk and cleared my head?"

"Why don't you grab a nap?" asked her mother. "You must be exhausted from your travels."

"Yes, that sounds perfect. May I?"

They deposited her in a room cluttered with items that might have belonged to her. There was a starmap that was incorrect on several entries tacked to the wall, a child's telescope that even an amateur would frown upon, and a shelf of books that ran up against the foot of a single bed.

As they left her alone in there, Reiki chose not to question it, plopped herself down on the covers and passed right out.

Reiki awoke with a start to find Jude snuggled up to her back. Dazed, she pushed away, while her clouded mind caught up with her body's act of self-defence.

There wasn't much room in the single bed to get away from him, so Reiki rolled over and put her back to the wall. The room was dark. It was past sunset. She felt disoriented still. It made her want to vomit.

Jude was either awake, or it was her stirring that did the job, for he reached out to set a hand on her arm.

Reiki shuddered. There was only one person she wanted touching her arm, and that was Arthur. How to explain this to Jude in a way that made sense?

Jude, oblivious to Reiki's inner turmoil, pressed on. "I really appreciate you coming back to us. It's been tough getting on without you."

"Tough?"

"You're a rock in my life, you know. No matter when I'm angry or sad, you're always the same. Sometimes I feel like a volcano and you're the ocean that has to cool my lava."

Jude traced a fingertip to Reiki's shoulder and moved to run it along her collarbone. She got an arm in the way and gently pushed him back.

"Hold on, let me do it. You used to love it when I did that."

"No way," said Reiki. She folded her arms across her chest.

"You trust me, don't you?"

Not really. How did one tactfully explain to their fiancé that they wanted to be left alone?

"You're crowding me, Jude."

"Don't you want to kiss? Don't you find you miss me deep inside?"

"No. I don't remember you or anyone here. I just want–"

She wanted to be home. Home was where Arthur was.

That's when it occurred to her. The version of her that Jude loved had died in that car crash. She was going to have to break off the ridiculous engagement. Jude's soon-to-be wife had passed away in the accident.

"I'm sorry. I can't do this." Reiki got to her hands and knees and clambered to the nearest floor space in reverse. She edged past Jude and took to the hall without even stopping to put on her shoes. Jude caught up with her outside where she jammed the elevator button.

"Whoa, whoa, not so fast. Why the hurry?"

Reiki dumped her thoughts on him in one chaotic stream. "I can't marry you, Jude. I'm not me and the me you thought you knew went away and isn't coming back. I've got to get out of here. I need to get home."

"You're building a wall that doesn't exist. Let yourself feel for once."

"What?"

Where had she heard that before? Why was it so familiar?

"Say it, Reiki. Say you love me."

"Jude, it's too much for me. I can't remember an us. You're still a stranger to me."

"A stranger who still loves you and ran a thousand miles for you."

"It's over. I'm sorry, but we're through."

"B-but..." out came the puppy dog eyes. Reiki turned and concentrated on the down-button so she wouldn't have to look at them.

"I'm sorry," she said.

"Two weeks." Jude's voice cracked with emotion.

"What?"

"Two weeks is all I ask. I can convince you in that time you were meant for me. It's what you would do if the situations were reversed."

The elevator arrived, but Reiki made no move to board. Jude was right. If Arthur had forgotten her by some miracle, he'd likely try to leave her and chase all those better options he had. Reiki knew she would be prostrate on the floor, begging him to give their relationship a chance if that were the case.

The elevator doors closed, and Jude seemed to take that as Reiki's answer, because he happily spun her around to face him and wrapped his arms about her.

When Reiki closed her eyes, she could almost picture him as Arthur.

"You'll do it? You're giving me two weeks?"

Unable to open her eyes and face the reality, Reiki nodded.

Two weeks of this torment. Arthur, please wait for me.

CHAPTER 27

FREEZE ME, THAW ME WITH YOUR LIES

Reiki still dressed and took that walk she wanted. Resigned to being stuck with Jude for the evening, she allowed him to take her hand as they strolled. Now that Reiki was certain of her love for Arthur, she might even let Jude kiss her and not bat an eyelash. In the two weeks she had agreed to, no romantic advance could hope to make her heart waver.

They passed under the shroud of night as guards tried to enforce order. The air was alive with the sound of bells and sirens, smashing windows, and the occasional gunshot. At one point, they chanced upon a mob starting a bonfire in the street from the fixtures of some abandoned restaurant. They gave that one a wide berth, watching as guards rushed in from all angles.

"Jude, are we safe here? Maybe we should go back."

"After you see the place we first met."

Jude took Reiki to a park where five teenagers skateboarded even at this hour. They went to stand by a copse of trees, hidden in the shadows, and watched the kids practice stunts.

Jude pointed at the skateboarders. "I used to do that. You were sitting right here when I first saw you. You'd just come off a relationship, so things were slow at first."

"Do you remember what words we first said?"

"I think it was something along the lines of 'wanna grab ice cream?' or some such. You were on that like ants to a picnic."

Reiki laughed. Even now she'd say yes to free ice cream. At last, she was meeting a part of her past that made sense.

"There's no one looking this way," murmured Jude.

"Don't be gross," said Reiki. She stepped out of his grasp before he could plant a kiss on her neck. "We're not making out before that two weeks, so forget it."

Her words drew a smile and a chuckle from him, but Jude backed off.

"Come, let's get you home before it gets too late."

They stayed up late while Jude recounted their times together. From the advantage of a third person's point of view, the Reiki being described sounded book-smart, but willing to tag along with Jude on his escapades. It made her secretly wonder what she'd seen in him while they passed the time away. Perhaps the sex had been as good as Jude claimed.

Reiki was late getting up in the morning, and her parents were at work. She made herself breakfast, but stopped in puzzlement when she found herself about to place a saucer of milk on the floor.

"Why was I about to do that?" she asked aloud.

A knock at the door broke her train of thought. Reiki went to admit Jude into the apartment.

"Reiki. Go get dressed," he said. "We'll explore town a bit, then I'll show you the trail we took on our first date as a couple."

That meant finding comfortable shoes, but all the shoes in her closet were too fancy for hiking. Reiki cursed at her past-self's lack foresight in stocking up on footwear.

She ended up buying clothes and shoes on the way, though Jude chafed with impatience to get started.

More strange places followed that day. Reiki met the tree where they first kissed. She managed to recognize it, which surprised her. She didn't remember kissing there, but it was some progress to remember anything.

They ended up watching the sunset, sitting on the edge of a metal bridge overlooking a cement valley in Hillvale's industry centre. Warehouses and industrial complexes hugged both sides of the trough, with smokestacks that sparked and made them look like large green hornet nests. Men worked below Reiki's feet, clearing away gravel in preparation for a night of production.

"Nephir Avenue," said Jude. "You used to love it here. This bridge is going to be for a railroad. One day, the train will run from the station in Credd to here."

"Is that valley some kind of river? I see gates to control water flow up ahead."

"A river, yes. Wait and see."

After sunset, street lights illuminated the last of the men leaving the trough. A viscous, blue fluid spewed out of giant pistons that made a bass grinding noise like giant trash compactors. The fluid formed a river that traced the contours of the concrete valley and headed for the control gates.

Recollection stormed back. It was a liquid nitrogen weir. The men would use poles to stir the compound to keep the water component from completely freezing as it flowed past the locks and battered an array of fluorite crystals. Somewhere along the line, they'd end up with gaseous fluorine, which powered demesnes like Hillvale where oil was hard to get.

The river soon became obscured in a thick cloud of fog. Workers in oxygen masks took up the task of stirring. They made little cyclones of heat as they worked. It was stunning to watch the red clouds of warm air dancing over the freezing waters, forming short-lived eddies of turbulence. Reiki was entranced just staring at it.

"Hah, you always did like that. I could leave you here for hours sometimes and come back and you hadn't moved."

"Jude, it's beautiful. I see a mirror of the formation of a galaxy inside."

He sat beside her and put an arm around her shoulders. For once, Reiki didn't pull away. Jude's showing her this was a fair bit of genius—he deserved a break from her standoffishness.

She did lean away when he tried to kiss her, but he laughed goodnaturedly.

"Reiki, if you loved me, would you let me kiss you?"

"Of course," she said, already suspicious of where this question was leading.

"If you loved me, what would you give to keep that love?"

"Jude. Stop." She frowned at him.

Laughing, he gave up his relaxed pose and leaned forward to set his elbows on his knees. "No, no, work with me on this. What would you do for love?"

Reiki sighed and decided to play along a little further. "If I loved someone, I'd do anything for them."

"Would you kill someone to save them?"

"What? No. Of course not." Though, realizing she meant she'd not help a lover, Reiki relented. "Well, if they were being threatened and I could help, it would be a different story."

"Not a threatening person. I mean..." Jude paused a moment, eyes lost in thought. "If I was accused of a crime, and you loved me, would you lie to set me free?"

"If I loved you that much," said Reiki. "And I don't, by the way, so you'd best not be guilty of any crimes."

"I'm being theoretical here. So you'd lie to get me out of a crime is what you're saying."

"Jude, what is this about?"

"Even if that lie meant an innocent man had to die?"

"No way I'd do that."

Jude leaned back again. "Yep. You haven't changed a whit. Same old Reiki in there, just a new shell."

"Oh? And what do you mean by that?"

"You never understood love before, Reiki. You still don't now. But don't worry. I'll teach you. When you were changed, your heart went all cold inside, but I'll heat it back up."

"What, changed?"

There was something important in what he said. Reiki just knew it.

"You used to say your ex-boyfriend transformed you in

some way. But he's off running the demesne, now, so he's forgotten you. Reiki? Are you okay?"

Memories were pouring back now and filling the void. Places and numbers danced in her mind. Old fears and woes, fellow students, and friends of friends. Lastly, searing pain. Pain to make even burning to death under the rocket look pleasant.

"Reiki, please. Please talk to me. Tell me you're alive."

Reiki nodded, opened her eyes, and frowned as she spoke.

"You lied to me, Jude. Those weren't my parents, and we were never engaged."

"What?" cried Jude. "Of course they're your parents."

They got to their feet, and Jude backed a step away from her.

"I remember now. I remember what my real parents look like, and that they live in the suburbs. I remember that they would have had my pet cat, and, most of all, I remember that when you proposed to me, I broke up with you."

Jude looked over Reiki's shoulder in surprise, and she whirled to see Arthur Galenden, of all people, emerge from the shadows. He had a pistol strapped about his waist under a swordsman's jacket in House colours. His face looked a mask of cool and collected as his gaze settled on Jude. And his aura burned tall above him.

Heat splotches told Reiki other people followed not far behind. Guards, she hoped. Come to arrest Jude for such a conspiracy. She turned back to face him and found him staring aghast. He offered no words of explanation for such heinous deeds.

"Speak, Jude. Tell me why you did this to me."

"Reiki!" Arthur called her name and she turned back to face him.

She was torn. Arthur had lied to her as well–paid people to follow her, manipulated her, and had possibly been sleeping with Xandri on the side. In many ways he was just as bad as Jude.

Silly goose. Arthur never laid a finger on you until you came to terms with your feelings for him.

Arthur had shown he was capable of change. Forget what other crimes he'd committed. Reiki reaffirmed her choice and stepped toward him.

She was stopped by Jude who put an arm around her waist. Reiki felt the tip of a gun on her temple. She held very still.

"Hold it, lover boy," said Jude when Arthur made to draw his pistol. "Try anything fancy and neither of us gets Reiki."

"Jude!" she cried. "Have you gone mad?"

"Let her go, Jude," came the warning from Arthur.

"Sure thing, guy. Just as soon as you drop your gun over the edge. Slowly. No sudden moves."

"Arthur, don't," said Reiki. "He's bluffing."

Jude laughed. "I never bluff. If I can't have her, neither of us gets her."

"You wouldn't dare," said Arthur.

"You're not calling me out, are you?"

The gun made an ominous click sound that sent shivers of fear down Reiki's spine. Given Jude's history, he just might do it. He was even giggling to himself as he held her. She had to talk reason into him.

"Whatever happened to the two weeks?" she asked.

Reiki also motioned for Arthur to be calm, hoping Jude couldn't see. "How will we spend time together if you've killed me?"

"Reiki, I would never kill you," he murmured.

"Then, kiss me and have done with," she said. "Kiss my heart warm like you promised."

Kiss me and lower the gun so Arthur can save me.

Arthur glanced to his sides as guards materialized from the shadows around him. In the middle of them came Iliara and Hendry. She wore a striking red gown that looped over one shoulder. She also bore a glove, upon which sat a plump-looking falcon. Hendry bore a pistol as well, though he came without House colours, opting for his usual leggings and a woollen jacket.

For a moment, everyone seemed to freeze in surprise. Even Jude stopped giggling. It fell to Arthur to make the first move.

"Hendry," he said. "You told me you were running to get help. Not her."

"Sorry, guy. I can't let you get yourself tied up with Reiki."

"Tied up?"

"Ya, guy. She changed you. Broke you. I've gotta do this to save you from your own folly."

Arthur looked baffled. "Hendry, that's preposterous."

"Jude," said Iliara. "Kill her, now."

"No way, babes," said Jude. "Reiki's mine. Stars take you all."

A fight broke out then, for Arthur tried to reach Reiki, but the guards grabbed him by the arms. Iliara released the falcon into the air as Jude began to pull Reiki backwards.

"Let's get outta here, my love," whispered Jude. "We'll get down from here and disappear into the factory district. They'll never find us."

"Jude, look out!"

Reiki ducked as she cried out the warning. Iliara's falcon swept in from the side of the bridge and managed to strike Jude in the head in a flurry of feathers and claws.

Jude stumbled off balance. He teetered on the side of the bridge before falling over the edge. Reiki dived to grab him, but she only got a pant leg and was unable to hold him. Down he went, to vanish into the nitrogen waves.

Arthur had broken free of the guards and started running for her, but Reiki knew what she must do, and she would have to act quickly or Arthur would try to stop her. She had no idea if she could negotiate the kind of temperature liquid nitrogen would be at, but if she didn't, Jude was as good as dead.

"No! Reiki!"

She stepped over the edge before Arthur could reach her—stepped over the edge and met with unforgiving chill.

CHAPTER 28

RIVER FROM A
WARM HEART

Ferra observed the bizarre scene from her hiding spot on a factory rooftop. She saw the dark-haired man fall into the river, and Reiki dive after him. The man she assumed was Arthur ran to the edge, flanked by the other guards and watched, completely ignoring the falcon that banked into a sharp turn and landed on Iliara's glove.

Iliara shifted her weight like a runway model. She opened her ruby lips and uttered two words.

"Take him."

The guards gathered around Arthur began to pummel him.

"Easy there, guys," said Hendry. "Don't kick him in the face like that. You'll ruin his dashing good looks."

That's when Ferra signalled to the four guards with her and crept down the stairs. She patted her pocket to make sure the tiny revolver was still there. Iliara had her six remaining loyally paid-off guards with her. The four with Ferra had defected back to Kajo and all had scores to settle with Iliara. Revenge was what led them to follow Ferra even though they five were outnumbered.

And they had one special trick. The electrorifle recovered from Iliara's assassination attempt.

By the time they reached ground, Iliara's guards had beaten Arthur unconscious and were dragging him off the bridge by his arms. Iliara remained where she was. Hendry stared over into the darkness on the side Reiki had dived.

They could rush now and shove Iliara over the edge. But Iliara might find a way to survive that. Ferra considered the mathematical possibility far too high to make it worth the risk, so instead she got up to speaking distance, which gave Iliara's guards time to get out of sight.

Five versus two. Much better odds. Ferra made to speak, but the whine of the electrofile sounded, and Iliara whipped around.

"Ferra–"

It was all Iliara had a chance to utter before the guard with the electrofile shot her point-blank in the chest. Iliara went down, and the falcon fluttered away.

"Stars!" cried Hendry. "What have you done?"

Iliara looked to be moving. She must have blocked most of the shot with her powers. Ferra nodded to the guards who surrounded her and laid into her prone body with their guns. For a moment the only sounds were gunshots, and the only motion was Iliara's twitching leg.

"I think we got 'er," said a guard.

"Holed up her leg good and proper."

"I nailed her in the eye. Ain't no one gettin' up from that."

"Guys, the electrorifle's down. The core's burned out."

Ferra cursed under her breath. Without the rifle, they had no way to be certain Iliara stayed down. They would have to haul her to an incinerator and burn the body to be sure. If only they'd brought butane or a bucket of hydrochloric acid.

"That was utterly amazing, young lady."

Hendry came running around the guards to meet Ferra. It was he who had caught Ferra's attention when he arrived at the fortress and gone straight to see Iliara instead of an official. In some ways, Ferra supposed she should thank him for leading Iliara out of her safe zone.

"I'm of House Galenden. So pleased to meet one as beautiful as you."

"Huh?" Ferra blinked. No one had ever called her beautiful before. She found the term puzzling... repugnant, almost.

"Yes, I mean you, you pretty thing." Hendry tried to take Ferra's hand but she stepped away from him. "Your hands are so lovely, please let me kiss one."

"No," said Ferra. "Get away from me, you creep."

"I can't. I am stunned beyond reason by your loveliness."

Hendry put his arms out to gather Ferra into a hug. And what was Ferra to do, except defend herself from such advances? She pulled her revolver out of her pocket and shot Hendry in the face.

When he fell, Ferra stood over the body and shot twice more. Maybe she'd chuck him into the incinerator with Iliara just to be thorough.

The cries of the guards surprised Ferra.

"Augh! She's got my–"

"Fire!"

Limbs thrashed and guns fired, but it was too late. Iliara had regained her feet.

Her red gown was in tatters, and her once beautiful legs were marred in scoring from shotgun pellets. What had been long, flowing hair was matted in slick blood that ran from Iliara's left eye and down to her jaw. Ferra was glad the hair stuck to Iliara's cheek, covering that eye, because it would surely be a grotesque sight to behold.

Iliara took a step towards Ferra, so she fired the revolver. The shot glanced off Iliara's protective field, so instead, Ferra aimed at a metal post near the bridge. She judged out the angles and fired a shot that ricocheted and narrowly missed. The third shot, at a stone counter-weight, grazed Iliara's calve by striking from an angle Iliara hadn't been concentrating on shielding from.

Seeming to realize that the closer the she got to Ferra the easier the shots were getting, Iliara fled. Ferra pointed the gun at Iliara's retreating form but lost out on what would have been a killing blow. The gun was out of bullets.

Iliara was still due a trip to the incinerator. Ferra paused to reload before setting out after her.

Iliara took to a metal staircase that led up through the nitrogen condensation plant that fed the river, and Ferra dashed after her. She reached the top and pointed her revolver around, but there was no sign of Iliara.

On top of the plant, fans and air filters buzzed on their metal stilts. Residual unprocessed moisture had formed icicles which hung from the overhead cables that linked all the air-intakes. Lighting came from only half a dozen fluorescent lights that flickered with age.

Ferra moved forward and bent slightly to pass underneath the nearest rattling fan. There would be a million hiding places in this giant field of intakes and vents. The only saving grace were the droplets of blood Iliara was leaving behind.

"Iliara. Won't you come out? I will make your death very quick. No need to suffer."

A flash of red cloth drew Ferra's attention, and she fired. It was a direct shot, since she didn't have time to calculate a bank-shot. Iliara blocked and flitted off between a pair of rusted cogs attached to a roof-based flute.

Ferra moved on. Her heels made gravelly clacking noises on the rooftop, but the rattle of all those fans covered the sound.

"Iliara, don't you want to know why I'm going to kill you at least?"

Ferra paused and listened. The response came muffled from the left.

"I tried to help you, and now you're picking on me," said Iliara.

The concept was laughable. Ferra smirked.

"Help me, yes. By leaving me to rot in jail. You know who got me out? It was Reiki. Pictures of her hugging me on the front page of a million newspapers embarrassed the Academy and freed me from court martial. So, what did you do to help me, Iliara?"

"I would have tried to help. The time wasn't right."

Ferra studied the layout of the intake vents and figured on a likely hiding spot. She kept walking as though she was unsure where Iliara was.

"Think about it, Iliara. The person I tried to kill saved me. I was due for twenty-five years in prison, and she got me out. She didn't have to, but she did. You should have done something, but you didn't. That makes Reiki a good person. You know what that makes you?"

There was no reply. Iliara must have started to worry about the proximity of Ferra's voice. No use hiding her movements anymore. Ferra swung around a corner and found Iliara sitting on the ground in the predicted hiding spot between two low vents.

Iliara had her back to the corner and faced Ferra with her knees drawn up for protection. It was a well-chosen spot. Ferra would be unable to bank a shot at her unless she could convince Iliara to get up and walk forward a little.

"You didn't answer what that makes you, Iliara," said Fera with a snarl. "It makes you scum. Now stand. Face your death like a warrior."

"Ferra, we need to talk."

Ferra fired a direct shot that Iliara managed to block.

"This word 'talk' makes me nervous. Shall we try again?"

"I've done a lot of bad things, Ferra. I've done even worse things to cover them up. Atrocities, really. To stay ahead of them, I murder people. But I regret them." Iliara looked at her hands which she looped over her knees. "I regret each and every one of them. Ever since Doli died, I've not been able to sleep at night."

"Cry me a river," said Ferra.

"You have no idea how many times I've wanted to change. But an opportunity comes up, and I just go right back to the way I am."

"My arm grows tired while your empty talk clogs my ears."

"Oh, Ferra. Won't you please let me go?"

Iliara put her hands together and offered a pleading look. Ferra narrowed her eyes and pictured her like a horned demon waiting to pounce. Not easy to shoot someone when staring them in the eye. Better Iliara stay a monster.

"This is the end, Iliara. I'm putting a stop to your reign of fear. Then, I'm going to find Reiki and tell her she's safe from now on. She both freed me and forgave me. I owe her a debt that I mean to repay."

Iliara offered a toothy smile and began to laugh. The motion caused her injured eye to leak from behind the matted hair. Ferra tried to fire a warning shot, but the gun merely clicked.

Ferra backed up as Iliara rose to her feet. Lights dimmed and flickered as a storm of energy began to gather about Iliara's splayed fingers.

Ferra jammed her hand into her pocket to grab fresh bullets. They smelled smoky before she even got them loaded. When she squeezed the trigger, more futile clicking noises erupted. Iliara must have used her powers to bake the gunpowder into something non-reactive.

All that talk had been to stall Ferra so Iliara would have time to perform such a feat. Clever indeed.

Snake-like, energy crawled along Iliara's arms. A tremendous storm of power coiling to strike. The scent of burning cloth and ozone made Ferra's eyes water. She shielded her eyes and pointed the useless gun.

"What happened to that bag of lies about demons chasing you?"

"Oh, that was true. I'm running from my past." Iliara raised her hands into bolting position. Thin spider-lines of electricity arced from one hand to the other. "What I didn't say was that I'm still far ahead of my demons. So far ahead they'll never catch me."

The energy jumped for Ferra, and the world went dark. As she collapsed to the cold ground, Ferra's last thought went outwards.

'Guess I won't be repaying you, Reiki.

CHAPTER 29

OF POISON AND LIQUID NITROGEN

"Check," said Lady Galenden as she moved her piece into attack position on Lord Muldret's Namika. She smiled as she sipped at her tea.

It was a weak attack–he would easily defend against it. That was okay. All she wanted to do was distract him for a few more minutes.

They were upstairs in the palace, having a bit of a respite. The members of the other Great Houses were downstairs in the throne room deliberating what to do with Wendiah. Since getting up from her sick bed, the girl had dared petition the Houses to allow her to take the throne in her father's stead.

Wendiah had been sent to her room in the tower so the Houses could deliberate. House Galenden and Muldret had abstained from the vote. The fate of Ged was up to the remaining three.

Or so everyone thought.

"In about five minutes, the fluorine gas will vent into

the throne room," said Muldret. He stalled on responding to Patricia's move and took another bite of cake.

"The other three Houses will be decimated," murmured Patricia. "The people will blame Wendiah. She will be put to the gallows."

"Naturally, our two Houses will rise above the chaos," said Muldret.

"Or, actually, my House. Yours won't fare very well."

Muldret followed her gaze to the cake. He set the fork down and pursed his lips.

"Well, old goat," he said. "It seems great minds think alike."

"What?" she cried. "Impossible."

"A bit of hemlock in your tea. Your death will be pretty spectacular. Wish I could be there to see it."

Muldret clutched a hand over his chest. He opened his mouth to spew dark bile, struggled once, then slid off his chair.

Lady Galenden stared at her teacup in horror at first, but she calmed herself and sat down. No help was in reach. She had seen to it in her efforts to keep Muldret from surviving.

"I guess I outsmarted myself. Ah, the irony."

Lady Galenden began to chuckle.

She was still laughing when the first of the convulsions took hold.

The water was shockingly cold when Reiki touched down. Cold enough to make it feel like an icy hand gripped her heart. She floated there a moment, unable to do much more than shudder while her body adjusted to the temperature.

This water has to be around negative seventy, Reiki thought as she tried to paddle her arms and legs and felt lumps of ice resisting her. Her dress ballooned around her and tangled her legs, preventing her from surfacing. Her lungs burned for air, but all she could see was blue slush and bubbles.

Panic seized her as she struggled to disrobe. In her haste, Reiki tore some of the lining, then gave up and ripped the dress to shreds. She surfaced for a much-needed breath of air and heard fighting sounds coming from above the bridge.

Arthur, please be safe.

Reiki dived again and searched for Jude as she flicked her shoes off and slipped free of the last few fibres of her dress. No sign of him in the dark and murky waters. She surfaced for another gulp of air and dived farther down river.

At last, Jude's arm came into view. Reiki grabbed at it and pulled him into a hug. She kicked her way to the surface with him and threw everything she had into swimming for the bank.

Compared to the water, the shore was a warm summer's day. Reiki got out of the river and laboured to drag Jude along after her by the collar of his jacket. She paid little heed to the sheets of ice that crackled and tumbled from her bare skin. Or to the workers who were running to meet them. Jude was her main focus, with his eyes closed under frost-laden eyebrows.

"Jude," she breathed. "Please don't die."

Even if she didn't want to be with him, the thought of

him dying was unbearable. She had loved him once. Deep inside, Reiki thought maybe she still did. Just no longer in the way he wanted.

Reiki set her lips over Jude's and tried to breathe life into him. She pumped at his chest, following the CPR books she now remembered reading and tried to force more water out of his lungs.

But the water had frozen there, and no heart beat in his chest. Jude had gone beyond anything Reiki could do, though she was at it until the workers interceded.

Hands grasped her shoulders and drew her away. Almost forty workers had descended upon her while she worked. Two of them had grabbed her.

"Stop, miss. The guy's gone."

"He can't be. I gotta keep trying."

Reiki slipped out from under their wet gloves and tried to get back to Jude, but they looped arms around her waist. She fought them, but her kicks and punches clipped nothing but air. At length, she exhausted herself and allowed them to close ranks around Jude's body.

Someone passed Reiki a set of overalls. She scrambled to put them on while the workers checked on Jude.

One stood up, looked at her, and shook his head sadly.

Something inside of Reiki snapped, but she knew she wouldn't cry until the shock wore off. There was also Arthur, who had yet to make it here. Something must have happened to him.

Reiki ran for the stairs to the bridge and stumbled on them in her haste to make the top. When she got there, Arthur and the guards were gone. Yellow, glowing foot prints indicated a scuffle.

Foot prints led in two directions. One direction showed male-sized boots dragging a body. Two others were female and met at a corpse that turned out to be Hendry before trailing off toward the nitrogen condensers.

Reiki picked the trail of the men and ran off in the hopes of rescuing Arthur.

CHAPTER 30

FACTORY OF DESTRUCTION AND DEATH

The tracks led Reiki to a closed up factory. It was a three-storey brick structure with little square windows in groups of nine and plenty of rain overhangs and ledges marred with years of pigeon excrement. Lights glowed in those windows as though there was a beat club dance party going on inside.

A single guard stood outside near a wooden billboard that read, "Property sold to Reinergy Guild."

That was the name Arthur had chosen for Reiki's microguild. She now owned a factory in Hillvale? When, exactly, had Arthur been planning on sharing that news with her?

Reiki forced herself to calm down. First she needed to rescue Arthur. Then, she would kick his ass for hiding things from her.

The guard was emptying his bladder against the sign,

and Reiki thought to sneak past him for the doors but she was caught several metres before she could make it.

"Ahoy, little girl. C'mere a bit."

Reiki stared at the guard in surprise as he did himself up. She could dash for it now. He wouldn't have time to unsling his rifle, aim and hit her. But then he'd run and tell Iliara. Maybe she should stay and offer to pay him off.

Shades! My purse is at the bottom of that river. Scratch the pay-off idea.

"Oi, sweet'un. Looks like Mistress 'liara cut 'erself a sweet spot from the deck when she got embroiled with you."

Reiki glanced him over. Boy, could she use that rifle he carried right now. Maybe she could buy it off him if she ran back and dove for her purse.

"By all the shooting stars, you all look super cute. Turn around, would ye? Lemme see that caboose."

"Do you talk to your wife like that, sir?"

"Naw, she all get lippy nonstop. Now turn around, put on a show, would ya?"

Reiki complied, though she was careful to measure for an opening as she spun. She'd only get one chance to strike. And since she was untrained in fighting, she would need to make the most of it. A knee to the groin would probably do the trick.

"Phooeee, no wonder 'liara gon' get jealous over the likes of you."

He boldly reached out and unzipped Reiki's overalls. She let him do it, as a new plan formed in her mind. The guard slid his hands around her waist, so Reiki hugged him back. She put one hand near his heart, one on the back of his head, and threw her full powers into freezing. It was something she'd never tried before. Even when freezing the width of the Salthan river, she'd not touched the limits of her psychothermic shifts.

The guard jerked and stiffened. His arms went solid around her... when Reiki stepped back, they snapped off. Thrown off balance, he toppled backwards and shattered into frozen bits of flesh.

The sight was too much for her. Reiki knelt beside him and retched.

There was little in her stomach to bring up, so she dry-heaved for some time before she managed to still her wildly beating heart. And hurriedly, before nausea could overtake her again, she struggled to fulfill two more chores.

The first was the gun. She knelt to collect the guard's rifle. The shoulder strap was useless—it had gone brittle from the cold, so it broke up under her fingertips. His ID had survived because it was protected by his wallet. Reiki glanced at it and memorized his address since she owed his widow reparations.

Jobs complete, Reiki turned her gaze upon the factory.

Arthur was conscious when the guards tied his wrists, though he feigned being under. They tossed the rope over a horizontal beam and down to his arms, so he'd have plenty of slack if he could find a way to shimmy up the support pillar with his knees. They left him there and convened in the middle of the building.

The inner area of the building consisted of two floors, the second of which was a ring, so that the centre of the factory was open to the roof. Shipping crates of all sizes adorned the room, much resembling an eerie industrial circus where the spotlighting came from dim, moth-covered utility bulbs laced along the ceiling.

Arthur took a moment to eavesdrop on the guards' discussion.

"Mistress 'liara been gone a long time. You all figure she run into some kinda trouble?"

"Guy, ain't nothing that can kill her. Relax. She'll show."

"Hope she let us get some sport before she up'n'kill that hottie she's after."

"Oh, yeah. Score us some rodeo time before we put her under."

As if on cue, the doors banged open, and there stood Reiki. She wore baggy blue overalls, had her hair all askew, and carried a rifle that she held as one new to rifles. Still, with confidence, she pointed it at the guards and threatened them.

"Let him go, or I'm going to get unhappy."

The guards dived for the cover of crates and drew their rifles. Reiki seemed to reconsider her position and ran for the crates against the walls. The guards fired at the open doorway, but scored no hits.

"Fan out. She's hidden somewhere on the left."

The guards' attention was away from him. Arthur strained at the ropes, but there wasn't enough slack to get free.

He gave up with a sigh. *Face it, Arthur. You're too weak to save her. You're both going to die here because you couldn't even lift a hand to help yourself.*

No! He strained harder. One of his wrists was a little bit loose. If Arthur could pull a little bit harder...

Reiki yelped in surprise, and there was a gunshot. Arthur heard more scuffling and running. She lived yet.

Who am I kidding? We've already lost.

"I always win." The phantasmal memory of Jude teased him. Oh, how Arthur longed to wipe that sneer off his face. How he longed to go to Reiki and hold her. Whisper to her that she was safe. He wanted to be anywhere but here.

The guards reconvened in the centre, and Arthur watched them wordlessly point out their target. Reiki was about to get ambushed. It was his last chance.

I've gotta do this to save you from your own folly.

Hendry, that's preposterous.

Skin rubbed raw under the ropes, but Arthur continued to twist his arm. In a moment, his wrists would bleed. Maybe the lubrication would help.

I can't let you get yourself tied up with her. That's just how we do things, chap.

With a yell, Arthur freed his arm. He stopped to breathe between clenched teeth. Everyone else who thought to interrupt had best get in line. Reiki was his.

Reiki discovered a ladder going up. She knew the guards were closing in on her and realized they would follow her up once they figured it out. But for now, up was the only direction that made sense.

The ladder was hidden behind tall crates. Exposure was minimal, so Reiki took the risk and climbed it to gain the second floor, where ancient workbenches formed an office-like decor.

Reiki got on all fours and crept to the edge, so she could peer down to the ground floor.

The guards were no longer visible, though she heard them calling to each other. Arthur was gone too. Reiki blinked. He must have slipped off at the first distraction.

"Arthur's escaped," she breathed. "I gotta get out of here."

But the glow of heat told Reiki someone very warm was drawing up behind her. She whipped around to see Iliara.

Iliara looked to be in significant pain from the wounds crisscrossing her arms and legs under shredded fabric. Blood flowed from those gashes to the point where Reiki was unsure of the original colour of Iliara's gown. Her skin was pale, where it wasn't streaked in blood. It was like the Star of Death had crawled into a corpse and chosen to animate it.

Reiki pointed her rifle and squeezed the trigger, but the gun just made a dry "click" noise. The safety might be on or something. Reiki was unsure.

Meanwhile, down below, yells arose and a single gunshot sounded.

Reiki glanced down to the factory floor to make sure that cry wasn't Arthur. Iliara pounced upon her during that distraction. She wrenched the gun from Reiki's grasp, bent it along the barrel, and cast it aside.

"Iliara, no—"

Reiki got no further. Iliara leaned forward and back-handed her.

Stars swam in her vision. Reiki fell from her crouch, and Iliara placed iron-strong hands around her neck.

"I could kill you right now," said Iliara. "One snap of the fingers, and no more Reiki."

She held Reiki down one-handed, and used the free arm to slap her again. A tooth dislodged and went flying out of her mouth. Below, another gunshot sounded.

"But I'm not going to kill you," said Iliara. "I'm going to smash your face instead. When I'm done with you, you'll look so horrible Arthur will never want to touch you."

The next blow must have knocked Reiki unconsciousness because her next coherent thought was being shaken awake.

"Don't you dare pass out on me, you little red toad. I've only just begun to hurt you." Iliara picked Reiki up by the neck and dangled her over the edge. "This fall won't kill you, I think. You'll lie on the ground with a busted up leg. I'll come down and get you and drop you again, maybe. We'll keep doing that until you learn to hop like any other toad."

"Iliara!"

It was Arthur. He stood on the floor with a rifle in each hand, one of which he pointed at them in accusation.

"Arthur." Iliara's face changed, and for a moment she looked almost child-like to Reiki. Just... a deadly smiling child that was about to drop her from a great height.

"Don't do it, Iliara," said Arthur.

"Oops."

Iliara released her, but only carelessly, so Reiki was able to grab the edge of the platform. Iliara stared at her with a beatific smile plastered on her maimed face. She raised a leg aimed for Reiki's left hand, but Reiki moved it and grabbed the ankle when it came into reach.

Reiki channelled all of her freezing powers into that leg, calling deep into her reservoir until she knew there could be no cold left in her. Iliara never even twitched. She toppled forward, and her leg snapped off in Reiki's hand. The body fell to the factory floor, where it shattered with a sickening crunch.

Hands slick in Iliara's frozen blood, Reiki was unable to pull herself up. She slipped from her handhold and tumbled backward.

Arthur caught Reiki and broke her fall. She blinked in surprise.

"I told you if you ever fell, I'd be waiting to catch you."

Reiki buried her face in his shoulder and began to cry.

CHAPTER 31

THE LEDGER

They stood there for several minutes while Reiki wept quietly. Arthur heard the bells of the eighth hour toll while he held her in his arms. At length, she calmed down and spoke to him.

"You have any money? I left my purse on the bottom of a nitrogen river."

Arthur nodded into Reiki's hair. "Taxi? Back to my hotel room?"

"Come."

She took him by the hand and walked outside. Once they passed the scraps that remained of some unfortunate guard, Reiki quickened her pace. She was at a near run by the time they reached the street, laughing and swinging Arthur's arm with a stunning freedom from restraint.

"Oi! Over here," she called.

Arthur had forgotten that this strange city still used horse and carriage for taxis. He helped her board and settled in beside her.

"Downtown-South," said Reiki. "I've got to get home."

She bounced in excitement on the way, grinning so

much that Arthur noticed her missing a tooth. When he made to ask her about it, Reiki grabbed his head in both hands and kissed him.

They were at it for some time. Arthur took no notice of the city lights scrolling past until the tall buildings of the urban centre drew into view. He realized, right then, that he needed to do something very important, but hadn't planned well enough for it.

"Driver, hold," said Arthur. He paid in gold, disembarked, then turned to help Reiki down.

The streets were jammed with traffic, and the sidewalks still heavily populated in commuters. A pair of street performers were in the middle of a silent comedy sketch as Arthur led Reiki away from the cars. She seemed to figure it out the moment she saw the jewellery store, for she put up resistance.

"Wait. You can't," she said.

"Mmm?"

"We haven't discussed Xandri. Or your mother. Or us."

Arthur turned and touched her cheek. "Reiki. You're the only woman for me. Please don't make me wait another day, or even another hour to do this."

She lowered her gaze and gave a slight nod. Arthur hurried her inside since stores would soon close.

Once past the threshold, Reiki settled on the first display case, but Arthur charged right up to the clerk. He slapped a bank note for a large sum on the glass case between them.

"I need your largest, most expensive engagement band."

"Right this way, milord."

They had several rings in the same price range, so Arthur picked out the one with the fattest diamond on it and motioned for Reiki to join him. When she failed to notice him, he joined her at the display case she studied.

"I don't need to keep looking," said Reiki. "I'm in love with that one."

"Huh?" The ring she indicated was a paltry one fifth the price of the good rings. Arthur drew her out of earshot to the clerk and tried to explain. "Why are you looking at those tiny stones? I've got you a much bigger and better one."

"Silly boy," she replied as she wrapped her arms around him to kiss him on the nose.

"Ah, the princess cut," said the jeweller. He was standing by the display case waiting to measure for it, and even had the box ready, perhaps having divined which one of them would win the ring debate. "It's one of the newer cuts. First done in Rion about ten years ago, but gaining in popularity."

The measuring seemed to take forever, and Arthur ended up promising to bring it back for refitting. He took up the precious box, held Reiki by the hand and took them outside, where he looked for somewhere fitting to ask.

Unfortunately for him, the two street performers seemed to have Arthur's number pegged. They ran over and began to circle him. The downy pillow feathers they cast in the air looked almost like a late-spring snowfall.

Reiki giggled. When her eyes met Arthur's, she burst into laughter. It cleared the vexation from his spirit, and he found a smile tickling his mouth. Her voice was like rainbows.

"If you're not going to ask, could I go home and change?" Reiki pinched at the pant leg of her overalls. "I'm not really dressed for this."

Arthur gave up and knelt. She obediently took up

position on his knee. Feathers rained on them, and passers-by stopped to watch. Even traffic seemed to slow down and draw in a collected breath.

"Reiki, will you..." Arthur's voice cracked as he realized the magnitude of what he was about to ask. Reiki studied him wordlessly. And wind teased the curls of her hair. The look made his throat go dry. All at once, Arthur's hand began to tremble, and he found he couldn't get the box open. It was her impatience that saved him from an embarrassing gaffe.

"Yes!" cried Reiki. She snatched up the box amidst a mighty cheer from the crowd. She held it aloft, and turned once, beaming at everyone in sight. Then she flew into the crowd, apparently forgetting that Arthur was supposed to slide the ring on her finger and those other rules he thought went with proposing.

Arthur followed her and found Reiki with her arms wrapped around an Orionite woman about her age.

"I've missed you, Kwan," said Reiki.

"It's about time you returned," the woman replied. "And this boy's a keeper. I can tell."

Ah, Reiki has friends here. Arthur would get to meet a whole other side of his future wife. He found himself looking forward to it.

"Arthur, come."

Reiki took him by the hand swept him away from the crowded sidewalk. Cheers and feathers rose after them.

Through darkened streets and gritty alleys they ran. Reiki's laugh was so infectious Arthur found himself laughing despite worries about getting lost. They came to some kind of nightclub with a burnt-out sign. Reiki charged right in and announced their engagement to the room.

"Loretta! I'm getting married."

The room cheered like a group of old friends. Reiki ran to the stage and jumped around gleefully while holding the singer's hands. Arthur made his way to the bar and leaned against it. He watched a transformed Reiki in amusement.

"So, you're the lucky guy?" The barman offered a warm grin.

Arthur smiled ruefully. "If I can keep up with her."

The barman reached out a hand. "The name's Charlie. Miss Reiki's a real special girl. You'll take good care of her for us, won't you?"

"I'd better, or she'll beat the tar out of me."

"Here, it's on the house," said Charlie. He set a glass of beer on the bar, and Arthur drank of it deeply.

Beer was not the kind of thing Arthur normally got to enjoy in high circles, but he could get used to it. And the drink calmed his nerves, which was good, because Reiki had one more surprise for him.

She took him upstairs, out a window, then up a fire escape to the roof of the bar. Out of breath at last, she fell into his arms.

Arthur managed to pry the box out of Reiki's fingers. He re-assumed proposal form in the hopes of getting it right this time, but she distracted him by kissing him from her perch on his knee. They were at it for some time with the little box pressed into their hands, but the rumble of thunder got their attention.

From the sky, a man appeared. He wore a bright blue cape and a straw hat that set off his dark complexion. He fell, as if parachuting, and landed before them, toes only brushing the roof. There, he rested, cape billowing under a wind Arthur couldn't feel.

"Kajo," said Reiki.

"Kwan told me she found you," said the leader of Hillvale as he doffed his cap for Arthur.

"Iliara is dead," said Reiki. "She was hiding bank accounts from you."

Reiki proceeded to rattle off names, dates, and numbers. There were hundreds. Arthur had no idea what they were all for, only that Kajo listened raptly to each fact and figure Reiki spat out.

When it was over, Reiki leaned on Arthur for support. Her eyes looked tired, but satisfied. He supposed she must have used the rest of her energy on that deep recollection.

"I saw the report from the Academy," said Kajo. "You're to get a medal of valour for bringing the rocket back."

"I don't deserve a medal. All I did was point the nose up. Give it to Janan. He earned it."

"And you have a new name. On the second moon trip, you'll be Captain Reiki Starsong."

Arthur nodded. The name was very fitting. And captain, of all things. A huge promotion.

But Reiki wore a rueful little smile, and Arthur realized she was about to turn it down.

"Thank you, Kajo," she said. "But I don't think I want go back. I'm already the first woman on the moon–there's no part of space left for me to conquer. I have a guild to run now. Besides, by the time they're ready to relaunch, I'll be taking care of a bunch of little Arthurs."

Kajo briefly studied the box in Arthur's hand as he

seemed to consider the import of her words. He looked at the two of them and smiled.

"Congratulations. Hillvale owes you a great debt." Kajo flew off, but hovered in the air for a few more parting words. "Oh, and Reiki. May happiness follow you wherever you go. You deserve it."

"Bye, Kajo," called Reiki. She stared into the night sky until Arthur got her attention by coughing and holding up the ring. "Oh. Sorry."

She held out her hand, and he looped it over her finger.

"May you never leave my side, Reiki Starsong."

"Arthur, wherever you are, I am home."

Printed in the United States
By Bookmasters